Looking Real Good
Copyright © 2020 by C. Morgan.

Editor: Eric Martinez
Cover Designer: Ryn Katryn Digital Art

D1516980

DEDICATION

To my awesome readers! I'm so blessed by you guys. Never in a million years would I have thought I could spend my life telling stories and reminding people that love is always the answer. And I'm only able to do it because of you. Thank you. Thank you. Thank you a million times! I love you guys.

C. Morgan

CHAPTER 1

LUKAS

My public-relations consultant flicked off the lights in the conference room. She held a remote in her hand and pointed it at the projector at the far end of the conference table. She clicked through a couple of slides, each one lighting up the room in the predominant color of the slide. Red, blue, white, green. Finally, she stopped clicking, and she read the words aloud on the presented screen.

"The negative shift in media and public opinion toward tech billionaires," she said. Lisa's tone was monotonous but assertive, and her gaze slid toward me as if to double-check that I was in fact paying attention.

I nodded for her to continue.

Lisa, my PR consultant and younger half-sister, clicked past the index page of the slideshow she'd created to inform me just how out of favor I had fallen. According to her, wealthy men and women like myself were being seen more like villains than successful business people. She'd been breathing down my neck about how I needed to do better.

Better than building my own empire from the ground up? Better than providing a stable work environment for my employees with full-ride benefits and generous salaries? Better than the property and the mansion I owned? Better than pulling myself out of the slums and becoming one of Seattle's wealthiest and most eligible bachelors?

Not that I had time to date.

We'd bickered about this nonsense for weeks now—possibly months. She wouldn't relent, and neither would I, so she'd not so subtly sabotaged me in my own damn conference room this morning with a slide show she'd prepared. Her intention, it seemed, was to showcase how disliked I was.

It was a great way to start my Monday.

A picture of dozens of families leaving a rundown apartment somewhere downtown filled the screen. Lisa didn't flip to the next slide. She turned to me with one hand on her hip. She set the remote down on the conference table and stared expectantly at me.

"Yes?" I asked.

"Your kind are seen as responsible for this." She gestured at the screen. "Money-hungry elites are driving up rents in big cities. Consequently, low-income or *no*-income tenants and their families are driven out onto the street with nowhere to go. The consequences of this are severe, Lukas."

"I haven't evicted anyone."

My half-sister carried on like I hadn't even spoken. "Perhaps not directly. Regardless, other millionaires and billionaires are portrayed as making fortunes and then failing to give back to their communities. They're instead choosing to continue lining their pockets. They disregard any and all negative repercussions of them pursuing yet more wealth and—"

"Lisa," I said dryly, "are you trying to tell me I'm a jackass?"

My sister blinked impassively at me. "Perhaps."

"You've been telling me the same thing since we were kids."

"And I was right all along. Imagine that?"

I scoffed without humor.

Lisa sighed. "Lukas, just let me get through my presentation, okay? I know you don't want to sit around and listen to this, but please try to learn something from it. I'm not telling you this as your sister. I'm telling you this as your PR rep. I'm doing my job. You know, the job you hired me to do?"

I sighed. "Fine."

Lisa flipped through a couple more slides. They flashed images of more people being evicted from low-income housing apartments and townhomes. Next came pictures of wealthy CEOs, many of whom I knew in the flesh, who had bank accounts as overflowing as my own. She stopped flipping through slides and landed on a picture of my face.

I recognized the picture. It was of me sitting in my office in this very building. Across the top of the image were the words "Success at Whose Cost?". In the picture, I wore a bespoke dark gray suit and a smirk. The Seattle skyline sat behind me against a backdrop of blue skies. The article had not reflected well on me, and Lisa had been doing damage control over the last three months since it had been published.

"That was a good suit," I said as I stroked my chin.

Lisa huffed. "Focus, Lukas. Articles like this have swayed public opinion. You're being lumped in with bankers, oil barons, and Wall Street tycoons. Tech CEOs like yourself are the new whipping boys in the court of public opinion." She moved through a few more slides, all of which were pictures of me. "The fell swoop that led to your decline was when you demolished the old building that used to stand right here so you could build this office tower in the historic district. Yes, you have a nice view, but the people who were born and raised here never wanted this building here, Lukas. It's an eyesore."

"An eyesore? Have you looked at this building, Lisa? It's the definition of modern and exquisite architecture."

"It's obnoxious."

"You're obnoxious," I muttered.

My sister sighed and dropped the remote control on the table, leaving the final image of my face on the screen. "You're being accused of everything from gentrification to negative environmental impact."

"Oh, come off it. The building that was here before I started development was a vacant health hazard. The mold and asbestos were off the charts. That alone was enough to get rid of it. It was infested with rats and vermin. It was lowering property values in the neighborhood. And you want to talk about a health risk? Teenagers were breaking in all the time, breathing that shit in. If anything, I did this community a favor by eliminating a dangerous environment."

"You're missing the point."

"What is the point then?" I asked sharply. I was getting tired of this nonsense. I had other things to do.

"The press is against you right now. You need to polish your image."

I arched an eyebrow as my attention slid back to the ten-by-ten-foot image of me shining on the screen at the far end of the conference room. "Looks pretty polished to me."

My half-sister rolled her eyes. "Not your physical image. You're impossible, you know that? You need to polish people's perception of you."

I liked grinding her gears. "Perception?"

She nodded. "Your bottom line will drop if public perception continues to be negatively affected by the negative press. Here, for example." She clicked through a few more slides and paused at a familiar chart. It displayed last quarter's profits which had started to dip despite a recently launched upgrade. "Your profits should have been in an upswing after your last upgrade. But they're not."

"Because people don't like me?"

"And they don't trust you."

"I'm not a politician," I said, straightening my suit jacket. "I'm a businessman. Since when did my success equate to being trusted and liked?"

"Since forever. Look, Lukas. You hired me because you knew something wasn't working and you needed help. This is my forte. I'm the professional here and I need you to trust me. I'm your sister. I want to help you—even though you already have more money than any one person could spend in an entire lifetime. Or eight."

I stayed in my seat as my sister turned off the projector and moved to the door, where she flicked the lights back on. I squinted and shielded my eyes as she packed up her things into her work bag.

She dropped into the chair beside me. "Did any of that get through to you?"

I didn't answer her question. Instead, I returned one of my own. "I assume with all the effort you put into this to change my mind that you have a game plan?"

"Of course, I do."

"Let's hear it then."

Lisa sat proudly and lifted her chin a little. She and I had an unconventional history compared to a lot of siblings. We shared the same father but different mothers. At twenty-eight, she was two years younger than me, and just like me, she was the outcome of our father's serial philandering. He lived in a rundown neighborhood that he treated like his own personal whore house. He maintained affairs with several women—some married, some single, some somewhere in between—and managed to keep his indiscretions under wraps until two pregnancies were tied back to him: mine and Lisa's mothers.

He got the hell out of Dodge after that so he didn't have to pay child support or be a father.

My sister and I grew up as neighbors. It was unconventional, sure, but it worked for us. Our mothers became allies after what our father put them through and, in turn, best friends. Sunday mornings were spent alternating between each apartment for breakfast and we'd have at least three dinners a week together as a family.

Things had changed a lot since then.

"The plan is for you to institute some kind of charitable-giving campaign," Lisa said.

"A giving campaign?"

"Yes, Lukas. A giving campaign. It's time for your business to give back to the community instead of just reaping the benefits. According to my research, CEOs are more favorable to their audiences when they take a hands-on role. Said audiences prefer when this hands-on charity work is done to help those in need within their own cities. So with that in mind, I want to show you a couple of proposals of some projects you could dive into."

Lisa pulled a portfolio out of her bag and flipped it open. There were dozens of charts in there, as well as more articles.

I pinched the bridge of my nose as she began laying them out on the table in front of me. "Lisa, I have other meetings today. Just tell me the bottom line."

Lisa glanced up at me. "What?"

"You tell me what I should do. Don't present me with all these options. Like you said, I hired you as my public-relations expert. I don't have time to hear out all of these."

My sister leaned back in her chair. "Fine. I have connections to a non-profit organization here in Seattle that does excellent work. I can set up a meeting with their director to fit your schedule."

"Talk to my assistant. I have a conference call to hop on."

Lisa started packing her things back up as I got to my feet and moved to the door. "Lukas?"

I turned back to her.

"I'm on your side, you know?" she said.

"I know."

I left my sister in the conference room and moved down the pristine hallway to my office. I closed the door behind me and went to stand in front of my floor-to-ceiling windows. Gazing down at the city streets below and the rooftops of the historic district, I thought about the things Lisa had said.

There was a time when I had nothing. My sister knew that better than anyone. She hadn't had anything either. Our mothers had struggled to put food on our plates. I remembered how it felt being sent off to school with two quarters in my pocket. My mother always asked me if it was enough. Could I buy lunch with fifty cents?

I always told her I could. And it was always a lie.

My first day of high school hadn't been easy with those quarters in my pocket, hand-me-down clothes, and a notebook I'd found at a garage sale with a kitten on the cover. I'd swiped pens from places that always had dozens of them in holders on their counters, like the print shop or the DMV. At the time, I'd thought I was going in prepared, but all I was walking into at school was four years of torture at the hands of merciless bullies who terrorized me for my clothes, school supplies, lack of a father, and how poor my family was.

I came home with more black eyes than my mother ever could have dreamed of.

And now?

Well, I'd worked hard to amass my billions. I'd sacrificed leisure time and relationships to build my software and find success. I had no intention of giving those billions away and leaving myself or my mother vulnerable again. She needed me more than anything, especially now.

CHAPTER 2

KAYLA

I secured my hair in a low bun before pulling my hairnet over it. I tucked the net up under the bun, slid two bobby pins behind my ears to secure it in place, and plucked my apron from the magnetic hook on the side of the industrial refrigerator. The soup kitchen was bustling this afternoon and they needed all hands on deck. I'd been more than happy to take the call from Rodney, the kitchen manager, begging me to come in for a couple of hours to help them get through the lunch rush.

Rodney had taken over washing dishes and was up to his elbows in bubbles when I brushed past him to make my way out onto the floor.

"Thanks again for coming in, Kayla," he said, flashing me a smile over his shoulder. He had a nice, bright, white smile, and he wore it often. His light brown hair was cut short on the sides and he was in need of a trim on top. Little strands poked through the top of his hairnet and stuck every which way, making him look permanently frazzled, which I supposed he was. Rodney was a busy man.

"No problem at all. You know I'm always happy to help." I tied my apron behind my back and started to adjust the strap behind my neck. These things were always far too long on me due to the fact that I was only five feet tall. My jeans were cuffed for the same reason—so I didn't trip over them. I had my working shoes on, complete with insoles to avoid foot cramping and aches. Even though Rodney had only asked me to come in and cover the lunch rush, I fully expected to be there well into the evening. That was how these things went.

The buckle on the neck strap of my apron wouldn't slide. I let out a frustrated growl and decided to take it off and try a different apron.

Rodney turned off the sink and dried his hands on the faded red towel draped over his shoulder. "Hold on. I've got you."

I turned my back to him so he could tighten the strap for me. His fingers were hot and still a little damp from washing dishes, and I wondered how long he'd been at it for. Hours most likely. Once he tightened the strap, he put both hands on my shoulders.

"Thank you," I said.

"You're welcome. Now get out of here before I try to talk you into dish duty."

I laughed and hurried to rush through the swinging doors. "You don't have to tell me twice."

The soup kitchen hall was *packed.* Nearly every seat at every table was taken, and there was a line against the far wall that wrapped all the way around to the double doors that led out onto the street. I was sure the line continued for at least a block, perhaps more, and I hoped deliveries from caterers were all on time and we wouldn't have any gaps in between putting out fresh dishes. I hated having to delay people who'd already waited for hours to put food in their bellies.

For some of them, it would be the first thing they'd eaten in days.

Everyone working the food line waved and called hello to me as I fell into the open spot at the mashed-potato station. A glass divider protected the food from the volunteers and the guests coming in to get food, and it was our job to serve everyone their portions. This kept things fair and equal, avoided potential confrontation between people in line, and followed health and safety guidelines.

A woman and her young son stepped up in front of me. The boy couldn't have been more than nine. He wore a ball cap with frayed edges on the visor and a jacket that was far too big for him. His eyes were dark brown and fixed on the steaming potatoes between us.

I grinned at him and his mother. "They look good, don't they? It's torture having to stand up here and serve them when all I want to do is stick my finger in them and have a taste."

The boy looked up at me.

I winked. "Don't worry. I didn't do it."

He smiled.

I slapped a hefty serving onto his plate and then his mother's. Their plates already had some steamed carrots and a scoop of corn on them, and they shimmied down the line to pick their protein. On the menu today was baked chicken and gravy. The gravy was clumpy and beige, not at all aesthetically pleasing, but it smelled like gravy, and that was sometimes as good as it got at the kitchens.

It was better than nothing anyway.

More people filled the place of the mother and her son. I offered smiles and friendly greetings to everyone who stopped in front of my station. I asked them about their day and asked a gentleman in a long coat and fingerless gloves how many people were still waiting in line.

"About three times as many who are eating in here," he told me with a crooked smile. He was missing three of his front teeth.

"How long did you have to wait?"

"I don't have a watch," he said. "I couldn't tell you. But I'd guess it took me an hour or so to get inside. Not bad at all. Not bad at all. Smells good, too. You make this?"

I laughed and shook my head. "No, and be glad for it. My cooking never turns out. I always put too much salt in things and I overcook it. This stuff here? This is the good stuff."

The man flashed me another one of his crooked smiles before carrying on down the line toward the chicken. The rest of the afternoon moved along in a blur. There were no pauses in the steady stream of people filing in and filling their plates.

There were a lot of hungry people out there to feed.

I didn't mind. I liked being busy, and I liked meeting new people. Volunteer work made me feel fulfilled. I could remember a childhood that didn't feel all that long ago when I'd been the one in need. I grew up in a rough area where people didn't have a lot of money. My grandmother raised me after my own mother gave me up and lost herself in drugs. Sometimes as a young girl, I used to wonder what it might have been like to have a mother in my life who loved me more than she loved her addiction.

Now as a grown woman, I could see how warped that thinking was.

Addiction stripped choices away, among other things. It wasn't that my mother hadn't loved me. Quite the opposite actually. She'd left me with her own mother because she knew she would fall short. She knew I deserved a fair shot and the only way I'd get that was with my grandmother.

And my mother had been right.

My grandmother was a kind woman who worked too many hours at a bakery six blocks away from our apartment. We made a happy home together, but the money never went far enough. Soup kitchens like this were familiar to me. I ate many meals at collapsible tables with strangers packed in elbow to elbow.

I even made friends in those places.

I'd met my best friend in one of the apartment buildings in the complex, for instance. She and I were thick as thieves growing up. We used to play kick the can with the other neighborhood kids. Sometimes, we'd change things up and have a game of capture the flag, but kick the can was our standard go-to.

I never won, but that wasn't the point.

Three hours had passed since I assumed mashed-potato duty. I was happy to take a break when Rodney tapped me on the shoulder.

"Hey, Kayla," he said, nodding toward the kitchen doors. "I finally have more coverage in the back to stay on top of the dishes. There was something I wanted to talk to you about. Can you spare a minute?"

I nodded and handed the spatula to the woman beside me manning the wax-beans station. I gave a coy look and asked if she was sure she could double-fist it.

She told me to get going so I could come back sooner and relieve her.

I followed Rodney through the kitchens to the back room where he kept a small personal office. It was from this space that he managed the kitchens. He was a one-man show staying on top of fundraising events, bottle drives, specialty menus, donations, and much more. He had stacks of papers everywhere, including on the one chair at his desk, and he gathered them up and stacked them on top of an already overwhelming pile on the floor.

"Sit," he said, nodding pointedly at the chair.

I sat.

Rodney leaned up against the wall across from me. "I have a partnership with the local school district to provide free lunches to hungry kids and I recently got word that their funding has been cut in half due to lower donations this year."

"That's horrible."

"Indeed. That means fifty percent of their kids will go without lunches if we can't get more money together to cover the losses. We'll have to rely on outside community groups to revive it. Even that's a stretch. We're going to need our own manpower to handle deliveries and such. I have volunteers willing to take that task on but I need some help on the ground level to reach out to these community groups and other local organizations to kind of get the ball rolling. I was hoping you'd be willing to lend a hand. It's never easy asking for money but you have higher success rates than anyone I've ever seen."

"It's the charming smile and the disarming sense of humor," I said not so humbly.

Rodney laughed. "I'm not going to disagree with that. I know it's a lot to ask and you're already a very busy woman. If you can't fit this into your schedule, I understand. I can ask someone else."

"Who?"

He scratched the back of his neck. "I hadn't gotten that far but I always manage to make something work, don't I?"

I smiled graciously. "Don't worry, Rodney. I can handle it. It's not too much. I promise. Besides, you know this is something I'd love to be involved in. Just to clarify, what do you need from me?"

"Money," he said simply. "I need you in charge of donations."

"All right," I said thoughtfully. My mind was already hopping to and from businesses I knew I'd be able to go to. "I have a couple of companies and businesses I can tap. I don't see any reason why I won't be able to come through for you."

He clapped his hands together enthusiastically. "Excellent!"

I stood up and rubbed my sweaty palms on my jeans. The soup kitchen was not an easy, breezy place. It was stuffy and warm, especially with so many bodies packed inside.

Rodney moved in for a grateful hug.

I let him wrap his arms around me and regretted it immediately. Rodney was a good man. I'd always thought so. But he also had a bit of a thing for me and he tended to get a little too comfortable too quickly when it came to things like this. I'd told him on rare occasions that things between us were strictly professional, and he'd agreed every time, but this hug lasted a little too long to be deemed professional.

I pulled away and patted him on the shoulder the way two buddies might when they met each other at a bar for beers and a game. I was about to excuse myself when my phone started buzzing in my back pocket. It made for an easy escape, so I ducked out of his office and slipped out of the emergency exit into the parking lot behind the soup kitchen.

There was a cool breeze blowing that chased away the lingering heat in my cheeks as I raised the phone to my ear. "Hello, this is Kayla Goodfellow for Good Fellow's."

My best friend Lisa's voice filled the line. "Kayla, do you ever check your call display?"

I giggled and pressed the back of my hand to my head to wipe away sweat. "Not all the time, no. Sorry. What's up?"

"Well," Lisa said slowly.

I could tell she was building anticipation. "Yes?"

"I have a proposition for you. It would involve us working together. I know you're super busy but I think this would be a good thing for all parties involved. Are you interested?"

"Am I interested? Of course, I'm interested in working with my

13

best friend! Give me details."

"Hear me out before you go all in, okay? We'd also be working with Lukas."

Lukas. Lisa's older brother, the billionaire extraordinaire, tech success CEO, cover of magazines, drop dead gorgeous Lukas?

I swallowed. "Oh?"

CHAPTER 3

LUKAS

Polly, my assistant, nodded along to what I was telling her about the new software development launch. Her lips were pursed thoughtfully, and her eyes were slightly narrowed behind her dark-framed glasses, and she held a red-painted finger to her dimpled chin.

I paused a beat.

Polly cocked her head to the side. Her blonde curls bounced just above her shoulders. "Is that all, Mr. Holt?"

I sighed. "The next time I'm boring you, feel free to tell me you're not interested, Polly. I never intend to bore you to death with my blabber, but I've been told I'm not good at picking up social cues that someone has lost interest in the subject matter."

Polly giggled. "I'm not bored with you, sir. Or your subject matter. I just… well, I don't really understand much of what you're talking about when it comes to software and programming and coding."

"Right."

She put a hand on my arm. "I swear I was listening."

Someone knocked softly on my office door. Polly released my arm and took a step back to stand beside my desk rather than behind it. She wrapped her arms around herself, and one of the buttons at the top of her silky pink blouse threatened to pop open as her breasts pulled at the fabric.

"Come in," I said as I lowered myself into my chair.

Lisa opened my office door and stepped in. She smiled at Polly.

"Morning, Polly," Lisa said cheerfully. Her attention turned to me and she put her weight on her right foot while she waited expectantly.

Clearly, I'd forgotten something. "Yes?"

"We're meeting the non-profit director I told you about in the conference room in five minutes."

Polly excused herself and closed the door behind her, leaving me and Lisa alone in my office.

"I hadn't forgotten," I lied smoothly.

"Sure you hadn't." Lisa paced behind my desk to stand in front of the windows. She looked down at the street before turning her gaze up to the sky. "You have the best views in Seattle, big brother. I'll give you that."

"I paid a hefty price for them."

"Of your own volition. Nobody forced you to."

"Never said they did."

Lisa smiled at me over her shoulder. "I have to admit, your office is the nicest one I've ever been in. The only thing I'd remove to make it better is you."

I chuckled. "Very funny."

"I wasn't joking."

A lot of thought and consideration had gone into appointing this office of mine. To say I was a workaholic would be a gross understatement. I lived and breathed this job, so I spent more time within these four walls than I did anywhere else. On some occasions, I'd worked straight through the night writing my own code.

On the far wall to the right were all my coding computers. Six monitors, three on the bottom and three on top, all concaved inward around a sleek, glass-top black desk. Little lights flashed and blinked on computer towers and other devices tucked neatly into the storage unit under the lowest row of monitors.

The rest of the office was minimalist and clean. The floors were glossy, light gray marble. My business desk sat in the middle of the room upon a dark blue carpet. The desk was mahogany and had two matching guest chairs on the opposite side from where I sat. Three ceiling lights hung low over the desk, providing ambient light at night that wasn't too bright and wasn't too dark. The walls were white, though most of them couldn't be seen because they were hidden behind floor-to-ceiling bookcases or filing cabinets.

By the window was a lounge area with four black leather arm chairs, a liquor cart, and a coffee table. I spent the least amount of time there.

"How much did it cost just to decorate this room?" Lisa asked as she strolled past the only piece of art in the room: a canvas oil painting of the south of France, a place I'd been to several years ago and wanted to revisit when the time was right. I'd purchased the piece from a local artist.

"That's a bit personal, isn't it?" I was playing hard to get but I liked the praise about my office. It represented how far I'd come and the man I'd grown into after all my success. I was no longer the broke, shattered, sad teenager I used to be. I was a builder of empires—a wealthy scion of Seattle.

My sister turned to me with a smirk that looked much like my own. "Oh please, Lukas. You're never bashful about discussing how much something cost you. You have six cars that all cost well over two hundred and fifty thousand dollars a piece. I know so because you told me."

"Well, it didn't cost that much," I told her.

Lisa rolled her eyes, shook her head, and went to the office door. "Come on. Let's go to the conference room. We don't want to be late for our own meeting."

I followed my sister out of my office and down the hall to the conference room. It was prepped for our meeting, most likely by Polly, who'd laid out three settings on the long white marble table. Each person would have a notepad, two pens, and a cup of water. A coffee machine in the corner of the room was midway through brewing a pot and the whole room smelled like coffee beans.

Lisa took a seat in front of one of the notepads and crossed one leg over the other. Her foot bounced and she fidgeted with one of the pens.

She was excited.

Why?

Five minutes passed, followed by five more, and irritation welled up inside me. I did not have time to wait around for people to squeeze me into their timetable. That wasn't how things worked. I fit people into my schedule, not the other way around.

I sighed.

Lisa, sensing my withering patience, perked up. "Did I tell you my mom got a new job?"

I ran a finger along my jaw. "No, you didn't. Where's she working now?"

"A dog grooming company. For the life of me, I can't remember what it's called but they're the highest rated luxury grooming company in Seattle. Mom's over the moon, of course. You remember how much she loves dogs and anything with whiskers really."

"I remember."

"Well, now she's practically drowning in them. Since she and I bought that duplex and moved in, she's adopted two. Can you believe it? How many years did she pine over getting a mutt when we lived in those shithole apartments?"

"Twenty, give or take."

"And now she finally has two." Lisa smiled. I could tell she was brimming with happiness for her mother. "Bruno and Gauge. I think I have pictures."

"Great," I said dryly. I loved my sister but I had no interest in looking at pictures of her mother's rescue dogs. Nevertheless, I sat and waited while she pulled out her phone and scrolled through pictures.

"Here they are," Lisa said, leaning forward to hold the phone out to me.

I took it and flipped through pictures of two dogs. One was gray and wiry with longer white fur around his snout. The other had short coppery fur and folded ears. "Cute," I said, assuming this was the word Lisa was fishing for.

"Aren't they? She just adores them and they bring her so much joy. I hear her let them outside every morning next door. They get her up early and keep her company in the evenings when I can't. It's a best-case scenario really. And the duplex has enough room for her to be comfortable, too."

Guilt nudged at my insides.

I could have bought Lisa and her mother an expensive property years ago, but I'd been too focused on myself and my own mother. I'd been so consumed by my mother's worsening health that I hadn't had much energy to share in Lisa's excitement as her consultant firm grew and she finally had enough money to buy the duplex for herself and her mother. They lived as neighbors, an ideal situation for my sister who cherished her mother more than anyone else, but they could have had a nicer place if I'd been in the frame of mind to help them out.

Lisa put her phone in her handbag. "How has your mother been, by the way? I tried to go visit her last week but they wouldn't let me in."

"She's fine." I glanced at my watch. The non-profit director was over ten minutes late. "She has her good days and bad days. Listen, I'm going to need to reschedule this meeting. I don't have time to sit around and wait for—"

The conference door swung open.

A young woman with long, wavy, dark brown hair shuffled in. Her arms were overflowing with paperwork and folders. Her purse had a long strap on it, and as she closed the door with her hip, it slid right off her shoulder to land in the groove of her elbow. The purse jerked her arm down, and in that hand, she held a travel mug of coffee. A bit sloshed out of the open mouth opening and spilled onto her light gray long-sleeved shirt.

"Shoot," she hissed, scowling at the stain. Her dark features pinched together and she finally glanced up.

My jaw nearly hit the floor when I got a look at her face.

"Kayla?" I breathed.

Kayla Goodfellow, my sister's long time best friend and the girl who'd grown up three apartment buildings down from us, grinned at me.

"Lukas Holt," she said, her dark brown eyes practically glittering as the coffee stain soaked into her shirt. "You're all grown up."

I looked her over. I couldn't help myself. Kayla had always been a short, wiry little kid. She'd been the kind of girl who wanted to keep up with the boys. She had the athletic ability to do so, but her legs had always been too short to keep up with me and my friends. She was still short as hell, but today, she wore a pair of black heels that gave her a few extra inches.

Kayla shuffled into the conference room and began putting her things down on the table. "I'm so sorry I'm late. I had to come directly from a project and I didn't have time to change. If I had, believe me. I'd have put more effort into what I was wearing."

Lisa stood up and hugged her best friend. "I think you look great."

I also thought she looked great, but I didn't say a damn thing. She wore a pair of black skinny jeans with her heels and gray long sleeve. A black blazer was draped over the top of her purse, which she set on the floor as she took a seat across from my sister and me.

"What was the project you were at?" Lisa asked.

Kayla ran her fingers through her hair and shook it. A little bit of what I thought might have been dust puffed out of her locks. "My team and I were helping a family clean up and repair their property. If they hadn't gotten it done, they were facing some serious fines but there was no way they could manage it on their own. I had to hang around and wait for the inspector to show up, and of course, he was late, so by default, so am I. Again, I'm sorry. I know it's not a very professional impression."

Lisa waved off Kayla's concern. "Don't sweat it. We're all practically family here. Right, Lukas?"

I'd been unable to take my eyes off Kayla since she walked in. I felt suddenly embarrassed by my lack of control. "Let's get started," I said gruffly. "I have other appointments today."

I tried to pretend not to notice the way Kayla's cheeks turned bright pink.

Lisa shot me a dark look, but I ignored her.

CHAPTER 4

KAYLA

Lisa took a sip of water before continuing to explain to me how badly the press and the public had begun to see her brother.

I listened intently, but it was impossible not to keep shooting looks at her standoffish older brother. He'd always been a serious guy, even when he was just a kid, but there was something about him now that made him intimidating, not just serious. He had an air about him. He was accomplished, successful, and obscenely wealthy. Even though he'd never been easygoing to begin with, he now seemed removed and unapproachable. Distant.

But still dashingly handsome.

Lukas Holt had dark blond hair that wasn't long or short. He wore it slicked back, and the style was somehow careless and slick all at once, like he'd woken up and ran his fingers through it and it fell neatly into place. His eyes were blue and as sharp as his jawline. He was clean shaven and I could see the little scar on his chin that he'd gotten when he was a teenager after a fight in school.

Lisa and I had walked home with him that afternoon and cleaned him up, hoping we'd do a good job before his mother got home. He hadn't wanted her to know he'd been fighting. Of course, she saw right through all of us. As soon as she got home from work, she'd spotted the gash, scolded him for not calling her, and kicked me and Lisa out so she could clean him up properly.

The scar was nothing but a pale shimmer of skin now.

Lukas wore a perfectly fitted dark gray suit. Underneath was a crisp white shirt and a tie the same color as the suit. The suit accented his broad shoulders and tapered waist, and there was no concealing that he was fit as hell. The tall, lanky teenager I remembered was gone. He'd been replaced by a rippling god of a man and it was making it difficult for me to stay focused on the task at hand.

"So, are you going to tell us or what?" Lisa asked.

I blinked at her. *Shit. What did she just say? Tell them about what?*

"Um," I stammered, feeling and probably looking like a total ass. "I uh…"

Lisa giggled. "I know you're not used to big fancy conference rooms like this. Just forget about where we are. It's just me and Lukas. No need to give a full-blown presentation. Just tell him about your non-profit."

"Oh, okay." I could do that in my sleep. I licked my lips, cleared my throat, and sat up straight. "My non-profit is called Good Fellow's."

"Very aptly named," Lisa said pointedly to Lukas, who didn't bat a lash at her comment.

"Good Fellow's focuses its work at the micro-level individuals that make up our neighborhood. We deal in real impact at the community level all over Seattle. Over the last two years, I've set up a network of organizations that communicate to let each other know their needs and resources, creating a spider web of sorts so that everyone has a support system. Not only does it make it easier to find and fill the needs of the people we're trying to help, but it broadens our donations pool as well. We've seen an increase in donations over the last eighteen months since we got the network up and running, and in turn, the number of people we've been able to help has increased as well. I have some printouts with me if you want to take a look." She paused to flip through the mess of paperwork she'd brought with her.

"I don't need to see numbers," Lukas said evenly. "Lisa says if I team up with your non-profit, the public won't see me as the devil anymore."

Lisa rolled her eyes. "He's being dramatic. I never said they saw you as the devil. I just said you're falling out of favor and people kind of think you're a selfish asshole. I presented it professionally, of course," she added with a wink in my direction.

I laughed nervously. "Well, there is no downside to allying with Good Fellow's. We're the team on the ground and we never turn down help. Having someone with your access to resources would be incredibly beneficial to us."

Lukas ran a finger along his chin and rubbed absently at the scar there. I tried my best not to stare at his jaw muscles as they flexed while he thought things over. "Where would we start?"

Lisa took over. "I was thinking we start with a bang. Something to really get the ball rolling and announce to the city that you're getting involved with charity."

"Something like what?" I asked.

"A charity event," Lisa said confidently. "Something big enough where the media will show up and Lukas will get a lot of press. With any luck, this will start turning things around in terms of public opinion and favor, and you'll start to see the financial benefits of your software upgrades."

Lukas looked up at me. "Thoughts?"

"I'm on board," I said. "But if you really want to do this thing right, you should commit to a campaign that goes beyond a basic fundraiser."

He arched an eyebrow.

"Don't get me wrong," I added hurriedly. "We can always use the money, and a fundraiser of this proportion is sure to get us a pretty penny in donations, but this is what most wealthy people do. They dip their toe in, raise a bunch of money just by showing up and smiling at the cameras, and then they feel like they've done their part. No offense, but that's not what we really need."

Lukas's eyebrow was still arched. He turned to his sister.

"Don't look at me," Lisa said. "I'm with her. It's easy to show up for the short haul and smile for the media. But we need to go deeper. We need to make real change and we need to be able to track it. Otherwise, what's the point?"

Lukas sighed. "Fine. What do you suggest then, Kayla?"

My name on his lips almost made me shiver. "We need to go a step further. I can help you learn and understand the plight of the people we're trying to help. After that, you might be able to see other means of assistance beyond just donations."

"I understand their plight already," he said.

"Well, sure, to a certain extent—"

He cut me off. "To a certain extent? Have you forgotten how we grew up? We lived and breathed that plight. I have no interest in reliving that."

Lisa frowned at her brother. "Nobody is saying you don't understand. But times are different, and so are people's struggles. I think all Kayla is saying is that it might be useful to start at the ground floor."

Lukas prickled. "You're the one who suggested this whole thing, Lisa. Maybe I should just leave you in charge. What do you think?"

Lisa shot me an apologetic look. I glanced down at my hands and tried to be invisible. This was not the Lukas I remembered. He had a short fuse, and he was defensive. Were there struggles in his past I'd never even known about that made him like this?

"I think you're being rude," Lisa said stiffly.

I reached for my handbag. "I should go."

"No, stay," Lisa said.

"I'll go," Lukas said, getting smoothly to his feet. He tugged at the sleeves of his suit jacket and looked down at me, his posture stiff and proud. "It was nice seeing you, Kayla."

I couldn't tell if he was lying or not. "It was nice to see you, too."

Hell, I couldn't tell if *I* was lying or not. *Nice* hardly seemed like the right word. Nothing about this felt *nice*. It felt tense and uncomfortable and I couldn't recall the last time I'd been so out of my comfort zone.

Lukas strode to the door and stepped out into the hall. I watched him through the glass wall until he disappeared around the corner, after which I let myself deflate like a popped balloon.

"I'm so sorry," Lisa said, reaching across the table toward me. "He's not always like this. I don't know what his deal is lately. I should've prepared you for—well, whatever this was."

"It's okay. You have nothing to apologize for."

"From where I'm sitting, it feels like I do. He can be a total ass sometimes."

I shrugged and collected my papers. "Maybe I caught him on a bad day?"

Lisa shook her head sadly. "I appreciate your optimism, but most days are like this now."

I didn't ask any questions. None of this was my business and I doubted Lukas would appreciate me poking my nose into his affairs, trying to riddle out why he'd turned into such a Scrooge.

If he wanted to work together, I'd still be open to it. I wasn't one for turning down much-needed money and assistance, especially from someone as influential and powerful as Lukas Holt. But if he was going to string me along and be a jerk the whole time?

Maybe I'd just have to find someone else to partner with.

Lisa got to her feet and smoothed out her high-waisted skirt. "You've had a long day. How do you feel about happy hour? There's a cute place around the block with killer Moscow Mules and chicken Thai bites."

I grinned. "You know I can never say no to Thai bites."

CHAPTER 5

LUKAS

I loosened my tie as I strode to my car in the underground parking lot beneath my high rise office tower. Seeing Kayla had gotten to me more than I could have imagined possible and I couldn't get far away fast enough. Lisa would be chomping on my heels if she spotted me in the office for blowing her friend off and getting pissy and I was in no mood to entertain that.

So I hopped in my Lykan Hypersport and revved the engine. I hadn't corrected my sister on her comment about my six cars worth two hundred and fifty thousand a piece when she took a jab at me. It hardly seemed right to point out that this bad boy had a price tag of three and a quarter million dollars.

And she was worth every penny.

I pulled out of the underground parking and sped through the historic district. I ignored the dirty looks from strangers on the street as I slid from fourth into fifth gear. The engine hummed and the steering wheel thrummed in my grasp. The power of the car dared me to open it up but I resisted. I wove through traffic, earned myself more than a handful of middle fingers, and sped out of the congested down-town core in favor of the long winding road along the Sound. A breeze blew in off the ocean that put white caps on the small waves and filled the air with salt. It was cold out but I cracked a window anyway. It rushed around in the car and filled my senses. Slowly, the heat that had tried to swallow me up in the conference room began to ebb away.

Kayla Goodfellow had sure grown into herself.

She was a beautiful young woman now. She'd done well for herself, too. She wasn't sitting tall and proud in an office tower like mine but she was passionate about her work. It showed in her eyes when she spoke about it.

And you shit all over her and stormed out like a child.

I grimaced at the thought.

I hadn't meant to be rude to Kayla, but the conversation had called up memories I never wished to return to.

There was a reason I hadn't opened that box.

But seeing her brought all those feelings of inferiority and anger right back to the surface, along with other feelings like lust and desire.

I had no right feeling those things toward my sister's best friend. Kayla was off limits.

But damn, did she look good in those jeans.

I cracked the windows a little more. Cold air hummed inside the car.

Kayla had always been pretty back in high school, but at the time, I'd been too focused on teaching myself how to code to really notice. Besides, she wasn't around often since Lisa and I never lived together. Sometimes, we'd all end up outside with the neighborhood kids. We'd play kick the can or other games before being called back inside by our mothers.

Speaking of mothers, I realized that I'd been subconsciously driving toward my mother's care home.

I hated the term "care home." What I hated more was the fact that my mother had to be in one. She wasn't an elderly woman, not even close. She'd just celebrated her fifty-fourth birthday two months ago and she'd stayed with me for two nights to get out and have a bit of normalcy. I wasn't sure which one of us had needed it more, her or me.

It hadn't gone how I'd hoped.

Leading up to that weekend, I'd been optimistic that things would go smoothly. I'd even entertained the idea that if I could handle it and her condition remained steady that I might be able to take her out of the care-home facility and have her stay with me every second weekend or so. In an ideal world, she'd live with me full time, but my work demanded that I was in the office five days a week minimum. Every specialist I'd seen when my mother's health started to decline told me I wouldn't be able to keep up with the level of care she needed anyway—even if I stayed home full time.

She needed the round-the-clock care the care home provided.

My grip on the wheel tightened as I remembered the day my mother was in her car accident. It had been a cool crisp fall day like this. It had rained that morning and the roads were slick with oil. She'd been on her way to meet a friend for brunch. Cindy, who'd practically been an aunt to me growing up, had called me when my mother was twenty minutes late for their brunch date.

It was unlike my mother to be late. She always used to tell me that there was nothing more disrespectful than showing up tardy. She used to get worked up when we were running behind leaving the house, whether it was for school, a dentist appointment, or Sunday breakfast a few blocks away with Lisa and her mother.

So when Cindy told me my mother wasn't there, I knew in my gut something was wrong.

I'd called my mother's cell phone seventeen times before I got a call from the UW Medical Center. They'd told me my mother had been in an accident and was in emergency surgery.

Nothing had ever made me feel like that before. The nurse on the phone asked if I could come in and suggested I get someone to drive me. She told me where to go once I got to the hospital, but everything after the words "emergency surgery" was lost on me. My brain went fuzzy, my ears filled with white noise, and a pit the size of my fist started to grow in my stomach.

There was nobody to drive me.

I'd gotten in my car and driven myself to the hospital. It was a miracle I didn't get a speeding ticket on the way.

My mother was in surgery for four hours, during which I sat outside the operation room, rooted to the same chair the entire time, terrified to leave in case something happened. In case she needed me. Lisa, who hadn't heard about the accident until it was somehow leaked to the press, showed up during that final hour of surgery and sat with me.

She'd been my rock that autumn afternoon. She held my hand, promised me that everything would be okay, and stayed there until the surgeon came out and told us the surgery had been a success. No words could explain the relief I felt as the surgeon led Lisa and me to my mother's recovery room. She didn't wake for a couple of days, but that was all strategy on the doctor's part. My mother suffered a massive traumatic brain injury that day. I was warned that she might have memory loss when she woke and the doctors wouldn't know the extent of the damage until that time.

I stayed by my mother's bedside and prayed to a god I wasn't sure I believed in that she would know my face when she opened her eyes.

Eighty-six hours after the surgery, I'd woken to my mother's voice calling my name and asking for a cup of water.

She'd remembered me.

Her prognosis hadn't been good, and recovery wasn't easy. But my mother was a headstrong woman. She worked hard to rehabilitate herself. I brought her home with me to live in my mansion while she worked on her health. Professionals came by every day: physiotherapists, chiropractors, motor-function specialists, therapists, and her friends. Everyone served a role in her recovery, and I lived and breathed for my mother's health for twenty-four months until she was independent again.

Then one morning when I came down to make coffee, I'd startled my mother in the kitchen. She'd screamed bloody murder when she turned around and saw me smiling at her and wishing her good morning. She'd rushed to the other side of the kitchen to put the island between us like she thought I was going to hurt her.

She had no idea who I was.

Her own son was a stranger to her. A threat.

If I thought too long about that morning, the feeling of devastation I'd felt in that moment would come back in full force.

I'd made appointments with the best doctors as her memory lapses grew more frequent. After several consultations and tests, a doctor pulled me into his office and told me my mother had a degenerative issue in her brain that would result in fast-moving dementia. There were suspicions it was accelerated or caused by the brain injury some years before but there was no way to prove such a theory.

I paid for the best specialists to save my mother's mind. Nothing worked.

So now she was in a home.

I parked my Lykan in the parking lot outside the care facility. It was an impressive building with perfectly manicured grounds and old English architecture. Several people were wandering the grounds as I made my way up the path to the front doors, through which was a lobby with dark green velvet sofas and a reception counter with a fish tank built underneath it.

I approached the counter and the middle-aged woman behind it. She rose from her seat with a smile. "Mr. Holt, what a nice surprise to see you in the middle of the week like this."

"I had some free time."

"Well, I'm sure Ally will be delighted to see you. She's been stable this week. She even joined some of the others for some lawn bowling when we had that beautiful sunny day. When was that? Sunday? Monday. Gosh, I can't recall. But she had a glorious time. You should have seen her. I might have some pictures somewhere around here if you—"

"Is she in her room?" I asked.

"Yes, yes, go on in. Pictures can wait."

I hoped my mother was having a lucid afternoon as I made my way down the hallway to her room. She had a corner unit, something I'd insisted on, with her own private little patio that overlooked the gardens. She liked to sit outside and listen to the birds with her morning cup of coffee.

I knocked on her door before opening it a crack. "Mom? It's me, Lukas."

Music was playing inside, a familiar John Denver tune. I opened the door the rest of the way and found my mother sitting in her rocking chair by the window. She blinked at me.

"How are you, Mom?" I asked as I moved into the room. It smelled like fresh laundry and egg salad. I spotted a plate with breadcrumbs on it sitting on the windowsill beside her. "Did you have an egg-salad sandwich for lunch?"

My mother nodded. She still hadn't placed me in her memory but I was used to it taking a minute or two for her mind to catch up.

Instead of telling her who I was, I waited for it to click. Doctors and nurses alike had told me over the last couple of years that this was the best approach. The worst thing to do was to make a person with dementia feel like they were forgetting something. It caused embarrassment, shame, and sometimes anger.

I never wanted to cause my mother any of those feelings even if it meant some visits were spent with her never piecing together that I was her son.

"Too bad I didn't get here earlier," I said as I sat down in the other chair across from hers. "I could have gone for a sandwich. What song are you listening to?"

My mother's blue gaze slid to the radio behind her right shoulder. "It's John Denver."

"You did always love John Denver, didn't you? I remember waking up to it on Sunday mornings. You'd be in the kitchen making breakfast for me and Lisa and her mother. They say hello by the way."

My mother's expression shifted. Her eyes brightened, and she smiled. "*Lukas*," she said warmly.

I smiled. "Hi, Mom."

CHAPTER 6

KAYLA

Our waitress for Happy Hour was a young girl who seemed barely old enough to legally serve us alcohol. She was a bubbly and somewhat scatterbrained person and it took her more trips than it should have to bring us our drinks and our shared appetizer platter of Thai chicken bites, pita crisps and hummus, and vegetables with ranch. Nevertheless, we eventually sat with the full spread before us, sipping our drinks on the enclosed and heated glass patio.

The mules had a powerful ginger kick. "These are fantastic," I said, licking my lips. "Really strong but delicious."

Lisa nodded and smothered a pita crisp in hummus. She popped it in her mouth and chewed with one hand in front of her mouth. Her nails were dark burgundy and glossy. I suspected she'd just had them done. "I know, right? I discovered this place recently. I've been trying to get Lukas to come with me one of these nights but he's always so busy with work."

Lukas seemed more than just busy with work. From where I'd been sitting during our meeting a short hour ago, it seemed like he *was* his work.

"I'm sorry again about him," Lisa said. She dabbed her lips with her napkin and slumped in her chair to sip her drink. "I really didn't expect him to act that way, especially in front of you. I thought a familiar face might..." She sighed. "I don't know what I thought."

"Stop apologizing, Lisa. I mean it. You have nothing to be sorry about."

Lisa fidgeted with her thumbs and tapped them against the side of the copper cup in her hands. "I can't help it. The jackass embarrassed me."

"What? In front of me? Come on, Lisa. Don't be silly."

"He should know better than to treat one of my friends like that."

I shrugged. "I think it's probably better that he treated me like that than a stranger, don't you?"

Lisa peered up at me. "Stop giving him the benefit of the doubt. He doesn't deserve it."

"You're right."

"That's better." She sat up a little straighter and gave me an assertive nod. "I think I'm just disappointed. He actually listened to me the other day when I finally had time to sit down with him and talk about all this stuff. His image in the public eye isn't good, Kayla. If he's not careful, he's going to become so disliked that he won't be able to go anywhere without people taking pictures of him and shouting at him. My brother can talk a big game but I know that would be hard on him."

"It would be hard on anyone."

"Part of me wonders if he deserves it."

That seemed harsh. Sure, Lukas had been an ass this afternoon, but did that mean he deserved for the whole public to look scornfully at him? I didn't think so. "I think he deserves a chance to do better."

Lisa chewed the inside of her cheek. "He's been hoarding all of his wealth since his software company went public. I don't think he's given a dime to any charities."

"Just because people have money doesn't mean they're obligated to give it away," I said softly. "Even if it is for the greater good. Humanity is..." I trailed off and took three gulps of my mule. "Humanity is flawed." That seemed like the best word to use. As someone who saw the seedy underbelly of this city more than most, I could attest that there were more accurate words than *flawed*.

Evil was one that came to mind. Along with *cruel, vile, narcissistic,* and *ignorant*.

But there were other words, too. *Inspiring, driven, courageous, determined,* and *good*. Not every person could be painted with the same brush.

"Well, my brother has more than his fair share of flaws. That's for damn sure." Lisa set her copper cup down on the table and went in for another pita crisp. "If he wants to keep his company's image positive, he's going to have to make some changes. He's part of Big Tech and the backlash against techies like him making millions upon millions of dollars is insane. They're driving up rents and making a killing without lifting a finger to make the world better. Tech CEOs like Lukas are the new media villains. I really don't want my brother to be lumped into all that. His reputation may never recover."

I felt bad for my friend. It was obvious that she was agonizing over this. "These are Lukas' decisions, Lisa. We can't make them for him."

"We just have to convince him to be charitable," Lisa said earnestly. "For his own good."

I licked my lips. In my experience, convincing someone to do something for their own good never went well. At least, it never went the way it was supposed to.

"I'm not in the business of pressuring people for donations," I said evenly. "Even if said people have billions of dollars and plenty to give away."

Lisa shook her head and wiped her salty fingers on her napkin so she could reach across the table and take my hand in hers. "It's not like that. You'd be doing Lukas a favor. Trust me."

"I don't know."

Lisa released my hand and leaned back in her chair. "All he cares about is his business and making more billions for his bank account. He doesn't date, doesn't have hobbies, doesn't do anything besides work. Oh, and taking care of his mother, of course."

His mother, Ally.

I'd learned about her car accident a couple of weeks after it happened. Lukas had sworn Lisa to secrecy and asked her not to tell anyone so he could handle things privately. He'd been that way since he was just a boy.

I'd also learned about the early onset dementia that was eating away at her mind. Lisa had told me in confidence a few years ago when things started to get really bad.

I couldn't imagine how difficult it would be to face the truth that your mother would forget who you were one day. The thought made my throat feel tight and that was all it was. A thought.

"He just needs to realize there's a whole other world out there," Lisa continued. "All he's doing by building this wall of money is isolating himself from people who care about him. There are worse things than poverty and I'm genuinely worried that this fear of his is costing him more than he realizes."

I popped a Thai bite and some crispy noodles in my mouth and chewed.

Lisa kept talking. "Maybe if we can get him involved in something that makes him focus on other people's lives and not his own, he'll be able to see that, too. He just needs a push, you know?"

I nodded, swallowed, and went back in for another piece.

I could see where Lisa was coming from. However, I had concerns of my own.

Lisa could be a forceful person. On more than one occasion, she'd pushed things too far and I could see the beginnings of one of those situations forming in an invisible thought bubble above her head.

"What did you have in mind exactly?" I asked.

Lisa pulled her chair up closer to the table and smiled. "I was waiting for you to ask me that."

Here we go.

Lisa gripped the edges of the table. "I have a plan that I think will motivate Lukas to see things my way. I've already made contact with a journalist who often writes about CEOs and social-justice issues. I'm in the works of setting up an interview between her and Lukas. A series of interviews actually. My hope is that these interviews will form a sort of blueprint of how a tech CEO can become a philanthropist. I'll document Lukas' first forays into philanthropy, and in the process, we'll humanize him and show the world, or at least Seattle, how good of a guy he is beneath all the ones, zeroes, and techy code."

I scratched my chin. "It sounds like it would make a good article. Is Lukas on board with the idea?"

Lisa winked. "That's what you're here for. To hook him into giving."

I grimaced. "No pressure."

"Once he gets the charity bug, he's bound to open up. You just have to find a way to make it interesting. That's all."

"Interesting?"

"Yeah, you know. Something to hook him and draw him in. Maybe a way to distract him from the fact that he's doing charity."

I frowned. "I don't know, Lisa. Charity work to me is interesting and fun. But I don't know if I can swing it to be that appealing to a billionaire."

"I have confidence in you. You're a professional and so is he. I'm sure you'll find common ground sooner than you'd expect. Besides, you grew up with Lukas. You know what he's like. How he thinks. If anyone can convince him to make a change for the better, it's you. I'm sure of it."

I appreciated my friend's confidence in me. I truly did. But I couldn't help but feel that she was overestimating my skills as well as her brother's willingness to try something new.

The Lukas I used to know was not the same man I'd sat across from in that conference room. That man was someone else. Someone hollow and materialistic. Lukas had always been a hard worker, sure, but a selfish or greedy one? No. He hadn't been either of those things.

The task before me was daunting. Part of me wished I'd never agreed to help out with this. I didn't like to mix work and personal life for a reason. Things like this easily became unnecessarily complicated.

What if I failed? What if I couldn't get Lukas to step up the way his sister needed him to?

Would she blame me? Would he resent me for pushing too hard? Would his image in the public eye worsen if he dipped his toes in the pool of charity and then got cold feet and bailed before any real progress was made?

The stakes were high.

"Should we order more mules?" Lisa asked, nodding at our empty copper cups.

I had an early start in the morning and should have said no, but my nerves were getting the best of me, and another drink sounded like the perfect way to ease the swells of anxiety in my belly.

I nodded. "Sounds like a good idea to me. Good luck flagging that waitress down, though."

Lisa twisted around in her chair. "She's gotta be around here somewhere."

While Lisa scoured the restaurant for our server, my mind wandered back to Lukas in his dashing suit and tie. His cool stare was burned into my memory and I began to wonder what the best way to get through to him would be.

Maybe all he needed was a gentle touch. Maybe being told what to do and how everything he was doing was wrong wasn't the way to go. Maybe he just needed someone to take his hand and show him how to be softer. How to care.

That would be my game plan. Kindness first, action second. It worked in my day job. There was no reason to think it wouldn't work for Lukas, too.

CHAPTER 7

LUKAS

I'd had a headache since I got up that morning. Perhaps I'd indulged in one too many glasses of whiskey upon getting home after visiting my mother yesterday. Or perhaps it was just the usual stress of daily life catching up with me. Two coffees, aspirin, four glasses of water, and a hearty breakfast hadn't helped.

The intercom on the old-school phone on my desk buzzed. A little green light blinked and my assistant's voice filled the speaker.

"Mr. Holt? There's someone here to see you. She says she has an appointment."

I held the button down beneath the green light. "What's her name?"

"Rebecca Mills, sir."

That name didn't ring any bells. "I don't know who that is."

"She has an appointment, sir. It looks like Lisa set it up. She's here with her and—"

My sister's voice filled the line. "Let us in, Lukas. Do you ever check your agenda? What's the point in making appointments if the guy you're making an appointment with never refers to his schedule?"

My headache doubled in intensity. *This is just what I need this morning.*

"We're coming in, Lukas," Lisa said cheerfully.

Well, that was that. I closed my laptop, leaned back in my seat, and listened for the telltale sound of high-heeled shoes coming down the hallway toward me. I didn't have to wait long to hear them. Maybe twenty seconds tops.

Another ten seconds later and my office door swung open. Lisa walked in wearing a lavender pant suit that I might have told her looked pretty on her if she hadn't already gotten on my nerves this morning. Her hair was shiny and nicely styled, her lips were pink, and she flashed me an excited smile as she stood back so another woman could enter the room.

"Lukas," Lisa said brightly. "This is Rebecca Mills."

I got smoothly to my feet and did up my suit jacket. Moving out from behind my desk, I extended my hand to shake Rebecca's. She had a firm, confident grip, dark and calculating eyes, and a red smile. She was an attractive woman, but she also exuded "don't mess with me" energy. Her black hair was pulled back in a tight and severe bun. Her cheekbones were as sharp as the tips of her pointed red nails.

"It's nice to meet you, Mr. Holt," Rebecca said with a silky voice. "I appreciate you taking time out of your busy schedule to meet with me. Lisa says you're a hard man to keep company with."

I shot my sister a look. "I hope she didn't tell you too much about me."

Rebecca laughed lightly and shook her head. "No, not at all. I prefer to hold out until the interview process."

I invited her to sit down. Rebecca sat, placed her purse on the floor between her feet, and fished a notebook and pen out of the bag.

Meanwhile, Lisa came and gave me a hug. When her cheek passed my ear, she whispered to me. "Follow my lead. This is what you pay me for."

I nodded and Lisa stepped back to walk behind Rebecca's chair and sit down beside her. I took my seat behind the desk and leaned back.

Lisa smiled. "I know you've been busy Lukas, so I'll refresh your memory. Rebecca is the journalist I told you about. She won a Pulitzer for her piece on oil executives and their reactions to climate change. Quite impressive."

"Quite," I agreed.

Rebecca smiled graciously at us. "We're not here to talk about my credentials. Besides, I'm changing focus from oil and energy to tech industries. I was intrigued by your offer about the series of interviews revolving around your foray into philanthropy. I think there's a really big niche for that right now. It will garner interest. I'm sure of it. The public is craving someone they can latch onto who will restore their faith in humanity a little bit. If I'm being honest, I'm looking for that too. The world is an ever-darkening place."

My gaze slid to my sister. A series of interviews? This was the first I was hearing about a series.

How many of these interviews were scheduled? Didn't Lisa know I hardly had time for the one sit-down appointment with Rebecca? So little time, in fact, that I'd forgotten about said appointment?

I massaged my temple and willed my headache to go away. It didn't listen. "A series of interviews," I mused, trying to appear informed in front of Rebecca and accusatory in front of my sister. It was a fine line to walk, but based on the way Lisa scowled at me, I assumed she got the hint.

Before I could say more, my sister cut me off. "Yes, a series of interviews. Don't you remember when we talked about your plan to document your introduction to charitable giving with Good Fellows?"

I let my hand fall from my temple. Good Fellow's. *Kayla's* Good Fellow's?

I had agreed to no such terms.

"Good Fellow's is a great operation," Rebecca said. "I've heard nothing but positive things about it. It's small, so I suppose I haven't heard much about it at all. But I'm looking forward to changing that. What made you choose Good Fellow's?"

I blinked impassively at the journalist.

Lisa crossed one leg over the other and turned herself a little to Rebecca. "Lukas wanted to join forces with a non-profit that worked at the ground level. He had so many opportunities to choose from that it was almost overwhelming. We sifted through everything, and when we came across Good Fellow's, it became obvious that it was the place we could make the most positive change."

One of Rebecca's dark eyebrows arched as she scrawled in her notebook. Presumably, she was writing what Lisa had said on my behalf.

I studied my sister as she continued speaking.

"Lukas is excited to jump into this new journey. He's very passionate about helping people and giving back to his community. Timing has never been better. After laying a foundation for the past several years, he's ready to get centered, put on an apron, and get to work."

Put on an apron? Who did my sister take me for?

Rebecca Mills asked about ten questions, all of which my sister answered gracefully. She spoke highly of me—too highly—and by the time the forty-five minutes appointment slot expired, Rebecca seemed ready to put a pin in things. She got to her feet, smoothed out her skirt, and collected her purse from the floor. She kept her notebook clutched in one hand as I stood and leaned across the desk to shake her hand once more.

"It was very nice to meet you, Mr. Holt," Rebecca said. "I look forward to sitting down to ask you more questions and hearing answers in your own words next time."

Lisa turned bright pink beside the journalist.

"Thank you for your time," I managed to say as I kept my irritation in check.

Rebecca exited my office and I buzzed my assistant to see her out. As soon as I knew the coast was clear and Lisa and I were alone, I rounded on her.

"What the hell are you playing at, Lisa?"

My sister stepped back and her eyebrows pinched together. "What am *I* doing? I'm saving your reputation, you ungrateful brat. I knew you would never agree to the interviews if I told you ahead of time, so I did my job, Lukas. You need me. You hired me to help you. And that's what I'm doing."

I waved her off. "You're blowing this whole thing out of proportion. If you insist on philanthropy, I can have my accountant cut you a check and you can handle things. How much do you want? Five hundred thousand? Eight? A million? You tell me. Let's just get this over with."

Lisa planted her fists on her hips. "You're delusional. That's lazy. It's not going to help at all."

I rolled my eyes. "Throwing a million dollars into charity isn't going to help at all? Maybe I'm not the one who needs to check my priorities."

"If you do these interviews, you'll be on the vanguard. You'll be the tech CEO leading the charge into philanthropy. You'll be a damn trend setter, Lukas! Do you realize how much of a difference you could make in people's lives if you just—just—"

"Just *what?*"

Lisa bit her bottom lip. "Cared about something."

"I care about plenty of things."

"You care about the bottom line." Lisa took a menacing stop forward. "Tell me I'm wrong."

I stared down the length of my nose at her. My sister had always been a trifle too dramatic for my tastes. Every conversation was a battle with her.

"You need to trust me, Lukas," she said. "This is what you hired me for."

"I hired you to make improvements, not complicate things for me."

"How is asking you to do the right thing complicating things?"

I rolled my eyes. We were running in circles here. "Fine, Lisa. Fine. Let's just do whatever you think is best. Whatever will get you off my back." My head pulsed and pressure was building behind my eyes. I just wanted this conversation to be over with.

"Fine," she said coldly. "I'll set something up with Kayla. Something simple. Minimal effort because I guess that's going to be your approach to this since you won't make money off of it."

"For fuck sakes, Lisa."

"You and Kayla can have some pictures taken. Rebecca will publish

43

her article with the pictures, and a few weeks after it's published and everyone loves you, we can switch to just cutting checks to charities for the tax deduction. Am I speaking your language now?"

"Don't get sour with me."

"Sour with you?" Lisa asked incredulously. She threw her head back and laughed like she was the villain of a superhero movie. "Oh my goodness, Lukas. You're the sour one! I've been doing cartwheels for weeks trying to figure out how to help you, and now that I finally have a plan—a plan that I know without a shadow of a doubt will be effective, I might add—you're acting like all I am to you is a huge inconvenience."

I prickled. That was not entirely how I felt.

Lisa sighed and shook her head at me. "I'm sorry. I don't mean to get cross with you. This has all just been a lot of work to put into play and I feel like you're not appreciating anything I'm trying to do."

"I'm a busy man, Lisa. And I don't appreciate being ambushed."

"Well, you left me with little options."

"Even so," I grumbled. "You've done this to me several times. If you weren't my sister, I'd fire you."

"And if you weren't my brother, there are a couple of things I'd like to do to you, too."

A beat passed and Lisa smiled wryly at me.

I smiled back. "I know you have my best interests at heart, so I'll try. Okay? I'll try."

"That's all I'm asking."

"But if things go bad and it costs me, it's on your head. Do you understand?"

Lisa nodded. "I understand. All you have to do is trust me. Have I ever steered you wrong before?"

CHAPTER 8

KAYLA

My online calendar taunted me as I added in yet another commitment: the Lukas Project.

Everything related to Lukas Holt and my responsibility of changing him from a bad boy tech CEO into a compassionate philanthropist success story was noted in blue. Food drives were yellow, soup kitchen shifts were orange, Good Fellow's commitments were pink, and budgets were green. Purple was supposed to indicate leisure and social time, but there wasn't much of that on the calendar.

I sighed and considered all the blue coming up in my calendar.

I'd spent a lot of time thinking of ways to ease Lukas into what I did for a living. Somehow, I had to find a way to show him that there was more to my work than dreary homeless shelters and canned-food drives, although that was a big portion of the gig. I doubted those would be the right ways to pull him into a new lifestyle however. I needed something vibrant. Something he could sink his teeth into.

Something fun.

"I have just the thing," I muttered to myself as I reached for my mug of lukewarm green tea. I took a sip and wished it was hotter but didn't bother getting up to add more hot water to it from the kettle. My office was a modest place, probably a quarter of the size of Lukas', but it had all the fixings I needed. I had an electric kettle to make tea any time I pleased, a water cooler, a sofa, an old desk I found at a thrift shop that I'd painted white, a relatively comfortable computer chair, my laptop, and the odd decor piece I'd brought from home to spruce up the place.

My office sat nestled between a coffee shop and a hair salon. Beside the salon was a tattoo parlor, and beside the parlor was a financial services company that, in my not so humble opinion, did more harm than good by giving loans to people who they knew they'd make interest off of.

It wasn't the best part of the city, but it wasn't all that bad either, which meant I could afford the rent without having to sacrifice safety.

I flipped through my calendar to Friday and smiled. There it was, the thing that might suck Lukas into charity.

I'd arranged a partnership with a local disadvantaged youth community organization to head out into the countryside on the outskirts of Seattle where we would spend time on a generations-old family farm. The game plan was to pick apples for some fun engagement and also learn about nutrition and growing your own food. I'd been busting my butt to make sure it would be an engrossing activity for the kids and I'd been in contact with one of the daughters at the farm, who often hosted days like this with community groups, elementary schools, and daycares.

I had not disclosed to her, however, that I was bringing along a guest.

A wealthy, handsome, headstrong, abrasive guest.

With any luck, he'd find the day at the farm enjoyable or at the very least satisfactory.

I thought back to when we were younger. Even back then when there were so many less things to worry about besides being back home by dinner, he'd been the serious kid. He spent most of his time indoors on an old computer he'd put together himself. It took him six months to collect all the necessary bits and pieces, of course. Things like that didn't fall into the laps of kids like us. We had to pick them up where we could. He spent a lot of time recycling cans and bottles he'd collect from the neighborhood to save up enough money to hit pawn shops or computer repair shops to see if the owners had any spare pieces they wouldn't need. Over time, he succeeded.

After that, we all saw a lot less of Lukas. Where he used to come out and play kick the can with us, he started to become somewhat of a recluse. Lisa saw more of him than the rest of us. Sometimes, she told me how much she missed her older brother. She told me she'd try to sit with him in his room sometimes but he'd be so absorbed in the work he was doing that he'd hardly notice she was there.

Eventually, she gave him what he wanted and left him alone.

There was one thing he did enjoy though, I recalled.

My mother worked at a bakery during those days. Sometimes, she'd bring home orders that were never picked up by customers. Other times, she'd bring home products that didn't sell and were on their last day before expiring. This meant my house always had something reheating in the oven, whether it was apple pies, peach cobblers, or cinnamon cakes.

It was on one of these nights that the apartment door was open. Lisa and I were in the living room playing with our dolls on the floor while my mother hovered over the stove, checking on an apple pie in the oven. Lukas came by to pick Lisa up and walk her back to their building, and he mentioned how good it smelled in the apartment.

My mother, being the angel that she was, cut him a slice of pie, spruced it up with some whipped cream, and handed it to him on a paper plate.

I smiled at the memory of how fast Lukas had devoured that slice of pie.

He'd practically inhaled it. My mother cut him another and sent him home with one for his own mother. Whether or not she saw that piece, we would never know. My mother used to joke that he probably ate it on his way back and swore Lisa to secrecy that no such pie ever existed.

Every time an apple pie came home with my mother after a shift at the bakery after that day, she sent me to his apartment with it. Lukas' fridge was often empty, and once it became a regular thing, he always made sure to save half for his mother. His gratitude had been obvious and I'd loved to see him smile. It was something I didn't see as much as I used to.

Had I even seen Lukas smile since that meeting with him and Lisa at his office the other day?

No, I don't think I had. He'd grimaced, frowned, scowled, pursed his lips thoughtfully, and brooded. But smiled?

No such luck.

Hopefully, our day at the farm would change things. I'd arranged for a bakery close to the farm to deliver freshly baked pies in the afternoon for everyone to enjoy before the education part of the day began. In my experience, people, especially kids, were more likely to pay attention when they had full, happy bellies.

There was no doubt in my mind the same principle could be applied to Lukas.

Maybe the pies would bring up some nostalgia for him and he would remember that it wasn't all bad growing up with no money. I'd always believed there were worse things than being poor. We had our mothers. Our friends. Each other. For me, that was more than enough.

But at some point, it had stopped being enough for him.

As if my thinking about him had summoned him, I looked up when my desk fell into shadow. Lukas stood outside my office door, reading my name painted beneath the words "Good Fellow's" written on the glass in yellow and blue paint. He frowned, reached for the handle, and tugged it open. He was wearing sunglasses—designer brand, I assumed—and a white shirt with a black tie. His pants were black, his shoes properly shined, and a silver watch glistened at his wrist as he removed his sunglasses and hooked them in the collar of his shirt. His eyes scanned my office before landing on me.

His eyebrows lifted as if surprised to see me there. In my own office. Working.

I swallowed and stood up. "Hi."

Lukas turned in a slow circle, sizing things up. He slid his hands in his pockets. "Where are your employees?"

"Oh, um, I don't have any."

He stared blankly at me.

I giggled nervously and hated how insecure it sounded. I cleared my throat and lifted my chin. "I don't have employees but I have volunteers who help out when I need it. Occasionally, I'll get an intern from a local high school who is interested in pursuing non-profit studies in college but those are getting fewer and farther between."

"So," he said slowly, his voice deep and gruff, "you handle all of this yourself?"

I wasn't sure what he was referring to when he said "all of this." My office was not all that impressive. Sure, I had a white board full of scribbles and commitments on one wall and a box of overflowing paperwork on my desk, but it was messy organization, and that still counted as organization.

"Yes," I said because it seemed like the only answer available.

He whistled, and I blushed.

Why did he make me feel so uncertain? I'd known him since I was just a little girl. I shouldn't be this flustered.

"I've been doing some research," he said smoothly. "I've seen the impact your organization has made on the community. Not to mention the good will some local companies have garnered from working with you. You have an impressive reputation here. I suppose I expected to walk in and find you barking orders at people in blue T-shirts with yellow ball caps that said 'Good Fellow's' on them."

The hint of something lingered in the corner of his lips. A smile perhaps?

You're not that lucky.

"I like to keep my overhead low," I said. I waved one arm around the office in a sweeping gesture. "Hence the nonexistent staff and small office in one of the lowest-rent districts in the city." I laughed nervously and kept some other things to myself. Like the fact that my salary was also budget conscious and I only made enough to scrape by. Every dollar available went to the people I worked my ass off to help.

Lukas nodded at the chair in front of my desk. It was a faded old thing made of wood that really belonged in a woodsy backyard or something, not a professional woman's office. "Do you mind if I sit?"

"Please do." I wished I'd invited him to sit before he'd had to ask. *Stupid mistake, Kayla. Stupid.* I sat down as well and watched the man before me. His eyes continued to scan the office, lingering briefly on my collection of books stacked haphazardly on top of my paint-chipped filing cabinet.

He looked conflicted.

Was he going to fire me before even giving me a chance to prove how good I was at my job? Had he decided not to go forward with Lisa's plan? Did he truly not care about the people in this city who desperately needed help from people like him?

I chewed the inside of my cheek until it was raw and my mouth tasted like copper. "What can I do for you, Lukas?"

His dark blue gaze landed on me and I wished I could disappear. He did not smile. "I wanted to talk."

I licked my lips. "Okay."

"About my terms."

"Terms?"

He nodded, and I lost his attention again as he continued to inspect every nook and cranny of my office. For the first time in my career, I felt insecure about the old ceiling tiles, the chipped and missing baseboards, and the dull clinic-blue walls.

CHAPTER 9

LUKAS

I didn't know what I'd been expecting when I decided to drive down to Good Fellow's Headquarters, but it certainly wasn't the one-woman show I'd walked into.

Kayla was singlehandedly running an entire non-profit, and she was doing it all from this little office.

"Office" was a general word. This room didn't feel like an office to me. It felt like a mashup between a financially struggling travel agency and a teenager's bedroom. Paperwork was scattered all over the place. There were holes in the pale blue drywall. The baseboards were chipped, broken off, or missing altogether. There was absolutely no artwork to be found and the only decor I could lay eyes on were mismatched personal items that I could only assume had been picked at random off the shelves of a thrift store.

It wasn't inviting, and it wasn't a suitable place to run such a huge operation out of.

This place didn't align with my expectations of Good Fellow's because of all the research I'd done. I'd found nothing but praise about Kayla's organization. Everyone in Seattle pretty much considered her an angel but there was nothing angelic about this place.

It was a hellish, low-budget nightmare. And it smelled like cardboard and stale tea. I spied the half-drunk cup of tea on the desk and chalked that mystery under the solved category.

Kayla watched me with apprehension. Her unease was written all over her face.

She'd been in my thoughts since she showed up in my office building the other day. She was nothing like the skinny girl who followed me around like a lost puppy when we were younger. Nothing at all. Now she was all woman. She had a strong gaze, pinched lips, and expressive eyebrows. She'd never been good at hiding her thoughts or feelings and those sharp brows of hers were the culprit. She was dressed plainly today in jeans and a white T-shirt but her beauty could not be played down.

Seattle was right. She was certainly angelic.

Not only was she physically attractive, but her big heart and generosity were appealing. How early did she come to work in this dive of an office? How many hours did she put in before she concluded she'd done a hard day of work and could go home to rest? What did rest look like for Kayla?

Was she the kind of woman who liked to run a bubble bath so she could sink up to her chin in the water with a good book and a glass of red wine?

Based on the state of this office, I assumed not.

"So are you going to tell me these terms of yours or not?" Kayla prodded.

I clasped my hands together. There were things I needed to get out in the open. Like, for example, how annoyed I was that both Lisa and Kayla had railroaded me. I leaned forward. "Did you help my sister come up with her little plan with the journalist?"

Her eyebrows lifted. The corners of her lips twitched. She broke eye contact. She gave herself away without having to say a word.

"I'll take that as a yes," I said.

"Lisa already had the plan in mind when she brought me in on the project. I swear. She ran it past me and I didn't think it was a bad idea."

I grunted.

Kayla bit her bottom lip. "But in the interest of transparency, you should know that I did agree to help by planning some activities that I thought might work well for the story Rebecca is writing."

"I figured as much."

Kayla fidgeted. She straightened out the pens on her desk, lined her laptop up so that it was parallel to said pens, and pulled her hands back into her lap. "I didn't want to cross any lines, Lukas. But I'm not in a very comfortable place. I'm trying to make Lisa happy and she's the one who hired me. But I'm also trying to make sure I don't—I don't know."

"Don't what?"

She shrugged and looked at her feet. "Piss you off."

I sighed, got to my feet, and smoothed out my tie as I walked around her desk so I could lean against it and look down at her. Kayla tilted her head back and her lips parted ever so slightly.

The sight of her looking up at me like that was maddening.

"I don't want you to feel like you have to walk on eggshells around me," I said.

Kayla frowned but didn't say anything.

So I continued. "Look, I'll go along with this little game you and my sister have concocted because I don't have much of a choice right now, but don't expect me to suddenly give my fortune away. I'm not Bill Gates. I've come by my money through hard work and ambition. I'm *never* going back to the days of having nothing. Ever."

Kayla swallowed.

I crossed my arms over my chest. "So I'll go through the motions. I'll jump when you say jump. But you're wasting your time if you think this is going to end with me having some kind of change of heart. This isn't a movie. It's real life. I'm not the guy you and my sister want me to be."

Kayla's brow furrowed and her stare hardened. She got to her feet and put her hands on her hips. "I'm not forcing you to do anything, Lukas. I'm just trying to help. If you'd prefer to work with another charity, that's your prerogative. But you listen to me. If you're going to work with me, then you're going to have to check your bootstraps mentality at the door. I'm here to help the people who need it. I don't have time to convince you to be a better person, and to be perfectly honest, I think it's absolutely ludicrous that you've come all this way to try to convince me that you're not who I think you are."

"Excuse me?"

She gestured around her office with an incredulous laugh. "Can't you tell I'm just as busy as you are? I have my own priorities. You aren't one of them. Lisa wanted a favor and I have the means to help but that does not mean I have to cater to your every whim and smile and nod when you talk down to me. I won't stand for it."

This wasn't going how I expected. My temper flared as she continued to glare daggers at me. Who did she take me for?

"There's nothing wrong with the person I am," I said darkly as I stood from where I leaned against her desk.

She continued glaring up at me with her hands on her hips.

"I'm the personification of the American Dream, after all," I said.

Her lips pressed into a thin line. "Not everyone's dream is so generic, Lukas."

I scoffed. "Generic?"

"You heard me."

"There's nothing generic about what I've done with my life."

Kayla shrugged and turned her back on me.

My temper pricked like a strummed chord on a guitar as she sat down, opened her laptop, and proceeded to work.

"It sounds like you're trying to convince yourself of that fact, not me," she said simply.

"You're stubborn," I grated.

"Maybe I learned it from you. We grew up together, after all. Not that you seem to remember that. You've been treating me like—"

"Like what?"

"Like your chew toy," she said with frustration. She slapped her laptop closed and got back to her feet.

I almost grinned. So she wasn't as unbothered by me as she wanted me to think.

"You have no idea who I am now," she said boldly. Her eyes danced back and forth between mine and her hands balled into fierce little fists at her sides. "I am not someone to be taken lightly. Success comes in different shapes and sizes. Just because you have a glitzy office and a stupid shiny watch and I don't does not mean I'm not exactly where I want to be, Lukas. Do you hear me? I've worked just as hard to be here and I refuse to let you walk all over that in your stupid expensive shoes and your—"

I grabbed her chin. Kayla fell silent. Her eyes widened with surprise. Her body went rigid. But she didn't pull away.

"Stop talking," I growled before I leaned in and grazed my lips across hers. Her breath hitched in her throat and her eyes fluttered closed. Her long dark lashes cast shadows on her flushed cheeks and she smelled like vanilla.

I pulled her close and sealed my lips over hers.

Kayla drew a deep breath. Her hands raced up to the front of my shirt. She gathered it in those little hands of hers as I lifted her off the floor and set her on the desk. I stepped between her thighs and cupped the back of her neck as the kiss deepened.

As her lips parted and she let me explore her mouth, I tried to figure out how I'd gone from furious to desperate for her in a matter of seconds.

CHAPTER 10

KAYLA

My body was rigid with shock as Lukas stood between my legs and kissed me like he needed to taste me to breathe.

The boy I'd had a crush on since I was a little girl was kissing me. *Lukas Holt is kissing me.*

My thoughts whizzed around my brain at a million miles an hour. *How is this happening? Is this real? Is this a trick? Is he playing me?*

It took several seconds for me to completely give in to the kiss and start taking what I wanted. I forgot I was in my office, forgot the door was unlocked, forgot anyone could walk in at any time and catch me on my desk with a billionaire's tongue halfway down my throat.

But the kiss set my nerves on fire.

His big strong hands gripped my thighs. He squeezed and worked his way up to my hips. His fingers rested in the groove there, his thumbs pressing against the fly of my jeans. He reached up and grabbed the waistband of my pants to pull me closer to the edge of the desk. All the while, he kissed me like nobody had ever kissed me before.

He stepped in closer and I felt the press of his bulge against me. My eyes snapped open. Lukas slipped his hands under my shirt. His touch wandered up my spine and paused at my bra.

"Wait," I breathed.

His hands stilled. We broke apart and I put my hands on his chest as I bowed my head and stared at his feet.

"We can't," I managed.

My cheeks burned furiously as I slid off the desk. I put my back to him so he couldn't see my embarrassment and shook my head. "We have to keep this professional, Lukas. I have a reputation to protect."

I could hear him breathing heavily behind me. I looked over my shoulder. His stare was icy. Just seconds before, his eyes had burned with lust. Now, all I saw there was anger.

"Fine," he growled. He moved out from behind my desk, marched to the door, and wrenched it open.

"Lukas, wait."

But he was gone.

I collapsed into my chair and pressed a hand to my forehead. What the hell was that? I couldn't believe he'd just kissed me.

No, not just kissed me. He'd wanted more. *A lot* more.

Did I want more? I wasn't sure. The way my body burned for something I couldn't have suggested that perhaps I did want what he was offering.

But I couldn't take a bite of that apple.

The way he'd left spoke volumes. While the kiss was a dream come true, his departure left something to be desired. Lukas ran hot and cold. That much was obvious. I had to be careful. Otherwise, I'd end up in trouble. He wasn't the kind of guy who was looking for a relationship, and even if he were, it wouldn't be a good idea.

For one, it would be a conflict of interest of sorts since we were now working together.

Secondly, I wasn't sure Lisa would love the fact that I had the hots for her brother. She knew how attractive he was, and she knew he had a certain effect on the women in his life, but I doubted she thought I had ever looked twice at him. He was her brother, after all.

But oh man, had I looked twice. Three times. Hell, I'd looked a thousand times over. How could I not? He was perfect.

I couldn't risk anything coming between me and my best friend.

Lisa was protective over Lukas and always had been. He was her brother, and with everything they'd been through as kids, she was particular about the girls he dated—or didn't date based on our conversation over drinks last night.

Either way, I'd seen Lisa's jealousy when it came to her brother and I wanted no part of that mess.

I glanced at the time on the clock above the door. "Shit!"

I was going to be late for my volunteer shift at the soup kitchen.

I leapt out of my chair and dashed for the door. Before pushing outside, I reprimanded myself for being so scatterbrained, went back inside, grabbed my purse and keys, and turned off the lights. I locked up my laptop in my safe, made sure all my files were put away, and locked up behind me as I stepped outside. I forgot to switch the Open sign to Closed and had to unlock it again to do so.

Finally after locking up again, I rushed onto the sidewalk and looked down the street. My bus was just coming around the corner. I hurried up to the bus stop, adjusting the strap of my purse on the way, and got there just as the bus pulled up. The brakes hissed and the doors popped open. I climbed the stairs, used my pass, and found a seat near the front.

Public transit saved me even more money. A car might have been a nice luxury with all the running around the city I did but I didn't have the money to pay for insurance *and* gas. So a public transit pass it was.

The ride on the bus was quiet. If I rode at night, it got rowdier, but I used this quiet time to rest. It was a twenty-five-minute ride from my office to the soup kitchen, just enough time to recharge and get ready for the next four hours serving food and cleaning dishes.

However, rest was hard to come by. My lips still tingled from the kiss and I was pretty sure the pine scent I kept catching a whiff of was Lukas' aftershave lingering on my cheek.

I daydreamed about what might have happened between us had I not stopped him. How far would it have gone?

Would he have undone my jeans? My heart skipped a beat at the thought of him slipping a hand down the front of my pants. I imagined that expensive watch of his getting snagged on my zipper. Him tearing my panties away in frustration. My sighing breathlessly and lifting my ass off the desk so he could—

The bus came to an abrupt stop and I realized it was, in fact, *my* stop. I scrambled to my feet and got off the bus to make the mad dash down two city blocks to the soup kitchen. Luckily, there was no half-mile-long line of people outside. Instead, there were about twenty people in line. I said hello, smiled, and waved before slipping inside and making my way to the back room and kitchens so I could get a hairnet and apron.

I put my purse up in one of the volunteer lockers, tucked my phone in the back pocket of my jeans, and found a hairnet and apron. As I was tucking the last loose strands under the net, a pair of big arms encircled me from behind and gave me a big hug.

Rodney smelled like dish soap and onions.

"How've you been, Kayla?" he asked cheerfully.

I slipped out from his arms. Rodney had always been a hugger. I turned to him as I fixed the last bits of hair sticking out near my forehead. "I'm good. Busy. You know how it is. How are you?"

Rodney rubbed the back of his neck and gave me an uncommitted shrug. "Same old, same old. Every day blends into the next around here, you know? But it's good. It's good."

I could feel Rodney watching me as I tightened my apron behind my back. I wasn't sure if he tried to hide the fact that he had a crush on me or not, but if that was the case, he was doing a poor job of it. I'd had a hunch that Rodney had a crush on me since my third or fourth week volunteering at the kitchen. He was a little too comfortable with me. He liked to hug me every chance he got, and on rare occasions, he'd even taken my hand and spun me around like we were a lovesick couple dancing in the middle of a candlelit dance floor.

He was a good guy. A simple guy. The last thing I wanted to do was hurt his feelings or make it weird for us to work together. We made a good team. He was the brawn and I was the brains. We laughed easily when we were together and it was infectious. If someone was having a bad day at the kitchen, we'd sick ourselves on them and our silliness was likely to brighten even the darkest of moods.

"Hey, uh, Kayla?"

I turned to him. "Yes?"

"I was wondering if you had plans after your shift tonight. I think I'll be able to get out of here a little earlier than usual and there's this great Vietnamese restaurant that opened around the corner. Well, I don't know how great it is personally, but I've only heard good things, and I've been meaning to try it for a while now. I like food. You like food. So it just makes sense, right?"

I laughed. "Are you asking me to dinner, Rodney?"

"Yes, I am," he said with a lopsided grin.

I chuckled softly as I passed him on my way to the saloon-style doors and put a hand on his arm. "I'm sorry, but I'm so busy with work right now that I need every minute I can get in front of my computer. I appreciate the offer, though. Why don't you see if someone else wants to go? I bet Carl or Bev would go with you."

Rodney pouted. "Bev is fifty-two."

"So?" I played dumb.

Rodney's disappointment slipped away as he shrugged off my rejection. "You know what? You're right. I'll ask Carl and Bev. They're decent company."

"That's the spirit."

"Not as decent as you, of course."

I flashed him a smile. "Well, of course not. Nobody is as decent as me."

I left Rodney chuckling in the kitchen and wondered if I'd let him down too easily. He was only going to keep trying if I left room for him to think there was a chance for us—which there was not.

My tastes leaned more toward unattainable men with bad attitudes and big strong hands. Men like Lukas Holt.

He'd been my wildest fantasy as a teenage girl. If I was being perfectly honest, he'd also been my sexual awakening as a young girl. Some of my friends were crushing on animated characters in some of their favorite films. Others continued to talk about the tall, dark-haired man in all black from the dinosaur movie who draped himself on everyone and everything and looked hot as hell doing it.

But me? I was crushing on the boy next door. And now I was *still* crushing on him even though he was an asshole.

He never should have walked into my office and put me in a position like that. And yet he had. And he'd left me standing in his wake all hot and bothered and flustered while he'd been able to walk out without the smallest gesture of a farewell.

I moved along the line behind the volunteers to find an open station dishing out assorted steamed vegetables that smelled like garlic and pepper.

Don't get ahead of yourself, Kayla.

I smiled at the first people to step up to my station and served them their vegetables. A young boy with dirty cheeks gave me a charming, gap-toothed smile, while an older boy, presumably his brother, removed his hat and muttered a shy hello.

I gave them a little extra and ushered them down the line.

Lukas takes what he wants. And he wants everything. I sighed. *You're not special. Not to a man like that.*

CHAPTER 11

LUKAS

"It looks like we've arrived, Mr. Holt."

I looked up from my laptop which was balanced on my knees as I rode in the back seat of the Range Rover. My driver, Art, a balding man with a thin frame and respectable posture, palmed the steering wheel and took a gentle right-hand turn. The tires rolled off the paved street onto a dirt road lined in apple trees.

The farm was nowhere in sight. The road stretched on before us until it narrowed to a point and met the blue sky. Kayla had warned me that it was a ways off the main road, about a quarter mile to be precise, which meant this property was of staggering proportions.

"What a beautiful apple orchard," Art said.

My eyes were back on my computer screen. If I wasn't so swamped with work, I would have driven myself. But the new software my team and I were working on was in beta testing, which meant I was drowning in extra workload. Beta testing always brought out the issues in code, as it was supposed to do. The last thing I wanted was to release software to the public that wasn't absolutely perfect. This was our opportunity to weed out bugs, rewrite and fix errors, fine tune and condense the code, and all the while make sure we stayed on schedule for launch.

So I'd opted to have Art drive me out to the farm so I could squeeze in an extra hour and a half of work on the way there and again on the way back into the city.

"Yeah," I said as my fingers glided over the keyboard. "Really beautiful."

Art chuckled softly. "Sir, you've hardly looked away from your computer."

"I'm a busy man, Art. I don't have time to admire apples, leaves, and some grass."

Art was quiet for a minute. "There is always time to admire such things, Mr. Holt. If you can't, maybe you're off course."

"Uh huh." I'd barely heard him. I was cutting and pasting, testing and running, publishing and deleting.

Art cracked a window and drove the rest of the way down the dirt road in silence so I could work. I appreciated it and didn't even notice when the Rover came to a slow stop. The tires crunched on gravel and dirt, and Art put the vehicle in park before announcing that we had arrived at our destination.

I submitted my work and closed my laptop to tuck it back into my work bag, which I slid under the back seat for safe keeping. I opened my door and stepped out onto the dirt. The air smelled sweet out there and I detected notes of hay and honey along with soil, grass, and cider. Perhaps the cider smell was coming from the ruby-red apples hanging from the branches of trees in the fields at our back.

"Is that Ms. Goodfellow, sir?" Art nodded in the opposite direction of the orchard.

I turned as I straightened out my suit jacket.

There she was. Kayla stood in front of a traditional red barn. The doors were wide open, exposing the belly of a modern and well-kept barn. Hay lay strewn about in little piles on a concrete floor, and a woman in overalls was walking to and fro, surrounded by children. She was showing them the pens in the barn. Based on the clucking sounds from the chickens and the other variety of farm noises, I assumed the barn was full of sheep, goats, donkeys, and pigs.

Kayla had her hair pulled up in a ponytail. She was smiling wildly at three children who were crowded around her, trying to get their hands on child-sized ball caps she was handing out. She laughed as one child pulled a hat down over his head all the way past his eyes to the bridge of his nose. Kayla crouched down and lifted the visor for him. She said something to him and he laughed before taking off the other way to run into a crowd of adults. Parents presumably.

Kayla wore a pair of jeans that fit her like a second skin. Her sneakers used to be white but had turned a muddy color around the soles. The staining had touched the ends of her laces, too. She wore a T-shirt that said Good Fellow's and so did all the kids.

I was suddenly acutely aware of the fact that I'd shown up to a working farm in a three-piece suit, loafers, and a tie.

What were you thinking?

I left Art at the Rover and approached Kayla. She didn't see me coming until I was practically right on top of her, and when she turned and saw me, her cheeks flushed a magnificent shade of pink.

"I hope I'm not late," I said.

Kayla shook her head. Her ponytail swung back and forth. "No, not at all. We're waiting on the hay wagon to come pick us up and take us out to the middle of the orchard." She looked me up and down. "You look nice."

"So do you." I meant it. She looked quite nice indeed. So nice that the sight of her pulled my memories right back to the kiss we'd shared in her office the other afternoon. Her thighs had felt so good beneath my palms. Firm and full. Her lips had felt much the same against mine.

"Come on. There's someone I want to introduce you to."

I followed Kayla into the barn where children were giggling while they fed carrots and hay to donkeys with swishing tails. We stopped in front of one of the pens, where a woman in a wide-brimmed black hat and a full black ensemble, including a shawl, was crouched down so she could peer through the lens of an expensive camera as she snapped shots of the kids.

"This is the photographer I hired for the day," Kayla explained. "Her name is Winifred. She'll be taking pictures of you today. Mostly candid. She'll be taking pictures of the children as well. We're going to send all the parents and guardians prints in the mail as a little added bonus so they can remember the day."

I wondered how much that was costing Kayla and her organization. Based on the condition of her office, I found it hard to believe she was covering the cost out of her own budget.

Winifred straightened up and tucked her camera strap over her shoulder so she wore it like a bag. She thrust her hand out. Every single finger bore a ring on it. Her nails were painted black. "Nice to meet you, Mr. Holt. Don't worry. You won't even notice I'm out there with you." She leaned in close and whispered. "I'm like a ghost when I work."

It seemed unlikely that she would blend in amongst the group wearing blue Good Fellow's T-shirts and matching ball caps, but I nodded anyway. "Sounds good to me."

Brakes squealed out on the gravel road in front of the barn. Kayla looked up and clapped her hands together. "That's our ride." She turned to the kids and their guardians, all of whom were still focused on the animals. "All right, folks! Let's head outside to the hay wagon and go pick some apples! Make sure you're with your buddy."

Chaos erupted around us. Kids scurried to find their buddy. Once they did, they grabbed hands and darted outside, where they formed a less than mediocre line at the back of the hay wagon being towed by a tractor. Several of them bickered about where they wanted to sit, but they all fell quiet when Kayla and I made our way over and Winifred took some not-so-subtle pictures of our backs.

The man driving the tractor nodded at me before looking me up and down. I shouldn't have worn the damn suit.

Kayla pushed open the latch on the swinging gate on the back of the wagon. There was no dropdown step, so she offered to lift the first child up herself. I watched as the boy, probably six or seven years old, held up his arms and beamed at her as she hoisted him up and set him down on the wagon. His boots, little rubber rain-resistant things with dinosaurs all over them, shuffled through the hay as he made his way right to the opposite end of the wagon to take a seat on one of the benches. There was seating all along the outer edges as well as six rows down the middle. He shimmied back so he could lean against the wooden guard rails of the wagon and his feet dangled off the ground. He started swinging them back and forth.

A child tugged at the hem of my jacket. I glanced down to meet the gaze of a little girl with brown pigtails and big green eyes. She had freckles across her little nose, and she wore a sweater beneath her rain jacket with a big gray cat on it. Its eyes were made of green sequins.

She lifted her arms expectantly and waited for me to pick her up.

I crouched down, picked her up, and set her in the wagon. Her boots left track marks of dirt along my hip and the thigh of my pants. She thanked me with a quiet voice and a small smile before rushing to meet the boy who was already on the wagon.

Kayla shot me an apologetic glance as she noticed the dirt on my pants. "Sorry." She giggled. "I hope that's not one of your favorite suits."

I laughed and shook my head. "I don't know what I was thinking when I put it on this morning."

A lie. I knew where my head was at. It had been bouncing between work and that kiss with Kayla. No wonder I'd dropped the ball and dressed like I was going to the office.

"I hope it wasn't too expensive," she said.

I shrugged. "It was."

Kayla covered her mouth and laughed. I laughed too and was struck with the question, how long had it been since I laughed like this?

We got the last of the small children in the wagon. The older kids, between ten and twelve years old, climbed up themselves and were followed by the guardians. Kayla and I hopped up last and I closed the door behind us. Kayla walked across the wagon to the tractor and gave the driver a thumbs-up.

We lurched forward and she braced herself with one hand on the wooden guard. She turned to the group with a grin. Her eyes were in shadow under the visor of her ball cap. "All right, guys. I hope you're all as excited about this as I am. I've been looking forward to it for weeks. Mr. Doherty here," she gestured behind her to the driver of the tractor, "is going to take us to his favorite spot in his orchard where he likes to pick apples. We have a whole hour out in the orchard today to pick as many apples as we want. I have a couple of surprises in store for you all this afternoon but you're going to have to exercise patience. Do you think you can do that?"

Her question was met by a chorus of *yeses.*

She caught my eye and grinned. In the sunlight, she looked like the angel Seattle said she was. She looked like the angel these kids needed.

As I looked around at the smiling faces, I wondered what lives these children really led. Kayla had said they were with an organization that helped disadvantaged youths and kids. Did this mean they came from poverty? Were their families in turmoil? Did they have safe, happy homes to return to when this afternoon was over?

The little girl beside me tapped my knee. She couldn't have been more than eight. I turned to her and smiled. "Yes?"

"Do you think they have candy apples out there?"

"In the orchard?"

She nodded.

I paused to look thoughtful. "You know, I don't think they will. If they come straight from the tree, they don't need caramel because they're already sweet. Just like candy."

"Really?" she asked with wide eyes.

"Really." I nodded earnestly. "You just wait and see. Take your time, find the perfect, bright red apple, and bite into it. It will be the best apple you've ever had."

For a moment, she looked like she didn't believe me. Then she sat up straight and proud. "I'm going to find the best apple in the whole orchard."

I leaned in close and nudged her shoulder with mine. "Not if I find it first."

Her bright-eyed excitement narrowed. "You can't have it. I want it."

"Well," I said, leaning back against the wood frame, "I'm taller than you. So I'll be able to pick the ones you can't reach."

She frowned. "I hadn't thought of that."

I chuckled. "Don't worry. If I find the perfect apple, I'll bring it straight to you. Deal?"

She beamed. "Deal."

I chuckled and draped an arm against the frame of the wagon. As I looked up to peer down the lane of apple trees flanking either side of the wagon, I caught Kayla's eyes. She was still standing, bracing herself with one hand, and based on the way she was smiling at me, I assumed she'd heard my conversation with the little girl.

She gave me a knowing nod and turned her back to me as she started talking to the kids around her about the nutritional value of apples. She'd make a good mother. I could see her in a soft robe with a cup of coffee in hand in the morning coming down a set of stairs with a sleepy toddler in her free arm. Her hair would be a mess, and she'd be yawning, and I'd meet her in the kitchen with a coffee refill and a piece of toast with peanut butter.

I blinked. Since when had I ever fantasized about being a father? I gave my head a shake.

Since when had I fantasized about being a husband?

CHAPTER 12

KAYLA

The tractor came to a stop. The wagon lurched but only a little, and the kids were on their feet as soon as we were no longer in motion. The parents and legal guardians got out first, followed by the older kids, and Lukas swung down over one of the guard rails. He landed soundlessly in the grass and met me at the back of the wagon to help the little kids get down. The girl he'd been teasing about apple picking refused to leave his side, and they wandered to the nearest apple tree, where Lukas scrutinized the apples diligently and told her they could most certainly be better.

"Never pick the first one you see," he told the little girl. "That's a good life lesson right there. Patience. Patience is key."

"Patience is key," the little girl repeated verbatim.

Lukas laughed.

I hadn't heard him laugh this much since he was a kid—and a young one at that. By the time he was eleven or so, maybe even ten, his innocence was long gone. He was painfully aware of how little he and his mother had and how hard he was going to have to work to provide better for them. And he had. Before that time though, Lukas had his carefree moments. Moments of teasing, playing, and goofing around.

Seeing that side of him resurface with the little girl, Angelica, was a sight for sore eyes.

Mr. Doherty climbed down from his tractor and led the group three trees down where there were stacks of silver buckets. He told all the kids to grab one for themselves. For the children that were too small, a parent stepped in to carry the buckets.

The farmer approached the nearest tree and showed the kids how to properly pluck an apple from its branch. "All you do," he said in a deep, warm voice, "is give it a little twist. You don't want the stem to come out of the apple if you can help it. Like so."

He gripped a red apple, twisted his wrist in a quick flourish, and pulled the fruit away from the branch with a soft snap. He held it up for the kids before wiping it on his plaid shirt and taking a bite. Juice sprayed his boots and his bite broke away from the core with a fresh popping sound.

"That's all there is to it," he said with a smile full of apple.

In less than ten seconds, the kids were rushing to grab their own buckets. Lukas passed them around and made sure everyone was equipped before Angelica decided to steal him for herself again.

She'd taken a liking to him. I couldn't blame her. There was a lot to like.

I watched as Lukas moved along the row of trees with Angelica. She hung off his every word as he talked to her about the farm and trees. She asked questions, and he answered, and on the fourth tree, he paused and looked down at her with an arched eyebrow.

I moved closer to hear what they were saying.

"I think I might have found it," Lukas said softly.

Angelica gazed up at him the way a child might at a mall Santa Claus. "Found what?"

"The perfect apple."

"The perfect apple?" she gasped.

Lukas nodded earnestly. "Would you like to see?"

"Yes, please."

I smiled at her manners and folded my arms as Lukas crouched down and lowered a shoulder. He scooped her up, balancing her in the groove of his elbow, and stood, holding her high so she could see what he'd seen.

He pointed at an apple nestled in the branches. "That one there. Do see you see it?"

Angelica nodded.

"Can you reach it?"

She nodded again.

"Stick your hand in there and twist it off like Mr. Doherty showed you," Lukas told her. He stepped closer to the tree. The branches nearly swallowed him whole. They tugged at his suit jacket but he didn't seem to care.

Angelica reached in. The leaves rustled and I giggled softly as she struggled but finally emerged victorious with a bright red apple clutched in her tiny hand. She held it up the way an athlete might hold up a football after the winning touchdown.

Lukas threw his fist in the air to celebrate with her. He took the apple, wiped it clean on his shirt, and passed it back to her. "Take a bite. Tell me if you think it needs caramel."

Angelica considered the apple before taking a small bite out of it. All she got was skin. Lukas threw his head back and laughed.

I bit my bottom lip and cursed my ovaries for screaming like teenagers in a mosh pit.

Angelica bit again, this time breaking away a decent portion of apple. Her eyes widened with delight and she went in for more.

Lukas was still chuckling. "Is it good?"

She held the apple out to him. He took a bite out of the other side. I loved the way his jaw flexed as he chewed. Angelica watched him with the same awe I felt. He swallowed, his Adam's apple sliding up and down his throat, taunting me seductively. He licked his lips and nodded appreciatively. "I don't think that needs caramel at all."

"Me neither," Angelica said matter-of-factly.

"Shall we find more for you to bring home?" he asked.

I wanted to linger and watch the pair of them for the whole duration of our hour out in the orchard but I didn't have that luxury. I was working.

Before breaking away to join the others, I spotted Winifred snapping pictures of Lukas with Angelica. There was no doubt in my mind that people would find him an easier man to connect with after seeing those pictures.

The kids loved picking apples. Some filled their buckets so full they could hardly carry them and adults had to carry them on their behalf. Lukas ended up carrying two buckets and complained about how heavy they were to any child who would listen. Even as I worked and talked to the kids about nutrition and how important it was to do our best to make mindful and healthy choices where we could, I was distracted by him.

He poked fun at those he knew could take it and spoke warmly to the ones who seemed a little more sensitive. He plucked pretty leaves from trees for the littlest children to play with and got down on their level as they scoured for bugs in the dirt.

He was softening before my eyes. I saw nothing of the gruff, tough, broody man he'd been just days before. His behavior touched and impressed me and I found myself pulled to him. Wherever he was, I wanted to be, and I wasn't the only one. Some of the other parents seemed to like being around him, too. His energy was magnetic. Compelling. Warm.

Trouble, I told myself. *He's trouble.*

And he was off limits. We were working together which meant there would be no indulging in any hanky-panky. More importantly, I had Lisa to think of.

Lisa.

What would she think if she knew I was drooling over her brother like this? She'd probably call me weak-willed or something like that and remind me that Lukas was an ass. She'd tell me I deserved better or something along those lines. Or perhaps she'd be happy for me.

I gave my head a shake. That was a preposterous thought. Lisa would not want me falling for her brother.

Falling?

Stop it, I thought sharply.

My mind was getting ahead of itself and I was thankful when the hour in the orchard ended and we all piled back in the wagon with twenty pounds of apples to our names. We rode back to the barn where our lunches were waiting for us, along with my surprise pie delivery.

I shot Lukas a glance as he tried to steal a couple of apples from Angelica's bucket. She was having none of his shenanigans and slapped his hand away every time he got close. Lukas glanced up and we locked eyes. He flashed me a devilish smile before leaning back and draping his arms over the sides of the wagon.

Trouble indeed.

We arrived back at the barn and everyone moved to the picnic tables on a grassy spot beside the building. Guardians brought out lunch bags filled with sandwiches, vegetables, fruit, and milk cartons, and all the kids sat down to eat.

Meanwhile, I moved through the rows of tables and talked to them about the nutritional value in their lunches. I asked them to hold up their vegetable, whatever one it may be, and explained the importance of making sure vegetables were always on their plate during a meal. Some kids had eaten their veggies already and held empty fists in the air.

This made Lukas chuckle and it was hard for me to keep a straight face as I continued my educational part of the day. When I spied him cutting the crust off Angelica's sandwich, I almost melted. By sheer will alone, I kept going.

I was saved by the sound of a truck arriving. I glanced at the dirt road where a delivery van had just pulled up and I grinned.

"All right," I said, clasping my hands together. "Do you remember when I said I'd arranged a surprise for later? Well, this is it."

The driver got out of the van and opened the back doors. Inside, stacked upon plastic crates, were boxes of freshly baked apple pies from a local bakery down the road.

The kids bristled with excitement as the pies were passed around to the tables along with plastic cutlery and paper plates.

"So there's something special about these pies," I said, continuing to walk up and down the rows of picnic tables. All eyes were on me, including Lukas'. "All of these apple pies were made with apples from this orchard. So the apples you picked today are the very same ones in these pies. Pretty cool, huh?"

I was met with a chorus of excited agreement.

I glanced at Lukas. He was cutting slices for everyone at his table and passing them around. Winifred was off in the far corner, snapping pictures, and I knew Lisa would be thrilled to see them all. How long had it been since she saw this version of her brother?

Lukas cut off a piece of pie and took a bite.

I watched out of the corner of my eye as he chewed and savored the morsel. He closed his eyes for a moment, like he had when he was a kid eating the pies my mother brought home from her bakery. Then he swallowed and nodded. The moment was entirely his own. He went in for another bite, and another, and each one brought the same look of pleasure and contentment to his face.

It was making me think naughty things. Very naughty things.

Licking my lips, I forced myself to turn my back on him. This was not the time or place to have sexual fantasies about my best friend's older brother.

While everyone ate their pie, I shared information about the Doherty farm and how many generations had worked it. We talked about the apples and the cider they made there and how not all farms made money from animals. We talked about the changes in the seasons and what that meant for farmers.

Within a half hour, I was done with the discussion. I knew I couldn't hold the children's attention for much longer, and I didn't want to bore them to death, so we ended the day with the kids dispersing amongst the nearest rows of apple trees to play and have fun before we headed back into the city.

I sat down to rest my feet after cleaning up the plates and lunches.

Lukas came and found me. He had a plate of pie in one hand and wore a cheeky smile as he took the seat beside me. He put the plate down and slid it toward me. "You were working so hard this afternoon, I noticed you never sat down to eat lunch."

My stomach growled and I hoped he didn't hear it. "It happens more often than it should."

He nodded at the pie. "It's delicious. I snagged it for you. Angelica tried to wrestle me for it but I'm bigger and stronger. So, you know, you're welcome."

I giggled. "Wow, I'm impressed. Way to stick it to an eight-year-old."

He laughed.

CHAPTER 13

LUKAS

Art had dozed off with his seat reclined in the Rover. I approached the SUV with a smile and rapped my knuckles on the driver's side window. He woke with a start, looked around with blurry eyes, and frowned at me before turning the ignition so he could roll the window down.

"I didn't mean to startle you," I said.

"It's no bother, sir. Are you ready to go back to the city?"

I glanced over my shoulder at the group. Most of the kids were making their way back to the bus they'd arrived on. Kayla was outside the bus doors doing a headcount while parents and legal guardians boarded. The only person not getting on the bus was the photographer. Winifred had already gotten in her own car, a red Volkswagen Golf, and driven off.

"I think I'm going to stay behind and ride in on the bus," I said.

Art blinked and peered past me at the faded yellow bus. "Are you certain, sir?"

"Yes. Thank you. Enjoy the ride back into the city, Art. At least you won't have to listen to me typing away the entire time."

Art grinned and fiddled with the touchscreen. "I think I'll listen to my audio book then."

I stood back with my hands in my pockets as he pulled away and the tires kicked up dust. I lingered there at the edge of the road, my ruined shoes stained from the grass and the dirt.

The view was incredible. The sky was still vibrant and blue but some clouds had rolled in, threatening to rain later this afternoon. The apple trees varied in colors of red, orange, yellow, and green. I'd seen oil paintings this colorful but it had been a long time since I noticed such beauty in nature.

I'd been cooped up in the city for too long. Sure, I had great views from my office, but they were nothing like this. I stared out at a vast jungle of concrete and glass every day. It smelled of carbon emissions, takeout restaurants, and garbage. Occasionally, I caught the whiff of fresh-baked bread from a cafe down on the street but those moments were few and far between. The sounds of traffic drowned out other more pleasant sounds. Like the sounds here on the farm of birds chirping, children laughing, and leaves rustling in the gentle autumn breeze.

Yes, I needed to get out of the city more often. Maybe I'd been working too hard for too long. I'd forgotten how to take time off— forgotten how good it felt to breathe fresh air.

The bus honked its horn and I turned around.

Kayla waved me over. "Are you coming or what?"

I jogged over to the bus and she laughed at me. "What's so funny?"

Kayla shrugged and got on the bus ahead of me. "You running in a suit and loafers on a farm," she said pointedly. "That's what's funny."

I followed her up the three steps and we took a seat side by side in the front row. She looked over at me in surprise. "What?" I asked. "Is this seat taken?"

She shook her head and kicked her feet up on the bar in front of us. "Nope."

The bus driver closed the doors, and seconds later, we were rolling away from the farm and down the dirt road. Kayla checked over her shoulder that everyone was settled in their seats.

I nudged her hip with mine to get her attention. "I think your day was successful. It looks like everyone had a great time."

She smiled and settled lower in her seat to get comfortable. "I think so too. I know Angelica certainly enjoyed herself."

"Cute kid."

"She's a troublemaker."

"No," I said, shaking my head in disbelief. "She's an angel."

"Because she liked you and you were giving her a lot of attention."

"Isn't that what all kids want?"

"Yes," Kayla said with a knowing smile. "But unfortunately, it isn't what all kids get. Today just might have been the highlight of the entire fall season for her."

I frowned. I didn't like the sound of that.

Kayla sighed and closed her eyes. "She's one of the children on the school lunch program I work with. A few of the kids out here with us today are. It's been a struggle to make sure we have proper funding to feed the children who are sent to school with no meals from home."

"Her parents don't have the means to feed her?"

Kayla shook her head and cracked one eye open to peer over at me. "A lot of these kids' parents don't. That's why they're in this group. Sometimes, all they have to eat in the day is the food the lunch program provides. It's important that we keep up with the demand. Otherwise, children go hungry." She stifled a yawn and gave her head a shake. "Sorry."

Kayla was obviously exhausted.

"It's all right," I said. "Rest. We have a long drive ahead of us."

Kayla nodded and closed her eyes.

I gazed out the window as we left the dirt road in favor of the paved one. The drive became smoother and Kayla nodded off. She slumped sideways in her seat until her cheek found my shoulder. I hid my smile and continued gazing out the window as the apple orchard gave way to fields of hay and rolling hills of grass.

It felt good to have her so close. It was a kind of intimacy I hadn't felt in a long while. Years, even. Her hair smelled like her shampoo, citrus and honey, and there was a lingering scent of hay around her that wasn't at all unpleasant.

For the rest of the drive, I considered what she'd told me about

Angelica and the other children who were part of the lunch program. It didn't sit well with me that there was such a high risk of these children going hungry for days if there wasn't proper funding.

I could do something about that.

I *would* do something about that.

The ride became less enjoyable as we arrived in the city. We made more frequent stops at red lights and the children were becoming unsettled. They wanted to get out and stretch their legs, and truth be told, so did I. I'd barely moved the entire drive for fear of waking Kayla up and spoiling the moment.

When we finally pulled up in front of the Good Fellow's office and the doors opened, everyone got to their feet. Children started brushing past us and Kayla woke. She sat up straight and rubbed at her eyes before shooting me an apologetic and timid glance. "I didn't mean to fall asleep. I'm sorry. That's so embarrassing."

"Nothing to be embarrassed about. You had a big day today. And I'm sure you were up at the crack of dawn."

Kayla nodded and put a hand on her stomach. "I'm looking forward to a cold drink and a warm meal," she admitted. "That pie feels like it was a long time ago."

We got off the bus last. Kayla thanked the driver and handed him a folded white envelope she fished out of her jean pocket. He thanked her as we stepped out onto the sidewalk, waved, and pulled out into traffic.

"What was that?" I asked.

"A tip," she said as she waved goodbye to the children and their parents as everyone began making their way to their cars or the normal public transit bus stop up ahead. "He drives his bus for the school district but offered to take us out to the farms today for free. He's our driver a lot of times, and if I have spare money in the budget, I like to throw a little something his way. He thinks it's from all the parents and guardians. Otherwise, he'd never take it."

Did her generosity have no end?

Her stomach growled loud enough that I heard it. She groaned pitifully. "Oh my goodness, I'm *starving*." She turned to me. "I'm glad you came out today. Lisa will be thrilled to hear how well everything went. And I'm looking forward to seeing Winifred's photos. I bet she captured some great moments."

"Come to dinner with me tonight."

Kayla blinked. "Sorry?"

That might have been a little forward. I chuckled and rubbed the back of my neck. "You're hungry. I'm hungry. I know this great place just a little ways down the street. We could walk over and be there in less than ten minutes. The food is great. Trust me. Let me treat you to dinner. It's my way of thanking you for a good day out of the city."

Her eyes danced back and forth between mine, and for a moment, I thought she was going to say no.

"I'm not sure, Lukas," she said slowly.

"I want to talk business. I did some thinking on the drive and want to talk to you about some ideas I have."

She arched an eyebrow. "Strictly a business dinner, then?"

"Strictly."

"All right," she conceded. "Fine. You lead the way. And you'd better pray this place doesn't serve fancy little portions. I want something big and heavy. Like pasta. Or a burger."

I laughed as she fell into step beside me and we made our way down the sidewalk. "You can order anything you want. I own a portion of the business."

"Of course, you do," she said with a knowing eye roll.

"It has its perks."

Dominion, the restaurant in question, was an elegant steak house positioned right on the street corner. It had a gothic edge to it with dark, moody decor, plush red velvet fabric accents, and ambient lighting. Kayla shot me a look when we walked through the front doors.

"This place is way too nice for me to show up in jeans and sneakers," she muttered.

I leaned toward her. "Another perk of owning the place? You can wear whatever you want and nobody bats an eye."

"I thought you said you owned a *portion*."

"I was being humble."

She wrapped her arms around herself and looked around at the customers in dresses and suits.

I shrugged out of my jacket, loosened my tie, and popped the first three buttons of my shirt open. "There. Now we're both messes."

Kayla smirked. "You are so out of touch if you think loosening a couple of buttons make you look like a mess."

A server saw us to our table in a private room at the back of the restaurant. Kayla said nothing about the personal service and dining area but she seemed to relax once we were secluded from the other customers. We were given menus and brought glasses of water. Kayla polished hers off in a matter of minutes as she scoured the menu. I didn't interrupt her decision-making process.

When she put the menu down, we locked eyes.

"So you said you wanted to talk business?" she said.

I clasped my hands together over the table. "Yes. First and foremost, I'd like to fund your school lunch program. To be clear, I'd like to fund it one hundred percent—annually."

CHAPTER 14

KAYLA

My tongue had become glued to the roof of my mouth. Lukas sat across from me and wore what seemed to be a mix between a satisfied smirk and a proud smile. He waited for me to say something—anything—in response to his generous offer, but I was rendered speechless.

"This is a good thing, isn't it?" he pressed after several beats of my silence.

I nodded and reached for my water. Finding it empty, I frowned.

Lukas slid his across the table to me. I tilted it back, drank greedily, and set the glass back down on the table. I watched moisture slide down the side of the glass.

"Are you sure?" I finally managed to ask.

Funding the *entire* lunch program for a whole year wouldn't be a small tab. He was biting off a serious expense. He could afford it, of course. He could likely afford anything he wanted. But that wasn't the point. Regardless of how much money a person had, it was still a staggering amount for one person to throw at a good cause.

"I'm positive," Lukas said. "And by annually I meant every year."

I drank more water.

"This makes you happy, right?" he asked.

I nodded as I drank. Water dribbled out of the corner of my mouth, rolled down my chin, neck, and into the collar of my T-shirt. "Uh huh," I said before swallowing and setting the glass back down. "It makes me happy. It's a little overwhelming. I didn't expect you to want to be so…"

"Children shouldn't have to suffer because their parents have no money," he said firmly. "Little girls like Angelica shouldn't go hungry when there are people with the means to feed them."

I wanted to crawl across the table, take his face in my hands, and kiss him.

Instead, I reached over and took his hand in mine. Surely, he'd been thinking about our childhoods. I knew he'd been sent off to school countless times with no food for lunch. I also knew he'd given some of his food away to Lisa on the days where she showed up to school with nothing but a piece of bread and butter. That was who Lukas was back then. He'd always looked out for his little sister and taken the brunt of any suffering in her place.

I saw that boy in him now.

"There's more," Lukas said, giving my hand a squeeze.

"More?"

"I want to use the farm we visited today and others like it to supply the program at cost. I think it's important, especially if we're going to do this under the Good Fellow's umbrella that all the profits stay within the community. We'll support local businesses and get all our supplies and products locally. It might cost a little bit more but I'm willing to absorb that in order to do this thing the right way. No ordering from out of state or country. We build our foundation here."

"That sounds incredible," I said. "I'm so glad you've found a way you want to get involved in giving back. I expected you to enjoy yourself today but I didn't quite anticipate this much of an impact. Thank you, Lukas. Seriously. You have no idea how many lives your involvement is going to change for the better."

Lukas ran his thumb over my knuckles and smiled. "And I'm glad my sister is a stubborn woman and forced me to follow through and reconnect with you."

I laughed. "She is stubborn. I'll give her that. I think it's in your blood."

"Perhaps."

My hand still rested in his. His thumb stilled upon my knuckles and I gently pulled back, drawing my hand back into my lap. Closeness like that was something we would have to be careful of, especially if we were going to work together going forward. We couldn't risk another moment like the one in my office. It was unprofessional and bound to invite complications into our project. I, for one, could not afford complications. My hands were already full with all of the responsibilities on my shoulders and it seemed safe to assume that Lukas had his own problems to worry about.

Our waitress arrived to take our orders. Lukas ordered several dishes with names I would never even try to pronounce, and I ordered a cheeseburger and more water.

After the waitress left with the menus, I bit my bottom lip and looked at Lukas. "I'm not one for fancy restaurants." I let the unspoken words hang between us. *I hope you're not embarrassed by me and my lack of class.*

"Sometimes, the occasion calls for a burger." He leaned forward with a glint in his dark blue eyes. "Do you remember that diner on the corner? Beside Lisa's building? What was that place called?"

"Lenny's Diner."

"Lenny's Diner," he said, sitting back in his chair. He chuckled softly and ran his thumb along the edge of the table. He looked thoughtful as memories resurfaced in both our minds at the mention of Lenny's name. "Is it still there?"

I shook my head. "No, he sold it about four years ago. It's a coffee shop now."

"A coffee shop? Doesn't Seattle have enough of those?"

I giggled. "More than a city needs. That's for sure. I've heard they have decent enough coffee, though. And pastries."

Lukas nodded absently. He looked incredibly handsome in the dim, moody lighting of the restaurant. Half of his face was cast into shadow and so was his throat. His jawline looked sharper than ever and his dark blond hair almost looked brown. I could see the beginnings of a five o'clock shadow forming.

He rubbed his jaw. "Those pies you had delivered this afternoon reminded me of the ones your mother used to bring back from her bakery. They were good but not quite as good as the ones her bakery had. Perhaps that's just the nostalgia talking."

"No, you're right. The pies she brought back were especially good. They had more cinnamon in them than the ones today."

"Cinnamon, huh?" Lukas chuckled. "Well, it was the best thing we used to eat back in those days."

I grinned. He wasn't wrong about that. On the days that were worse than others, our food options were pretty grim. "You don't miss the fried baloney or ketchup sandwiches?"

Lukas paled. "Don't remind me of such things before our meals arrive."

"Oh, come on. They weren't that bad. Every now and then, I still get a craving for the former."

"For fried baloney?" he asked incredulously.

"What's wrong with that?"

"Everything. Everything is wrong with that."

I shrugged. "Suit yourself. But you said it. Nostalgia tastes good."

He shook his head. "It does not apply to everything. Did you know I don't like potatoes because we used to eat so much of them? Three meals a day, day after day after day, of damn potatoes and wax beans. No, I can't do it."

It was my turn to smirk. "Peasant food is no longer good enough for you, Mr. Important?"

"Hey, it's not like that and you know it."

"I think maybe you're a little spoiled now."

He studied me before his impassive expression softened into a smile. "Maybe I am."

"Maybe?" I laughed.

"No need to rub it in."

I continued poking fun at him and enjoyed how he didn't prickle or get gruff with me like he had when we first started discussing how we might work together. He was no longer the tough and standoffish businessman. Tonight, he was showing me the colors of his youth. He laughed easily, teased me back, and brought up pieces of our child-hood I thought he might have forgotten.

For the first time, I felt close to him again.

There was a brief moment in time when I was quite young that things had felt just like this between us. Gender and attraction and chemistry hadn't come into the mix yet because we were both too young to feel or understand such things, so we were just friends. We got along well, played together, joked together, and all around enjoyed each other's company. But as time went on, things changed. He was a few years older than me, so looking back, it made sense that he tired of the same old routine with a girl the same age as his little sister. Where he wanted to buckle down and start making money, I still wanted to play and explore. I found the friendship I wanted and needed with Lisa, and Lukas found it with his computer.

The arrival of our food reminded me of how different my life and Lukas' were. The waitress set down a large tray that nearly took up the entire surface of the table. It was overflowing with dishes of seafood, pasta, hors d'oeuvres, and other things I couldn't visibly distinguish. Lukas began taking a little bit of everything and putting it on a small plate while I dipped a French fry in ketchup and popped it in my mouth.

He looked pointedly at my plate. "How are your potatoes?"

"Just call them fries like a normal person."

"I can't. Potatoes are potatoes to me."

"Don't ruin a good thing for me, okay? French fries are one of my favorite foods."

"You need to get out more, Kayla."

I threw a fry across the table at him. It hit him right in the chest and fell into his lap.

Lukas gave me a devilish smile. "Careful. This is an expensive suit."

"There's no way you're going to wear that thing again. You trashed it at the farm."

"Nothing a good dry clean can't fix."

Who was he bullshitting? I leaned forward, rested my forearms on the table, and arched an eyebrow. "So you're telling me that you'd pay to get this dry cleaned, and then you would wear it to the office for work? Or to a function?"

He shifted in his seat. "Yes, why not?"

"All right, I believe you. Wear it for your next interview with Rebecca Mills."

"I—" Lukas paused and looked away.

"You what?" I liked being the one doing the interrogating now. The tables had turned and I was in the driver's seat and it was giving me a rush. Sure, I knew I was being a little childish. What was more, I knew this was a bad strategy to play into when he and I were supposed to be keeping things professional. All this teasing and flirting had the air between us snapping and popping with chemistry. Wishfully, I told myself I was the only one feeling it.

Realistically?

I knew that wasn't the case based solely on the way he was looking at me. He looked at me like he was slowly unraveling my soul one strand of tangled Christmas lights at a time. And he was enjoying it.

Lukas sighed. "I think a wise man knows when to admit defeat. You're right. I doubt I'll ever wear the suit again."

"You should donate it."

He laughed. "I should've known you'd say that."

"Get used to it, champ."

His grin broadened. "It's been a hell of a long time since someone called me champ."

Over the rest of dinner, we teased each other about our childhood nicknames and all the silly things we did over the years. Lukas had been called champ by Lenny, the owner of the diner in Lisa's apartment building. The first time I'd ever heard him referred to by that name, I'd adopted it and started calling him it, too. Lukas never seemed to mind. In fact, he seemed to enjoy it. The nickname was used with affection and warmth and I was using it the same way now.

Lukas resigned himself to the fact that he couldn't fit another bite of food in his belly long after I'd already finished eating.

"Do you want to get out of here and go for a walk down by the Sound?" he asked. "It's just a ten-minute drive from here."

Every cell of logic in my body screamed at me to tell him no. Walking along the Sound at night was a bad idea. A very bad idea.

But the logical cells were soon overrun by the impulsive ones that screamed *yes*.

"That sounds nice," I said.

He fished his phone out of his pocket. "I'll call my driver."

CHAPTER 15

LUKAS

Art pulled over amidst the evergreen trees of Discovery Park. On our left was the dark expanse of the Puget Sound. The moon overhead, nearly full, glowed on the surface of the water like a giant white orb. Stars glistened overhead and upon the dark mirrored water, winking as if greeting Kayla and me as we got out of the back seat of the Rover.

Kayla breathed in the crisp fall air and wrapped her arms around herself. She hadn't brought a jacket, merely a thin knit cardigan, so I shrugged out of mine and draped it over her shoulders.

She thanked me with a smile and I noticed that the stars twinkled in her eyes, too.

Art told us he would wait for us there. He had a book with him on the passenger seat he was eager to read and I told him we'd only be forty-five minutes or so. We left him behind and found our way to the footpath along the Sound. About ten feet below, the water lapped at the edge of the rock wall upon which we walked. Had it been daytime, it would have been difficult to hear each other over the shrieking seagulls and ocean traffic sounds, but at night, it was pleasantly quiet. A hush fell over the Sound at this time as the city began tucking itself away to sleep.

Kayla hid a yawn behind one hand and gazed out at the water. Across the Sound, the lights of Bainbridge Island competed for attention with the starry night sky.

"I had a nice time tonight," she said as she tucked her hands in the pockets of my suit jacket. "Thank you for dinner."

"I'm glad you joined me. Eating dinner alone is never as enjoyable as sharing it with someone."

"Do you eat alone often?"

"I do," I admitted. "One of the demands of the job. But I enjoy my own company."

"You always have."

That was true. As a kid, I'd spend hours upon hours locked up in my room, working away on my computer. My mother never understood it. For a while there, I think it might have even scared her. She was always knocking on my door with a glass of lemonade, asking if I was going to go out and play with my friends that day. I'd remind her that I was thirteen and I didn't need to go outside and play anymore. My imagination was being put to proper use with the computer.

Over the years, I became more of a recluse, and she became more concerned. Now as a grown man looking back, I could see why some of my behaviors were red flags to her. She worried that I was giving up the tail end of my childhood—which I had—in favor of something indulgent and antisocial. She never could have known then that those tireless hours in my room as a teenager would be what led me to this future.

Hell, she didn't know now. Her dementia had stolen those truths from her years ago.

"What are you thinking about?" Kayla asked, bumping me gently with her hip.

"The past. I think I've thought about who I used to be more in the week since I reconnected with you than I have in years. A decade even."

She pursed her lips thoughtfully. "Is that a good thing?"

"I haven't decided yet."

A cloud passed in front of the sky and the Sound grew slightly darker. Kayla's eyes still caught the starlight as she gazed up at me. "I think if we'd had more as children, we never would have ended up where we are now. I think maybe this is how things were supposed to be so that we could make means of our own to help others."

I liked the way she looked at things. I'd never considered myself an optimist but that was certainly what Kayla was. She saw the good in people and things before she ever saw the bad. Whereas I proactively *looked* for the bad.

However, I never liked to think that things were how they were *supposed* to be. I didn't believe in that. Things were the way they were. There was no because, no explanation, no logical or explainable reason for it. There couldn't be. How could I find a reason that would appease my fury about my mother's dementia?

I couldn't because one such reason did not exist.

"What do you think?" Kayla asked. She stopped walking and turned to me. The moon peeked back out from behind the wisp of a cloud and she cocked her head to the side. "Do you think we would have turned out the same if we'd lived different childhoods? Grew up in nice houses on nice streets?"

I peered down the Sound. Up ahead, probably six or so miles, was my house.

"I don't know," I conceded. "Probably not. I doubt I'd have worked as hard if I came from something instead of nothing."

Kayla reached out and took my hand. Her fingers were tiny in mine and cold. "You didn't come from nothing, Lukas."

Her breath vaporized in the air and she smiled at me. Really smiled at me.

Before I knew what I was doing, I pulled her in close. Kayla let out a startled little gasp, but I silenced it with a kiss. She trembled in my arms until I cupped the back of her neck and the small of her back and held her like she was mine.

After that, she let out a breathless sigh and draped her arms behind my neck.

The kiss deepened and a cool breeze blew off the water. Neither of us felt it, even though it blew her hair around our cheeks. She clung to me fiercely, and for a moment, I thought things might get a little out of control.

But she broke the kiss.

"Lukas," she whispered.

"Yes?"

"We... we shouldn't do this. I've missed you. I didn't realize just how much I've missed you until today. But I can't let that affect so much between us. We've been friends for so long, but after seeing each other again, it's brought up some unexpected..."

Feelings? Urges? Desires?

"Chemistry," she said, choosing her words carefully. "We're both mature adults and we know this is inappropriate. Our jobs come first. And as a non-profit director, I have to be unimpeachable."

I swallowed the rush of need that had nearly consumed me moments before. "I understand."

She bit her bottom lip and looked down at her feet. "I'm sorry."

"Don't be. You're the one making the smart choices here." I paused and raked my fingers through my hair. I didn't know what I was doing. Why did I keep kissing this girl? Why did I keep trying to take something she couldn't give me? "I'll call Art and have him come pick you up and take you home. It's late."

"How are you going to get home?"

"I'll walk to my office tower. It's not too far from here."

"That's almost half an hour away. The clouds are coming in. It's probably going to rain."

"I like the rain," I said as I lifted my phone to my ear. Art answered the call and I told him which cross streets in the park to meet us at. I hung up and forced myself to smile at Kayla. "Come on. I'll walk you to him."

Neither of us said a word for the rest of the walk. My mind raced with self-loathing thoughts. I never should have let my heart get ahead of my brain. Kayla had rejected me once before. Why had it seemed like a good idea to try to kiss her again?

The connection between us was something I could not ignore. I'd never felt this way about a woman before. It wasn't like I hadn't dated since my company went public, but those dates hadn't felt like real dates at all. They'd been more like expedited hookups to fulfill my natural urges. If I was honest with myself, I knew I'd never had an interest in taking things any further with a woman because I figured all they wanted from me was my money.

But Kayla wasn't like that, which only made me want her more.

She was the kindest person I knew. She would never use someone for their money, even though she of all people was in a position to use said money for good. She knew right from wrong and she would never cross that line.

Hence why she stopped the kiss when she did.

The brake lights of the Rover flashed red when Art pulled over up ahead. We turned from the path, crossed the grass, and approached the car just as the sky let loose the first couple drops of rain.

Kayla slid into the back seat and I held the door open for her.

"Are you sure you don't want a ride back to your building?" she asked, eyes full of concern and guilt. "It's going to start raining."

"I want to walk. Might as well mess up the suit once and for all, right?"

She smiled, and I was glad for that. "Okay. We'll talk soon?"

"Soon." I closed the door and stepped back. The windows of the SUV were too tinted for me to see through, but I watched her pull away nonetheless.

Once the car was out of sight, I turned toward the downtown core and began my slow procession to my office tower, under which my Lykan was parked. All the while, I thought about Kayla, the kiss, and the soft sigh that had escaped her when I pulled her in close.

The sky was still heavy with clouds the following morning when I arrived at my mother's assisted living home. There was a new plant in the lobby, a palm-leafed, tall thing that looked like it belonged in Los Angeles, not Seattle, and it was full of white twinkling lights. A card on the front of it had a note about which family had given it to the home as a gift. I didn't bother going over to read it. Instead, I made my way to my mother's room, where I found her cross-stitching.

She looked up when I entered and smiled, and I knew right away that this was a good day to visit.

She knew who I was.

She beamed. "Lukas, you're all grown up."

"I am," I said as I pushed the door closed behind me. It clicked softly into place. "And you're cross-stitching. I haven't seen you do that in ages." I moved across the room and sat down across from her on a chair drowning in pillows and knitted blankets. "What are you making?"

My mother held the small circular cross-stitched picture up. It was a bouquet of flowers against a white backdrop. One stem hung limp from the rest, its petals sad and wilted.

"It's beautiful," I told her.

"It's a little messy. Could be better. Could be worse." She put it down on the table beside an empty cup of tea. "How are you?"

"I'm good."

"You have that look."

"What look?"

"The look of a son who wants to talk to his mother about something important."

How her mind could be ebbing away but still be so sharp, I would never know. I sighed. "Do you remember Kayla Goodfellow?"

"Lisa's friend? Of course, I remember Kayla. Sweet girl. Charming girl. A girl who was most definitely going places. How is she?"

"She's good," I said.

My mother leaned forward. Her chair creaked. The shawl over her shoulders slipped away and settled behind her. "And who is she to you now?"

"A friend, Mom. Just a friend."

"A mother always knows when her child isn't being honest with her."

My mouth twitched.

My mother pointed it out. "You see? I know you, Lukas. Now tell me what you came here to tell me. Go on. I'm listening."

I took advantage of her day of clarity and came clean. I told her how Lisa had arranged for Kayla and me to work together, and I told her how I'd been growing closer to Kayla and how I couldn't stop thinking about her. All the while, my mother listened with a knowing twinkle in her eye that was both rewarding to see and irritating. She'd always been a bit of a smartass, and on days where she was lucid like this, that quality shone through.

"I'm proud of you," my mother said once I'd told her about how things ended with me and Kayla on the Sound last night. "It's nice to see you finally interested in something other than money and financial stability. Can I give you some advice?"

"Please." The word sounded weak in my ears.

My mother reached out, took my hand in hers, and looked me in the eyes. "Follow your heart. There will always be more board meetings. More conference calls. More software to build and lines of code to write. But love? Dear boy, the real thing only comes around once, and that's if you're lucky. Don't let it slip through your fingers, David. You'll regret it one day."

David.

That was my father's name.

My heart went cold and hard in my chest. I pulled my hand free and leaned back. "Your advice is as good as ever."

She smiled and patted my knee. "Who are you kidding? You never listened to my advice a day in your life. That's why we never worked. You were too stubborn. And I was too—"

"Good for me," I said. My father had never been good enough for my mother and he knew it. That was why he'd left in the first place, and it was why he never came back.

And it was why I never missed him.

CHAPTER 16

KAYLA

"Can I try one of those?" Lisa leaned forward on her elbows to peer over at my plate.

I nodded and let her skewer one of the curried shrimp on my salad. She took a candied pecan and some greens as well, popped them in her mouth, and chewed gratefully while pressing her thumb and forefinger together in a symbol of perfection.

"Damn, that's good," she said, pointing at my plate with her fork. "I'm getting that next time."

It had better be good. The damn salad was costing me an arm and a leg. Who in their right mind could charge twenty-one dollars for a salad and still have a clear conscience? I wished I'd checked the price before I ordered but I thought I was on the safe side by ordering a bowl of greens and uncooked veggies. Apparently not. I would have to cut back somewhere else this week to make up for it.

"So Lukas told me he had an awesome time out at the farm with you and the kids the other day," Lisa said. "He wouldn't shut up about it actually. Kept going on and on about how he needs to get out more and how good it was to be out in nature. Nature?" She scoffed. "Who'd have thought Lukas would ever rekindle his love for the outdoors?"

"Stranger things have happened."

"Yeah, true, like Lukas wearing jeans. He wore *jeans* the other day, Kayla. Who is my brother and what did you do to him on that farm?"

I hoped my red cheeks didn't betray me as I sipped my water to buy myself time to respond. "I think it was the kids, not me. He bonded with a little girl named Angelica. He was really sweet with her, Lisa. You should have seen it."

"He told me about her. Said she was the reason he wanted to fund the lunch program. I can't believe how easy it was to pull off. I thought you'd have to work on him for days to get him to come around. Weeks even. But you did it all in one afternoon. See? I knew you'd have the magic touch."

Magic touch or magic kiss?

"In case you were wondering, his interview went well with Rebecca Mills yesterday," Lisa said matter-of-factly. She paused to take a bite of her lettuce wrap and dabbed chili sauce from the corners of her mouth with her napkin. "He was raving about the apple orchard and the educational value the field trip provided for the kids. He name dropped you like six hundred times."

I blushed. "Oh."

"That's a good thing, Kayla. Don't sweat it. Good Fellow's is going to get more free publicity from Lukas than you could orchestrate in a year."

That was one way to look at it.

"Anyway," Lisa continued, "Rebecca asked him what sort of action came out of the day at the orchard and he told her all about the school lunch program and his plans to fund it with local produce and food from Seattle-based small businesses. I have to ask, was that his idea or yours?"

"That was all Lukas."

Lisa grinned like a proud mother bear. "That makes me really happy to hear. I can't thank you enough, Kayla. Seriously. What you're doing for my brother and his reputation… well, I don't think I have the right words to express just how much it means to me."

Guilt rippled through my belly. "I'm the one who should be thanking you and your brother. Because of him, Rodney and I are going to be able to feed thousands of hungry kids. The best part is, I don't have to worry about finding where to get the money next year. Lukas is in it for the long haul."

"Maybe my brother isn't as far gone as I thought," Lisa said before diving back in for another bite of her lettuce wrap.

I wondered if that was true. I had seen a different side of Lukas this past week. But I'd also seen the disappointed side. Driving away from him at Puget Sound had not been easy.

Did things have to be this way between me and him? Was our only option to resign ourselves to the fact that we could be nothing more than professional colleagues?

Maybe it was time to put some feelers out there and find out.

"Hey, Lisa?"

My friend looked up at me. "What's up?"

"What would you think about Lukas starting to date again now that he's started to loosen up and he's not so married to his work?"

Lisa shrugged one shoulder. Her cardigan slipped free and she pulled it back up. "I hope he finds someone, but I'll be honest. I don't think it's in the cards for him anytime soon. He has a lot to be careful about like gold diggers and such. Once the articles start getting published, I expect things will get worse before they get better and women will start throwing themselves at him looking for a night out with Seattle's most eligible bachelor. I guess I'm just wary. Why?"

"Just curious," I said thinly.

"My brother isn't one for dating anyway. I don't think he wants something serious. He's enjoying the single life, you know? No attachments. No responsibilities. No commitments to spend a certain amount of time with a woman so she doesn't feel neglected. His lifestyle doesn't permit room for a girlfriend and the timing is bad."

Disappointment settled in place of the guilt I'd felt moments before. "Right, that makes sense."

"My brother is a fool anyway." Lisa laughed. "What girl in their right mind would want to date him unless they were in it for the money?"

"I couldn't tell you."

The girl who's known him almost his whole life and knows all his darkest corners and feels safe in his brightest rooms.

Lisa flagged down the server and put a fifty-dollar bill on the table. "I have to run back to the office. Thank you for meeting me for lunch. It was a nice break. I'll call you later, okay?"

"Lisa, you don't have to pay for lunch. I can—"

"Nonsense, I want to. Besides, Lukas pays me really well. So technically, lunch is on him."

Lisa got up, slung her purse over her shoulder, and bid me one last farewell before she hurried out of the restaurant and out of sight. She left me with a few bites of salad left and I told the server to keep the change when he came by. He was delighted by his twelve-dollar tip.

I left shortly after and hopped on the bus to ride down to my office. It was only a fifteen-minute ride from the restaurant and I was inside flipping the closed sign to the open side before one thirty in the afternoon. I tucked into my desk and opened my computer to start responding to emails.

There were over two hundred in my inbox that I needed to get through.

The feeling of overwhelm left me paralyzed. My mind hadn't been fully on work lately. And by lately, I meant since Lukas came back into my life and shook everything up like a snow globe, minus the magical feelings and perfect flakes of glitter. He'd shaken it up in a confusing, messy, stressful sort of way. I wasn't supposed to have any of the feelings that caught me off guard at random points of the day every time I thought of him.

And I wasn't supposed to think of him twenty times a day either.

Something was wrong with me. I'd turned back into that lovesick girl who'd pined over her best friend's older brother with the charming smile and bad boy attitude. He still had both of those things but a bit more class and flair now.

And money.

Twenty minutes passed and I only got through two emails.

I slumped forward on my desk and rested my forehead on the back of my hands. "I'm screwed."

My office door opened. I lifted my forehead from my knuckles and blinked up at Rodney, who stood backlit by the sunny afternoon with a grin on his face and a bottle of some kind in one hand. In the other were two plastic champagne flutes that looked like they were from the dollar store.

"Rodney?"

"Hey, Kayla," he said as he approached my desk. Out of the soup kitchen, he looked much less the ragged man that I was used to seeing. Instead of chunky black shoes with thick rubber soles, he wore a plain brown boot with no laces. He looked good in his dark green chinos and cream-colored polo shirt. He wore a thin brown jacket and looked the part of a successful entrepreneur instead of an exhausted kitchen worker. He set the bottle down and I realized it was champagne. "I'm glad you're here. I brought wine so we could celebrate."

"Celebrate?"

"Yes, *celebrate*. I owe you a big one. I can't believe you got the entire school lunch program funded! I knew you wouldn't let me down but I had no idea you'd secure this kind of funding. It's mindboggling and it's probably the most wine-worthy thing that's happened to either of us in a long time."

I smiled and closed my laptop. "I honestly hadn't thought about that."

"Probably because you're running yourself ragged going all over town making everyone else's day better. Please tell me you can spare a minute to have a drink with a friend."

I couldn't spare a minute. Not really. But then again, when had I ever been able to say yes to that question and be telling the truth?

"I'd love to have a drink with you," I said.

Rodney clapped his hands together enthusiastically. "That's what I wanted to hear. I only have one problem."

"And what might that be?"

He grimaced. "I forgot to bring a corkscrew."

Chuckling and shaking my head at his forgetfulness, I went over to the three-tiered table upon which I kept my electric kettle. In the top shelf, tucked away in a wicker basket I'd found that fit snug in the opening, were all my tea bags and fixings. In the second drawer were non-perishable snacks like individual bags of chips, granola bars, dried apricots, crackers, and trail mix that had been untouched for months because I'd eaten all the chocolate out of the bag. I crouched down and opened the bottom drawer which held my hidden mess. The junk drawer overflowed with random items including a tape measure, a bedazzled hammer Lisa had bought me eons ago as a grand-opening present when I secured the lease on my office, and other things like extra light bulbs, batteries, lighters, and miscellaneous debris. One such debris item was a silver corkscrew with a blue rubber grip.

"Aha," I declared victoriously when I found it in the back corner of the drawer. I popped up to my feet and spun to face Rodney. "We're in luck."

Rodney took the corkscrew and opened the bottle of wine. He poured us each a glass in our flute and apologized for the champagne flutes. "Originally, I was going to buy champagne," he said as he lifted his glass to his lips, "but the price tags were a little off-putting."

"I prefer red over bubbly anyway. Cheers, Rodney. To the kids."

"To the kids." He grinned. "And to the greatest non-profit director in the world, and an incomparable woman as well."

"I don't know about that." I tucked a strand of hair behind my ear. There he went, always making things a tad uncomfortable for me.

"I swear you could squeeze money out of a stone with those little fists of yours."

"If that was true, I'd have a much nicer office."

Rodney laughed. I'd always thought he had a nice laugh, even if it sometimes did seem a little exaggerated. "What are you talking about? You have a great office." He looked around and the corner of his mouth turned down. "Although I suppose a fresh coat of paint couldn't hurt. But hey, that's not why I'm here. I'm here to toast to your brilliant mind and persuasive skills. How did you convince that scrooge to give us money anyway?"

"I didn't—"

Movement to my left caught my eye. I shut my mouth and turned, only to find Lukas standing in the doorway that had framed Rodney minutes ago. The sun was still shining at his back, casting his face into shadow, but I didn't miss the glint in his eye as his gaze landed on me.

"Lukas," I breathed.

I couldn't read his face or hardly make it out in the shadows that fell across him, but I could feel his energy, and it wasn't warm and friendly.

I swallowed and nodded at Rodney. "Would you like a glass of wine, Lukas? Rodney and I—he's the manager and coordinator at the soup kitchen—were just going to toast to your donation and—"

"I'm sorry, but something came up," Lukas said smoothly. He simultaneously pulled his phone out of his pocket and held it up. "Duty calls."

With that, he turned his back on us and left.

Rodney tipped his head back and took a sip of wine. "See? Told you. He's a stone."

CHAPTER 17

LUKAS

Who was the guy in the cheap polo shirt in Kayla's office drinking wine with her? And why did his smug smile piss me off so much?

I jerked on the hem of my suit jacket, pulling it sharply against my shoulder blades as I strode purposefully to my Lykan parked at the curb.

I didn't like seeing Kayla with him drinking wine and smiling at each other—like how I wanted her to smile at *me*. And what was that asshole saying? Something about her being able to squeeze money out of a stone?

I stepped off the curb and walked around the hood of my car. The handles lifted automatically and I wrenched the door open. "Stone, my ass. I'm throwing hundreds of thousands of dollars their way and they're toasting to what?" I slid into my seat and turned on the ignition.

Was Kayla playing me? Was she only in this for my money after all?

Her efforts might not have been to line her own pockets. I understood she was working to help others but it still made me feel like a chump for believing she might have real feelings for me. Feelings like I had for her.

"You're a fool," I growled at myself as I slammed into first gear, checked my mirrors, and cut off an approaching taxi cab. He laid on his horn behind me and I wove around a couple of cars so I could leave the incessant wail of his horn behind me.

I made it seven blocks before my car speakers rang through the blue tooth on my phone. Kayla's name slid across the touchscreen display on the console. I sighed. It wasn't what I needed right then. What was she calling for? To apologize?

I considered letting her go to voicemail but decided against it. I was a grown-ass man. I could handle rejection without drawing into my shell.

I answered the call. "Hey, sorry to run out on you like that."

"Lukas," she said. It almost hurt how she said my name like a fluttering exhale. "I wish you hadn't run off so quickly. I wanted to introduce you to the man who came up with the school lunch idea in the first place. Rodney is a really nice guy. A little pushy," she added, "but nice. And Good Fellow's wouldn't be where it is today without his support."

Just what I wanted to hear, the girl of my dreams singing the praises of another guy who happened to be exactly the kind of person she probably deserved.

"I'm working a shift with him this evening at the soup kitchen," she continued. "How would you feel about joining me and seeing what it's all about? You could meet some great people, like Rodney and the other volunteers and our community of people we help."

I made a thoughtful sound in the back of my throat. "I don't know if tonight is good for me."

"Please? I'm telling you, you'll enjoy it once you get past the ugly aprons and the hairnet."

I heard Rodney mutter somewhere close by that the aprons weren't that ugly. And damn him, he made her laugh. Kayla's bubbly laughter filled the line and she told him that yes, the aprons were in fact quite ugly, but there was no room in the budget to replace them.

"Come on, Lukas," she pleaded. "Just a couple of hours?"

"Fine."

"Really?" she asked excitedly.

"Really."

"Great! I'll text you the address. Be there at six o'clock, okay? We'll get you suited up and find a spot for you."

"See you there." I hung up the phone. I didn't have any interest in serving people their food. I preferred to be the guy who wrote the checks. That was what Kayla and Lisa wanted, wasn't it? They wanted me to help. Well, logically, the best help was to pour money right into the ground-floor organizations that were making the biggest steps forward. It would certainly be more help than scooping box-mix pasta onto a stranger's plate.

However, spending a couple of hours at the soup kitchen would afford me the chance to scope out this Rodney character. Maybe some time with him would help me rule out whether or not he was competition.

The soup kitchen wasn't an impressive place at all from the outside. I parked the Lykan down the block and put money in a meter. Now I stood in front of the soup kitchen. To my right was a line up of people waiting to get their dinner. Some talked quietly amongst themselves. Some whispered back and forth conversations with no other partici-pants, only the voices in their heads. Others fidgeted with strands of hair, their hats, or whatever they could lay their hands on.

Not one of them made eye contact with me.

Again, I regretted wearing a three-piece suit. I had to stop showing up dressed for my office when I was working with Kayla.

You could take a page from Rodney's book and wear khakis and polo shirts, I mused to myself as I stepped through the front doors and into the soup kitchen hall. The thought almost made me laugh. There was no way I'd be caught dead in what Rodney was wearing.

I saw him before I saw Kayla.

Rodney stood at the front of the line for food. His hair was matted flat beneath his hairnet and he grinned and shook hands with every person who came up to get their food. It was impossible not to notice the fact that he knew every single one of their names.

Every. Single. One.

I gritted my teeth and wished he would make it easier to hate his guts.

I turned my attention to the people milling around the hall and settling in at the cafeteria-style tables to eat their meals. Dirty faces hovered inches above plates of food and forks shoveled corn and potatoes into open mouths. People didn't talk while they ate.

They were starving.

My gut tightened uncomfortably at the memory of being a hungry child. I knew exactly how it felt to have a belly aching with hunger and a light head from a lack of nutrition. I knew what it was to be tired all the time, to have heavy limbs, and to feel like the world had turned its back on you.

Because it had.

Except for the people like Kayla who were in this very room doing what they could to make things better for these folks. There had been people like her in my life when I was young and my mother and I would sometimes have to spend several meals a week in a place like this to keep ourselves from wasting away. My mother had never been too proud to wait in line. She'd kept her chin up and told me there was nothing to be ashamed of. Sometimes, you needed help, and if there were people holding out their hands willing to offer that, you smiled, thanked them, and accepted what they offered.

You did not let yourself falter and grow weaker all for the sake of your ego.

It had been a hard lesson to learn and accept. As I stood here feeling like an imposter, I wondered if the lesson had truly ever sunk in. Why did I feel so small? Hollow? And hungry for something that wasn't food?

"Lukas!"

I turned at the sound of hurried footsteps. Kayla was there, grinning like she wanted to be in this place as she tucked loose strands of hair under her hairnet.

When she reached me, she stretched out a hand and smoothed it across the lapel of my jacket. "I think you need to go shopping and buy some mundane clothes for when we're working together."

I arched an eyebrow. "My suits are part of my identity."

She laughed and waved the comment off. "Oh please, that would be like saying my hairnet is part of *my* identity, and that's just silly."

"I think it looks cute."

Her cheeks turned a pretty rosy hue and her cheek puckered as she chewed on it. "Thank you."

Rodney stepped up behind her and closed a hand on Kayla's shoulder. He leaned forward and extended the other hand to me to shake. I shook it. His grip was warm and firm enough.

"Nice to meet you, man," Rodney said. "I'm Rodney. Kayla has told me lots about you. What you're doing for the school lunch program?" He shook his head incredulously. "It's the biggest donation we've ever received. I'm very grateful. I know a lot of parents who are going to be relieved when they hear the news."

Kayla beamed up at me. For a moment, I thought she looked almost proud.

"Nice to meet you too," I said to Rodney. What I really wanted to say was *take your damn hand off Kayla's shoulder*. However, I suspected she wouldn't like that too much.

"The ripple effect will be huge," Rodney said, letting his hand fall from Kayla's shoulder. She looked up and over her shoulder at him as he spoke. "Hungry kids have a harder time in school. They can't focus without proper nutrition, so their grades slip. This causes tension between teachers and parents and so forth, and the last thing these families need is more strain in their household. Having a full lunch every day will turn things around for a lot of these kids. I hope you realize just how life changing this will be for a lot of people."

I wanted Rodney to be an ass so I could justify my distaste for him, but every word out of his mouth was kind and educated.

Prick.

He gripped Kayla's arms from behind and rubbed up and down as if we were standing in negative degree weather and he was trying to warm her up. The soup kitchen was a comfortable temperature. All this unnecessary touching was, well, just plain unnecessary damn it. "Pretty cool, huh, Kayla? Of course, you were instrumental in making this happen. You guys make a good team."

She smiled at me. "I suppose we do."

My eyes narrowed at his hands sliding up and down her bare forearms. He stopped, stepped up beside her, and draped an arm around her shoulders. She looked down as he pulled her in close, the way a teenage boy might tug his girlfriend inward. It sent her a little off balance, and to steady herself, Kayla braced a hand on Rodney's stomach.

My temples ached and I realized how hard my jaw was clenched.

Why did she keep this from me? It was obvious from where I was standing that there was something—whatever that *something* was— between her and Rodney. Otherwise, he'd never be so handsy with her or she'd have told him off. At least I thought she would. And she hadn't.

Kayla sensed the storm brewing. Her eyes shifted back and forth between mine. She took a step forward. "Lukas?"

Rodney's hand slipped from her shoulders when someone called his name from the swinging kitchen doors.

I leaned in close to her. "It's clear from where I'm standing that I've been manipulated by a pretty face. Well done, Kayla. You almost had me. But I'm done with this. You hear me? I'm done with it."

"Lukas."

Her words drowned in the voices of the crowd as I turned and pushed through throngs of people to get the hell out of the soup kitchen and away from Kayla and Rodney.

How could I have been such a naive fool? How could I have believed this was anything other than her working her ass off to get the money she needed for her cause?

I gritted my teeth as I broke outside onto the sidewalk.

The road to hell is paved with good intentions, I thought as the anger brewed deep in my gut.

CHAPTER 18

KAYLA

R odney stood beside me with his arms hanging slack at his sides as we stared after Lukas, who'd just vanished through the main doors of the soup kitchen.

"What was that all about?" he asked.

I shook my head in disbelief. "I have no idea. Hold on. I'd better go talk to him."

"Are you sure you want to talk to him by yourself?"

"He's angry," I said with a shake of my head, "not dangerous."

Rodney pursed his lips. "I don't like it. I should go with you. Just in case. You know, to be safe and—"

"Rodney," I said, stopping him from following after me with a hand pressed flat to his chest. "I appreciate the thought but it's misplaced. Lukas is..." I trailed off. What was the word I was looking for? Temperamental? Moody? Complicated? "He's just got some stuff in his past and it makes it hard for him to trust people. He and I go way back. It would be better if just I go."

Rodney looked for a moment like he wasn't going to oblige, but eventually, his shoulders slumped a little and he nodded. "All right, go. I'll hold down the fort here."

"You're sure?"

"I'm sure. Go on. We can't risk losing his donation."

The donation hadn't even occurred to me. All I'd been thinking about was Lukas and what I'd done to make him so upset.

You need to get your priorities straight, I chastised myself as I hurried around the rows of tables and burst outside onto the sidewalk. It was a crisp cool day and the sun had sunk down behind the high-rise buildings on the other side of the street, casting everything into cold shadow. I wrapped my arms around myself and looked both ways down the street in search of the tall blond-haired billionaire who made me crazy.

And crazy *for* him.

A car engine revved and I spun to a red light at the cross street. I spotted Lukas' car just as the light turned green. His brake lights winked out as he hit the gas. The tires spun on the asphalt. Somebody nearby swore loudly out their window at him and Lukas peeled away, leaving the smell of burning rubber in his wake.

Based on the direction he drove off in and the anger I'd seen in his eyes, I figured there was one place Lukas Holt would go right now.

His office.

I didn't realize until I was on the bus that I still had my hairnet and apron on. More than a handful of people shot me amused glances as I turned bright pink and tore the apron and hairnet off. I tucked them both in my bag, which I left on the empty seat beside me. With a tired and worried sigh, I slumped low in the seat and stared out the window as we drove past office towers, retail boutiques, salons, and shoe stores. The area continued to get nicer until I got off at the stop closest to Lukas' tower.

I stood on the sidewalk with my head tilted back and gazed up at the massive building.

This was such a different beast than what I was used to. My stomping grounds were low-income neighborhoods consisting of one-level homes with disheveled front yards, rotting fences, and collapsing front porches. Nothing was shiny and new. Nothing was taken care of how it should be. But this place?

It was a palace.

The building, all shiny reflective glass that looked dark and moody in the cloudy evening, shot up into the sky like a spear. The lobby was a massive sprawling thing with a giant crystal chandelier above the front desk and polished gray floors that were so shiny they looked permanently wet. Modern artwork hung on some of the walls, most in shades of gray and navy blue, and sleek furniture offered pockets of seating for employees in the building looking for a peaceful place to sit on their break.

I knew Lukas only used the top floor for his office. All the other floors? Well, I'd never had it confirmed but I was fairly confident all the businesses in this tower rented their offices from Lukas.

As I crossed the lobby and made for the elevators, I wondered what sort of staggering monthly income Lukas made from his renters alone. Undoubtedly, it was a great deal more than Good Fellow's saw in an entire year of annual income.

The elevator delivered me to the top floor, where I stepped off and set foot on a white marble floor shining under the ceiling lighting above. I strode across the lobby of Lukas' office to the reception desk, where his receptionist was typing furiously at her keyboard. She glanced up at me, smiled, and asked me to give her just a minute.

As I waited, I peered around what I could see of the office.

I'd spent time in this waiting room already when I came for my first meeting with Lukas and Lisa. It was a pleasant space but it didn't feel all that cozy. I supposed Good Fellow's was far from cozy, but the haphazard layout, colorful post-it notes all over the place, and the tea-brewing station made it feel a little homier to me. This place felt cold, almost sterile.

It needs plants, I thought decisively. The green would be a nice pop of color against the white floors and the cool gray walls. Some pots in jewel tones would really add life to the space.

I gave my head a shake.

Why was I internally decorating Lukas' lobby?

I heard high-heeled footsteps approaching and turned to find Lisa coming around the corner. She had a black leatherbound planner in one hand and she turned to the receptionist and peered at the screen, after which she scribbled something in the planner, tucked it under her arm, and turned to head back down the hall.

"Lisa?"

She turned to me, looking like she was all business, but as soon as she laid eyes on me, she smiled. "Kayla, what are you doing here?"

I met her with a hug and pulled away. "I came to find Lukas. Is he here?"

My best friend shook her head. "He's been gone for hours. I thought he came to see you. Did he not drop by Good Fellow's?"

"No, he did. It's just…" I trailed off.

"Just what?"

I sighed. "Your brother is a very complicated person to work with, Lisa."

At first, she was expressionless. Her facade shattered and Lisa threw her head back and laughed. "That's quite a diplomatic way of saying he's an ass."

The receptionist giggled and hid her mouth behind one hand after shooting an apologetic look at Lisa.

Lisa nodded down the hall. "Come sit with me in my office. I have time before I have a conference call."

"Isn't it a little late for calls?" I asked as I followed her to her office.

"When you're trying to communicate with people in other countries, sometimes you have to be flexible." Lisa opened the door to her office and let me enter first. She closed the door behind us and walked over to a set of white leather sofas by the windows. She gestured for me to sit. "Make yourself comfortable. Can I get you something to drink? Tea? Soda? Vodka? Pick your poison."

"No thank you. I don't think I can stay long."

Lisa moved to a cabinet built into the wall behind her desk, where she opened some cupboards and went about pouring herself a rye and ginger. One of the lower cabinets was actually a fridge and freezer, and once she had her ice cubes in the glass and her drink poured, she joined me on the sofas.

"Your office is beautiful," I told her.

She looked around, admiring her workspace. "It's easy to create a beautiful room when your brother is fronting the design bill."

"Sneaky."

She leaned forward and rested her elbows on her knees. "So tell me what he's done now."

I licked my lips. "He hasn't really *done* anything, per se."

"Don't play coy, Kayla. Just spit it out. Did he back out of the donation? Did he cut the funding in half?"

"What? No, nothing like that. We had a misunderstanding is all—about the lunch program," I added hastily. The last thing I needed was for Lisa to get suspicious of me and Lukas.

Lisa rolled her eyes and slumped against the back of the sofa. "My brother has been a tad touchy lately, hasn't he?"

I shrugged. How was I supposed to know if he was being more touchy than usual? Up until last week, I hadn't seen him in years. Now he was all I could think about and all I could see when I closed my eyes.

It was all becoming a little infuriating.

Lisa tilted her head back and took a sip of her drink. "Some days, he's happier than I've ever seen him, and others, he's spiraling down the drainpipe, you know? He's so lost and I want to help him but he won't let anyone in. He's so..."

"Stubborn?"

"Yes." Lisa nodded. "Stubborn. Like a mule. Sometimes I wonder if it's all because of his mother's condition. She's been getting worse, I think. Not that he talks to me about any of it, of course."

I chewed at the inside of my cheek. "How is Ally doing these days?"

Lisa eyed me over the rim of her glass. "Not good. Not good at all, I don't think. Ever since the accident, Lukas has been pulling away. He keeps things between him and his mother pretty much to himself. I know it hurts him to talk about it but I wish he'd just open up to me a little bit. It's like he thinks he has to go through this alone. I don't know how many times I've told him he doesn't. How many times I've told him that I'm here."

"You're a good sister."

Lisa shook her head. "I don't know about that. He specifically asked me not to talk to people about his mother, and here I am, gushing everything I know to you. Not that I know much."

"Let's agree that this conversation never happened then."

Lisa nodded absently and ran her finger around the rim of her glass. "He needs to let people in, Kayla. He can't keep doing this by himself. It scares me sometimes."

"What does?

"Thinking about how he'll handle it when Ally is gone," Lisa said simply. There was a heavy note of sadness in her voice. "It's going to break him, and if he refuses to let anyone help him through it? Well, I don't know if he'll come out of that grief in one piece."

My throat ached. I willed the emotions down. "Lisa?"

She glanced up at me with glassy eyes.

"Lukas has always been full of surprises," I told her.

She smiled softly. "You're not wrong."

I got to my feet. "I have to go track him down. I need to talk to him sooner rather than later. Do you know where he might be?"

"If he's not at work, he's either drinking alone in a bar or he's at home."

"Home, it is," I said. "Do you have his address?"

"I'll text it to you."

"Thank you," I said before opening her office door. I turned back and paused. "Hey, Lisa? Lukas is lucky to have a sister like you. Even if he doesn't act like it, he knows that's the truth."

Lisa rolled her eyes. "You don't need to say that just to make me feel better. Go on, go. We'll catch up later."

I left my friend in her office with her woes and made for the elevator once more. It spat me out in the lobby, which was busier than it had been when I arrived. The workday was over and people were socializing in the lobby. Nobody paid me any mind as I crossed the polished floors and descended the stone steps outside to the sidewalk, where I waited at the curb for the next passing bus and hopped on.

As I rode, it started to rain.

115

I hated riding the bus when it rained. The humidity was insufferable. And the smell?

Not pleasant.

I had to transfer two times and ended up on a smaller shuttle that circled around the Puget Sound and eventually made it closer to Lukas' address. I had entered the address Lisa texted me into the maps program on my phone and discovered that the closest bus stop to his house was still a ten-minute walk away.

So I got off the shuttle and started walking.

My clothes were soaked through by the time I arrived at the edge of his property. It was gated, but the gate was open, so I strode through and made my way down the winding driveway up to the mansion at the end.

The house was incredible. It was a sprawling single-story estate of contemporary Spanish design. The house itself was white with black trim around all the windows. His car, the Lykan, sat parked in the pull-through driveway under cover of a built-in carport. The structure was being overtaken by ivy plants that gave the place a whimsical feel.

I stepped up to the black front door and lifted my hand. Suddenly, I was afraid to knock.

There was no telling which version of Lukas I was going to get when he opened this door. I suspected he was upset about Rodney but I couldn't be sure. That seemed to be what set him off back at the soup kitchen. But it was impossible to tell with Lukas sometimes.

I'd just have to knock and find out.

I rapped my knuckles six times on the door, and I waited.

CHAPTER 19

LUKAS

"Hold on!" I bellowed down the hall toward my front door.

Now was not the time for visitors. I wondered who was knocking on my door at this time as I tore my towel off the rack and peeled my sweaty back off the workout bench. I'd been lifting weights and pumping iron and broken quite the sweat. Exercise seemed to be the only thing that helped me keep my head on straight when my anger was getting the best of me.

And lately, my anger felt like it had become part of my personality.

I wiped the sweat from my brow as I got to my feet and padded down the hall to my door in nothing but track pants and sneakers. It was raining outside. I could hear it pinging off the copper roof overhead. The sound was almost soothing.

I jerked the door open and draped my towel over my shoulder.

There, on my doorstep, was Kayla.

At first, she stared into my eyes and I stared back at her. Then her lips parted ever so slightly and a tight sound escaped her. Her eyes broke away from mine and did a slow up and down of my entire body, starting at my feet and working their way up only to fall back down one more time for good measure.

I crossed my arms and braced my shoulder on the doorframe. "What are you doing here?"

"I—I—" She closed her eyes and gave her head a shake. I tried not to smirk. I liked watching her squirm. Perhaps the key to getting what I wanted with her was to start wearing fewer clothes. She opened her eyes again and fixed them on me, this time refraining from checking me out. If it took effort, it didn't show. She'd collected her composure. "I was hoping we could talk about what happened at the soup kitchen."

"And what exactly did happen at the soup kitchen?" I asked.

"That's what I wanted to find out."

Of course, she was oblivious. Of course, she was going to make me feel like this was all in my head.

Damn her for screwing with me.

I arched an eyebrow. "I don't have anything to say about it."

"Well, I do," she said sharply. "So are you going to invite me in or are you going to leave me standing out here soaking wet in the cold?"

I sighed and stepped back. "Come in then."

Kayla squeezed past me like she was afraid to touch me. Chuckling, I closed the door behind her. She took off her soaking-wet sneakers, peeled off her jacket, and walked on the balls of her feet down my hallway to the back of the house where everything gave way to an open concept flow.

She didn't say a word.

People were usually rendered speechless when they entered my not-so-humble abode. The house was a showpiece and a daily reminder to myself that I was no longer the poor boy who grew up with nothing. Every collected piece of art from around the globe was a promise kept to myself that I would not settle and that I would see every corner of the world I'd always believed I'd never have a chance to visit.

Kayla wrapped her arms around herself when she reached the living room. "Your home is stunning, Lukas. I've never seen anything like it."

"Thank you."

Her compliment left me feeling out of sorts. Normally, I was proud to show this place off. I wanted the compliments. I wanted the recognition. I wanted the verbal reminder that I was enough.

But I didn't feel that way tonight.

I felt guilty.

Kayla let her purse fall from her shoulder. I moved to take it from her, but she shot me a look, and I stopped with one arm half outstretched.

"What?" I asked.

"I don't like what happened at the soup kitchen."

"Neither did I."

She put a hand on her hip and blew out an exasperated sigh. If her hair hadn't been matted to her forehead from the rain, I was sure she'd have blown it out of her face. "If I've done something to offend you, please tell me. Don't just storm out expecting me to figure it out on my own. My head is too full of things I need to remember, Lukas. Things I need to do. I can't anticipate your emotions when you won't tell me what's wrong."

I arched an eyebrow. "You sound like my sister."

"Good."

I rolled my eyes.

Kayla took a step forward. Rain dripped from the tip of her nose and landed between our feet. "I value your partnership and our friendship." Kayla's voice dropped a little lower when she said the word *friendship*, and my body responded with a feeling of tight anticipation. Lust.

I pulled my towel from my shoulder and held it in front of my crotch to hide the pitching tent happening inside my track pants. "What about you and Rodney then?"

"What about it?"

"How close of friends are the two of you exactly?"

Kayla laughed nervously. "We're colleagues, nothing more."

"Nothing?"

She shook her head. "Nothing. We've known each other a long

time. It's comfortable. Maybe at times a little too comfortable on his part but—"

I grabbed her arm and pulled her close. Kayla gasped and tried to back away, but I held fast, one of her wrists gripped in one hand while I put the other on her waist. "Being your friend has its perks if I'm allowed to touch you like Rodney does then."

Kayla's eyes narrowed. "You have the wrong idea, Lukas."

"Do I?" I growled. "Because from where I was standing today, it looks like I have a pretty clear idea." I moved my hand from her hip and trailed it up her side and across her chest. Her skin was still glistening with raindrops and I broke their perfect round dots upon her flesh with the tips of my fingers as I worked my way up the side of her neck. I pushed the wet hair from her forehead and she tilted her head back to gaze up at me. Her cheeks were flushed, her lips full and begging to be kissed. "What do you want from me, Kayla?"

"I don't want anything," she whispered.

"Lies."

"Let me go."

"Do you want me to let you go?"

Her eyes darted back and forth between mine. Her chest fluttered with quick, desperate breaths. Her mouth was saying one thing, but her eyes and her body were saying something else entirely.

"I want," she whispered. "I want..."

There was no more time for talking.

I yanked her up against my bare chest. The air rushed out of her lungs and I kissed her deeply. This time, there was no working our way up to the passionate, desperate kissing. This time, we started at full force. She ran her hands up my bare stomach. She clung to the waistband of my pants. I cupped the back of her neck and practically bent her backward as she suckled at my bottom lip and dared me to lose control.

I wrapped my arms around her waist when her knees went weak. I held her up and she whimpered against my lips as the kiss deepened. A soft moan escaped me, and she froze.

Suddenly, she gasped sharply and pulled herself away. This time, I let her go.

Kayla pressed her hands to her head and ran her palms over her already slicked-back wet hair. She shook her head and refused to meet my eye. "I think you have the wrong idea about our friendship," she said breathlessly.

I gritted my teeth.

This push and pull with Kayla was driving me mad. I couldn't stand it. I wanted her, but I knew she'd never let me have her.

It was exhausting.

"Fine," I grated. "You wanted to talk? Let's talk. I'm not interested in doing any more of your hands-on activities."

"But at the farm, you said—"

"I want to keep it simple. I don't have the luxury of time to dive into every little project with you. Farms and soup kitchens. Who do you think I am, Kayla? Let's just get this thing done and wrap it up with a pretty bow, and then you don't have to spend any more time with me than absolutely necessary. Sound fair?"

Kayla wrung her hands. "Lukas, that's not what I wanted. I'm just trying to understand—"

"I want a fundraising gala. Quick, effective, and done in one night. The press can be there if they want. I really don't give a damn. We'll have a traditional dinner and charge five thousand a plate."

Kayla's eyes widened. "Five thousand dollars *a plate?*"

"Wealthy people won't bat an eye at that. Aim high, Kayla. Don't assume to know the budget of a stranger. Besides, people will throw money at something if it makes them look good and gives them an excuse to show up in their best dresses and suits to rub elbows and gossip with other socialites. It's not that complicated."

Kayla pulled her purse strap up onto her shoulder. "A gala is possible but I tend not to throw them because they cost so much to host."

"I'll pay for it. All the tickets and donations will go straight to Good Fellow's. Deal?"

Kayla looked down and nodded weakly. "If that's what you want to do, we can make it happen. I'll start working on it right away."

She didn't look up at me when she brushed past and made her way back down the hall to the front door. I considered following, but the hint of sadness in her voice and her eyes made me feel like the ass I'd been, and I doubted there was anything I could say to take the sadness away.

So I let her leave, heard her close the door behind her, and resented the taste of regret that sat at the back of my tongue.

CHAPTER 20

KAYLA

"Are you sure there's no chance of rescheduling?" I asked desperately. I'd been on the phone for over twenty minutes with the event coordinator at the Ritz Carlton, who was steadfastly sticking to her guns and had told me nearly a dozen times over that no, there was nothing they could do to open up a ballroom for me to host my fundraiser.

"It's being hosted by Lukas Holt," I said, name dropping him for the tenth time that day.

"So you've said," the woman on the other end said. "Look, I know you're in a tight spot, but I can't call up the bride and groom who are using the ballroom that day and ask them to reschedule their wedding because Lukas Holt wants it for a fundraiser. I don't care who he is. I'm not doing it. My commitment is to my clients. We can fit you in at the end of January."

"That's too far away." I sighed. "I'm sorry to have bothered you. Thank you for your time and your help."

"Good luck."

I hung up the phone, slumped forward on my desk, and groaned.

I'd been working around the clock for the last few days trying my hardest to get my foot in the door with a venue for the fundraiser. A fundraiser that I wasn't even all that interested in hosting.

I hated fundraisers.

I hated the flashy decor and the centerpieces nobody could see over. I hated the gaudy jewelry and the tacky clutches decorated in rhinestones or, in the case of the guests coming to this particular event, diamonds.

The guests who came to these kinds of things never much cared for the cause their money was actually going to. All they cared about was a chance to be seen. They'd buy their way into the event so they could show off their glamorous dresses and designer suits. They'd pull up in their fancy cars and flash smiles at people they hated, who they would promptly talk about behind their back as soon as the chance permitted.

The young ones would end up in coat check to make out with people their parents forbade them to speak to. Others would take it up to a suite they'd booked for the night because they had better sense than to rely on a coat-packed storage room. Others would leave early, pile in the backs of luxury SUVs, and head home to indulge in each other.

And me?

Well, I'd be running around like a chicken with my head cut off, praying like hell nobody wanted or needed anything from me. The last thing I wanted to do was talk to these rich, egotistical, manic, self-ish, overindulgent, trust-fund dicks.

My office door swung open. I peeled my cheek off the back of my hands and lifted my head to see Lisa removing her sunglasses and tucking them in a small pocket in the lining of her designer purse.

She smiled at me and cocked her head to the side. "Looks like someone is having a long day."

"You have no idea."

"What's up, babe? Talk to me." Lisa pulled out the chair across from me and sat down. She set her purse on the floor and crossed one leg over the other.

She looked nice today. Her blonde hair was slicked back, a couple of strands hanging loose to frame her face, and she wore clean makeup with a bold burgundy lip.

Sometimes, I wished I had a reason to get a little dressed up for work. I couldn't help but feel a little insecure in my blue men's shirt that said "Good Fellow's" on the front and my faded jeans.

"Lukas switched gears on me the other day," I admitted.

"Oh?" Lisa cocked her head to the side.

I sighed heavily and nodded. "He doesn't want to do any more hands-on activities apparently. And here I was thinking the farm had gone so well."

"What does he want to do then?"

"Guess?"

Lisa stared blankly at me. "I don't know."

"Galas."

Lisa scoffed. "Of course, he does. Talk about taking the easy way out. Is that what you're stuck doing then? You're trying to plan a gala?"

"Yep. He said he'd host and pay for everything. I've thrown these kinds of things together before but not to this extent. He wants to charge five thousand dollars a head, Lisa. *Five thousand dollars.* Obviously, I can't just call the Comfort Inn and ask if they have one of their conference rooms available. I need a glamorous venue. Something chic and popular that people will actually want to come to."

"Have you tried the Hilton? Or the Ritz?"

"Both are booked."

Lisa pursed her lips thoughtfully and drummed her fingers on the armrest of her chair. "I might know a guy."

"What guy?"

"Just a guy," Lisa said dismissively. She leaned over to open her purse and pulled her phone out. She scrolled through her contact list and frowned at the screen.

"Can he help us?" I asked

Lisa nodded. "Yes."

I waited for her to dial, but she didn't. So I smiled. "Lisa, you don't have to call him. I'll figure something out. I just need more time, is all."

"No, don't be silly. I can help. Besides, he owes me." She pressed dial and lifted the phone to her ear. Whoever she was calling answered on the third ring. I heard a deep male voice say Lisa's name into the line. She looked down at her lap. "Hi, Stephen. Yes, I know it's been a long time. I hate to do this to you but I was actually calling to cash in on that favor."

She was quiet for a minute as this man, Stephen, said something to her.

I tried to look busy so she didn't feel like I was listening to every word she said, even though that's exactly what I was doing.

"Look," Lisa said. "I'm trying to get my hands on a venue for a fundraiser my brother is hosting. Yes, Lukas. Who else would I be talking about when I say my brother?"

I tried to hide my smile. Whoever this guy was, I suspected there was a bit of history there.

"Never mind," Lisa said. "The point is we're on a bit of a time crunch and we can't get a ballroom anywhere. So I want yours. The Saturday after next. Six o'clock until, well, until whenever the night ends. Our guests are not the sort of people you can impose a curfew on."

He said something on the other line that sounded a lot to me like "absolutely not."

Lisa held up a finger to me. "You owe me, Stephen. Remember? And you know I'm not one to ask for help but you're the only person I can go to right now."

He said something else that made her smile.

"Yes, well, times have changed," she said. "So are you going to give me the ballroom or do I need to go to someone else for help?"

He started talking about price.

Lisa shook her head. "I think you have the wrong idea, Stephen. I want it for free."

He didn't like that. I heard his voice rise and he started giving Lisa a piece of his mind.

She was unfazed. "I know it's not ideal for you, but trust me. This event will bring people in. If you have any suites open, they'll fill up, I promise. The press will be there. Your hotel will be featured as the beautiful backdrop of a spectacular evening for Seattle's wealthiest citizens. Don't tell me you can't see the value in that."

A couple more exchanges were made before it came clear that Lisa was coming out on top. Eventually, Stephen caved, and Lisa secured the ballroom for free with a triumphant smile. "You're a dear, Stephen. You have no idea how much this helps me out. Thank you so much." She ended the call and dropped her phone back in her purse. She wiped her hands together like she was a gymnast who'd just performed an incredible feat and was now knocking chalk off her fingers and palms. "Piece of cake."

I eyed her suspiciously. "So who is Stephen?"

"He's the owner of the Hotel Monroe."

My eyes widened so much so that I thought they might pop right out of my skull. "The Monroe? Are you serious? We're going to get the Monroe for the fundraiser?"

Lisa beamed at me. "Sure are, babe."

"That's the fanciest hotel in Seattle! And what, you say the right things and you're able to swindle the ballroom for free on a Saturday night? How is that possible?"

"Stephen—I mean Mr. Edmonds," she amended, "owes me a favor. And I'm a hard woman to say no to."

"Why is this the first time I'm hearing about you knowing Stephen Edmonds?"

Lisa shrugged. "He's a bit of a jerk. I don't like to bring him up in casual conversation. He's just the sort of guy you keep in your back pocket for things like this. I got him out of a pretty bad PR scrape a couple of years back and he told me he would make it up to me when I needed help. This seemed like the right time to cash in on that."

I leaned forward with a conspiratorial grin. "Is there more to this thing between you and Stephen than just you being his PR rep?"

Lisa shook her head. "No. Absolutely not. I don't like to talk about him because he's not worth thinking about. Don't get it twisted, Kayla. Sometimes, you keep people around because of what they can do for you. It's just good business."

I let the matter lie. Clearly, Lisa didn't want to talk about it. But letting it lie didn't mean I wasn't suspicious. Something had certainly happened between the pair. Whether it was just business or something more, I suspected I might never know.

"Thank you for your help," I said. "I felt like I was slamming my head against the wall trying to make something work. This is a huge load off my shoulders."

"My pleasure." Lisa got to her feet and retrieved her sunglasses from her purse. "Let me know if there's anything else I can help you with. I have a lot of connections, so if you need hookups with caterers for a glamorous event like this, I'm your girl. I could probably swing some entertainment, as well as bartenders too. You are going to do a full-service bar, right?"

"Of course," I said smoothly.

"Good. Make sure there's a specialty cocktail or something. The rich love a fancy drink they can post to their socials. Branding is in the little things."

"Right. Specialty cocktails. Anything else?"

Lisa shrugged and opened the office door. "I'm sure you have it under control. Email me what you have so far and I'll start working on the marketing. I'll contact the photographer from the farm and Rebecca Mills, too. No harm in having our own little media team snapping pictures and asking Lukas questions during the event."

"You'll have it within the hour," I promised.

Lisa left and I dove back into work, feeling relieved that we at least had a venue but feeling equally overwhelmed at everything else I still had left to arrange.

CHAPTER 21

LUKAS

The Monroe ballroom was as beautiful as ever.

I'd been to my fair share of weddings in this ballroom, all of which had been overdone, tacky, and obnoxious. But tonight?

The place was perfect.

The lights were dim and candles flickered on nearly every surface, creating a warm ambiance and inviting atmosphere. White plates sat on gold saucers, framed by gold cutlery upon burnt orange napkins. The centerpieces were elegant floral displays of rich fall colors: red, copper, gold, orange, and hints of yellow. The place had the feel of extravagance and minimalism all at once, and I knew immediately that Kayla had a hand in the decor.

Had she hired someone, it would have been as over the top as usual.

I stood in the entryway for a brief moment to get my bearings. There, across the ballroom, was the bar. Above it hung a long crystal chandelier which had been fed through with more floral arrangements that matched those on the tables, creating a woodsy aesthetic. The bar itself was elegantly appointed, and each and every stool in front of it was full.

The night was already in full swing.

The guests milled around in their best dresses and suits. Women walked arm in arm with their husbands, who stopped to discuss business with other men whose wives hung off their arms. The women would smile pleasantly but never open their mouths. Their heads would turn on swivels as they looked around and studied the crowd for familiar faces. Diamond earrings caught the light and glittered in competition with diamonds draped around necks and wrists and fingers.

Peacocks, I thought morosely. *They're all damn peacocks.*

"I need a drink," I concluded.

I began making my way through the ballroom toward the bar. On my way, I was stopped several times by the businessmen and their wives.

"Mr. Holt," a familiar and stout man with a bald head said, stepping in my path to the bar. "It's good to see you, young man. How have you been?"

"Doing well, sir," I said. His name was lost on me. His eyes, friendly and brown, were familiar, but I could not recall how I knew him. "And you?"

He ran a hand over his concealed belly beneath his suit jacket. "Quite well, quite well. This is a function and a half you have on your hands tonight. I must admit I'm a little surprised.

"Surprised?" I asked.

"Well, this hardly seems like your neck of the woods, son. A fundraiser? For a non-profit?" The man chuckled knowingly, and his brown eyes slid across the ballroom toward the stage on my left. "Perhaps there are other factors at play here?"

I followed his gaze until I saw who he was looking at.

Kayla.

She stood up on the stage by the podium. She was speaking to a hotel employee in black pants and a crisp white suit. He was a young man, probably no more than twenty-four, and whatever she was saying to him was making him smile.

She had a way of making everyone smile.

The stage lighting shone down on her and lit her up like she herself was part of the ballroom decor.

Her dress was simple and sleek. It was not like the gowns the other women at the gala wore. Where they wore puffy, sparkly, excessive dresses that needed to be picked up for them to walk, Kayla wore one that hung close to her body. It was silky and dark forest green. It looked familiar, but I must have been imagining it.

As I watched her, I realized she seemed uncomfortable. This was not a familiar environment to her. She held herself stiffly, like she was anticipating something going wrong at any moment, and even though she was smiling at the hotel employee, her eyes continuously darted around the room, looking for where she might be needed.

Then her gaze landed on me and she went rigid.

A jolt of electricity rushed through me. My fingertips tingled with the force of it. She was so beautiful and so off limits it hurt.

I gritted my teeth.

"Yes," the brown-eyed man said with a knowing smile. "Other factors indeed."

I grunted. "Sorry, sir. I was on my way to meet someone at the bar. Maybe we'll run into each other again later."

He let me leave without any protest and I made a beeline to the bar, where I ordered a whiskey on the rocks. As soon as the drink was in my hand, I took a greedy sip, followed by another, until the sharp sting of wanting the girl I couldn't have felt a little less sharp.

Conversation rippled around me.

"Did you hear about his daughter? Her husband has been having an affair for six years and she had no idea! Can you imagine?"

"That's his mistress in the red dress."

"She's not even that pretty."

I kept my head down and tried not to get sucked into the gossip transpiring between the two young women at my end of the bar. They had their backs to me and were watching the herd of socialites like two hungry lionesses.

"She must be so embarrassed."

"No wonder she hasn't shown her face yet."

"Do you think her father knows?"

"Do you think he cares?"

I moved to the other end of the bar to ignore the petty conversation. Here, I found myself between an older couple waiting patiently for their drinks and two middle-aged businessmen, both of whom were leaning on the bar with their heads bowed together as they chuckled about something.

"I didn't want to come to this damn thing," the taller of the two men said before he tipped his head back and drained the contents of his glass in a large gulp. "But the wife insisted. She claimed it would do us some good to put our money toward something that helps people. But you know what I think?"

"What?" The second man was shorter than the first by about half a foot. He had an impressive moustache that concealed his entire upper lip and he looked like the sort of man who liked to smoke a cigar at the end of a long day in a quiet room by the fire.

"I think these people we're supposed to be *helping* have done this to their damn selves. How many chances did they get to make a better choice? How many people tried to help them get clean? How long do they expect the rest of us hardworking people to fund their existence?"

Fund their existence?

The shorter man snorted into his beer before taking a swig. "I'd say you're onto something, Lewis. But watch your tongue in this place. There are softies about, trying to ease their conscience with their five-thousand-dollar plate and the raffle tickets."

"Ease their conscience." The man named Lewis chuckled without humor. "What have they to ease their conscience over? Hard work means wealth, Ken. Plain and simple. You know it and I know it. We worked hard for our money and we're expected to just give it away because we have a lot to go around? I didn't work this hard to give thousands of dollars to drug addicts and ex-cons who—"

I set my drink down hard on the bar.

Lewis looked over his shoulder at me while Ken narrowed his eyes.

"Something to say?" Lewis asked.

I faced them directly and rested one elbow against the bar. "If you're going to have such an ignorant conversation, I suggest you move to a dark corner where nobody can hear you making fools of yourselves."

People passing by paused as they heard my words.

Lewis straightened. "Excuse me?"

"You heard me," I said dryly. "If you didn't want to be part of the event, you could have stayed home and let your wife come out and enjoy her evening. I'm sure she would have preferred you weren't here, seeing as how you're flapping your mouth, embarrassing yourself quite publicly."

Ken eyed me. "From where I'm standing, only one person here is making a fool of themselves, and that's you, kid."

I arched an eyebrow. "You think the guy hosting the gala to raise money to feed starving children and their families is the one making a fool of himself?"

It sounded douchey when it came out of my mouth, but I meant it. This was the equivalent of them calling Kayla an embarrassment in my eyes. She dedicated her life to helping these people, and asshats like these men were what stood in her way a lot of the time.

I stepped closer to the two men. "You're not better than anyone simply because you have more. You're less than them if you have more and do nothing to help. When you reach the top, you're supposed to turn around and help others find success, too."

Lewis laughed. "Great, a socialist."

I rolled my eyes.

"The poor are given every advantage to get ahead," Lewis said. "They get tax breaks and benefits and financial assistance. But us? We have to work our asses off to keep our heads above water. Every time they get money, they snort it up their noses or inject it in their arms. They have nothing because they're weak and lazy, not because they got the short end of the stick. Educate yourself, young man."

"Weak and lazy?" I asked sharply. My temper flared. My blood rushed in my ears.

How dare these men call the people who were barely scraping by selfish and lazy? My mother had been anything but lazy when we lived in the apartment co-ops and survived by eating at soup kitchens or cashing in food stamps. My mother had a job. She worked her ass off. And these clowns probably spent the majority of their days on their yachts or with their feet up at their houses while their waitstaff did everything for them.

I moved in close enough that I could have reached out and grabbed Lewis by the front of his jacket. "The only weak and lazy people I see are the people like you," I seethed. "People who think they are owed their wealth and are entitled to keep it. You talk about how you've worked hard for your money. You're full of shit, Lewis. You and I and everyone in this damn room know for a fact you inherited millions from your father when he died. And you know what you did with those millions?"

Lewis backed up.

"You blew it on women and cocaine," I hissed.

"Everybody calm down now," Ken said, his voice thin with worry. "We were just talking. No need to make things personal."

"Oh, it's fucking personal," I said, never taking my eyes off Lewis. "I suggest you get your head out of your ass and go write a massive fucking check to Good Fellow's. At least your wife will think for a brief moment that you're a good man. Then you can walk yourself out of this ballroom and back to your car and get the hell out of here before I decide to take matters into my own hands and—"

"Lukas," a warm feminine voice cut me off.

I looked down to my right shoulder and found Kayla smiling up at me. Her cheeks were rosy, and even though she was smiling, I could see worry in her eyes.

"What are you three talking about?" she asked, her voice methodically controlled.

"Nothing," I said through clenched teeth. "The *gentlemen* were just leaving."

Lewis looked me up and down before breaking away from the bar with Ken hot on his heels. I watched them retrieve their wives in the crowd and make for the ballroom doors.

Kayla cleared her throat. "I hardly think swearing at and attacking the guests is going to help us raise money. What was going on? What did they do?"

"Come with me."

I grabbed Kayla's hand and led her out of the ballroom. She didn't try to pull away from me. She smiled at people we passed and promised we'd be back soon, but she had no idea where we were going. We broke through the ballroom doors, emerged in the lobby, and strode to the elevator. I jabbed the call button and waited. The doors slid open and we stepped inside.

I pressed the button for the top floor.

"Lukas, talk to me. Where are we going? Why were you so upset? Who were those—"

I rounded on her. "Stop talking."

With a soft chime, the doors closed, and we were alone.

CHAPTER 22

KAYLA

I was trapped in the corner of the elevator. Lukas caged me in and stepped in close. His face was a mask of anger and I knew it was a good thing I'd interrupted his argument with the two men at the bar when I did. Had I not intervened, there likely would have been an article published the following day about Lukas Holt throwing two fifty-year-old men out on their asses in front of the Monroe Hotel.

It would have been a scandal and a PR nightmare and I never would have heard the end of it from Lisa. Not to mention the damage it might have done to Lukas' already staggering reputation.

"Lukas," I breathed. His name was the only word I could think to say. My mind was a fuzzy, jumbled, white-noise-filled space.

"I'm tired of this runaround," he said. His voice was gravelly and deep.

I tried to speak. I tried to ask him what runaround he was talking about. But no words came out.

"I want you, Kayla," he said.

My heart hammered wildly in my chest.

He moved in closer. His eyes raked over the length of my body and I wished I'd had the foresight to wear a dress that didn't betray my arousal. My nipples hardened and pressed against the silk fabric as he closed in on me.

"And you want me too," he said, finally stopping when he was well within my personal bubble. He planted one hand on the elevator wall beside my head and stared down the length of his nose at me. "No more games. No more pretending."

"I'm not pretending."

"Don't lie to me."

I licked my lips.

What could I say to get him to give me space?

The better question lingered in the back of my mind.

Do I want him to give me space, or do I want him to take what he wants, consequences be damned?

"Look at me," Lukas barked.

My eyes darted up to his.

"Tell me to stop," he whispered. "Tell me to stop and I'll listen."

I swallowed.

He moved quicker than I anticipated. One minute, he was staring into my soul, and the next, he had a hold of the back of my neck. I didn't resist when he dropped his head, and his lips crashed against mine. He tasted like whiskey and something sweet and spiced, like chai. He smelled like musk and pine and citrus and I gave in to the rush of my own blood, pumping in a chorus of desire screaming at me to go for it.

Let him touch you.

I draped an arm over his shoulders as he craned my neck back to kiss my throat. His lips were warm and soft as velvet as he worked his way down my neck and across my chest. He lingered at the swell of my cleavage until a strap fell from my shoulder and exposed half of my breast. A deep, guttural growl escaped him.

My knees trembled and my thighs felt like I'd just done a three-hour spin class. He pinned me to the wall, his fist still clenched in my hair, and I gazed at the bright lights in the ceiling as he jerked the top of my dress down to expose the rest of my breast. He cupped me in one hand and pinched my nipple with his thumb and forefinger. A breathless giggle left me but it was stolen away when he sealed his mouth over my nipple and flicked at me with his tongue.

"Someone might catch us," I whispered. Every word hitched in my throat like it was getting caught on thorns. "*Lukas*, please."

"I don't give a damn if someone catches us."

"I do," I muttered.

He broke away and released my hair. I struggled to catch my breath as he shielded me from the door with his body. My breast was still exposed but he stared into my eyes. "I've been waiting too long for you to make me wait."

We crashed together again.

When the doors opened with a soft chime, Lukas blocked me from the view of the hallway as I pulled the straps of my dress back up. Luckily, nobody was there. He took my hand and led me down the hall to the Presidential Suite, where he swiped his card and shouldered the door open. He ushered me inside ahead of him and slapped my ass as I brushed past.

Hard.

It stung. I yelped. His deep chuckle followed me into the depths of the room as he closed and locked the door behind him. He didn't turn the lights on. All that illuminated the room was the moonlight streaming through the open curtains.

Neither of us went to draw them closed. The hotel had a glorious and unobstructed view of the city, and with the lights out, nobody would be able to see us.

At least that was what I told myself as I turned back to Lukas to find him shrugging out of his suit jacket and stepping out of his shoes. He undid his belt, and as his fingers worked, I stepped in close and began working on the buttons of his shirt. One at a time, I popped them open. Each one came free and taunted me.

One step closer to feeling him.

One step closer to tasting him.

One step closer to doing what I swore I never would.

The last button came free and I slid my hands up his shirt and over his shoulders. The shirt fell free and landed behind him. Finally, I could see him without having to pretend I wasn't looking. All of him. Every ridge of muscle, every rippling vein, every freckle, blemish, rib, and inch. He was magnificent.

Lukas caught my wrist as I ran a hand across his chest. "Your turn," he purred.

He released me.

I took a step back and stood framed in the moonlight pouring through the window at my back. I could take a hint. I dropped one shoulder and the strap of my dress fell. I dropped the other and the second strap slid free. A slight twist and a gentle roll of my shoulders sent the silky gown falling free, and it landed in a gentle gathering around my feet.

I stepped out of the green silk and stood before him in nothing but a pair of black seamless panties.

Lukas soaked in the sight of me. His eyes roamed the length of my body several times over before he discarded his pants and closed the distance between us in four long strides. He stopped inches away and reached upward. His hand hovered in front of my face, tracing the air around my jaw and hovering over my lips.

All I could hear was the sound of my own uneven breaths.

"Touch me," I whispered. "Please."

Lukas' thumb grazed my lower lip. I closed my eyes as his touch trailed across my cheek and down my neck. He traced my shoulder and my collarbones. He grazed my nipples and cupped my breasts and came back up to hold my chin so he could pull me in for deep, desperate kisses.

I needed more. I needed everything.

"More." The word left my lips in a half growl, half plea. I hooked an arm around the back of his neck and pulled him down to me.

Lukas obliged by gathering me in his arms and picking me up. I hooked my legs around his waist and felt the rock hard swell of his cock pressing against the fabric of my panties as he carried me to the bed. He threw me down none too gently and I laughed before he descended on top of me, cutting off my breathless giggles with a fierce kiss that set my veins on fire.

His kiss left my lips and trailed down, down, and farther still until he settled between my thighs, a pleased sound rumbling in his chest as he pulled my panties aside. For a brief, panicked moment, I realized what we were about to do.

There was no going back after this.

If there was a time to say no, it was then. It was all I had to do. One little word and it would be over and we wouldn't have taken things too far.

We wouldn't have betrayed Lisa.

But the word never left my mouth and Lukas' tongue glided up the length of my pussy, tasting me, savoring me, making me *feel* what I had not felt in a long time.

I gripped the blanket beneath me. "Oh," I whimpered. Lukas sealed his lips over my clit and suckled. My grip on the bed tightened and my body took over. "Oh *wow.*"

He chuckled against my pussy and I wished I'd been able to keep my mouth shut. The last thing Lukas needed was a bigger ego.

But holy *hell*, did he know what he was doing with that mouth of his.

He teased, licked, and suckled until I writhed on the bed. He slid his hands under my ass so he could hold my waist with me resting upon his forearms. It gave him control. I shouldn't have been surprised he wanted control in the bedroom. I was more than willing to give it to him. I let him turn me slightly on my side, let him push my leg back, let him plunge a finger inside me while he rolled his tongue over my clit in the most exquisite rhythm.

My body tensed.

Lukas pressed another finger inside me. Pressure mounted. My vision blurred and my heartrate accelerated. I forgot what we were doing was wrong and forgot that I had to be quiet. A cry of pleasure broke free as I came. Lukas didn't stop what he was doing until I relaxed on the bed, breathless and spent, wondering why I'd let my life get so busy that I no longer had room for sex.

Sex was glorious.

How had I forgotten?

Lukas slid off the edge of the bed and stood. He turned from the bed and bent over to pick up his pants. In the pocket, he found a condom. He flashed it at me with a devilish smile before tossing it on my stomach and leaving it there while he stripped out of his boxers.

I couldn't tear my gaze from his cock when it sprang free.

He grabbed me under my knees and dragged me to the end with him, letting my ass hang off the edge and supporting me with a knee under my right thigh as he stroked his cock. He plucked the condom from where it rested on my stomach, tore it open, and discarded the wrapper on the floor. He rolled the rubber on and dropped his hips to rub the length of his cock up and down my swollen pussy.

"I've been thinking about this for weeks," he growled as he planted his hands on the mattress on either side of my head. "And it wasn't nearly as good in my head as this is."

"Just shut up and fuck me," I managed to say.

The look of sheer lust on his face made my insides tighten.

Lukas gave me what I wanted. He slid inside me. I was wet and needy, and even though he was bigger than I could imagine, I took him. It hurt only briefly, and he waited for me to adjust to him before he began working his hips in a slow thrusting rhythm.

I gripped his forearms on either side of my head as he plunged in and out of me. My ass still hung half off the bed, and the momentum of his thrusts worked with the balancing act. I was forced up against him every time he drove down.

The combination was exquisite. My toes curled. I couldn't lose control this quickly. I had to hold on. I had to keep it together.

But what he was doing felt so good. Too good.

My back arched and my nails bit into the skin on his forearms. Lukas dropped lower and I met him with a kiss. His breath was sharp and hot against my cheek when he nudged my face to the side to pinch my earlobe between his teeth. A fluttery sigh escaped me that made him growl in response.

The sound pushed me over the edge.

I stifled my cry in his shoulder when I came. He bucked harder and deeper until he too lost control. His thrust slowed as our orgasms ebbed away, and he pulled back to look down at me.

I swallowed and closed my eyes when he pulled out and went into the bathroom to clean up.

Lying alone on the bed, my afterglow didn't last long before my mind went into overdrive.

We weren't supposed to do this. He was my best friend's brother. He was off limits. It didn't matter how good the sex was or whether it was the best sex of my life. What mattered was the damage this affair could have on other people and our reputations.

Our careers.

I sat up and raked my fingers through my hair as I let my legs dangle off the end of the bed. My toes were cramped after being curled. I wiggled them, but that only made it worse, so I hopped off the bed and stood flat footed while I listened to the water run in the bathroom.

Feelings floated around in my belly that I knew I shouldn't have. They were too strong. Too misplaced. It made no sense for me to feel the way about Lukas that I did. The risks were too high. What if he didn't feel the same way? What if he was only using me to work with Lisa and improve the way the public perceived him? Was I just a means to an end?

I hurried to put my dress back on and fix my panties and hair.

I didn't want another short-term hookup. What happened tonight could not happen again. If I was going to be smart about this, I needed to build a wall between us. Otherwise, one of us was going to be damaged when all was said and done, and I doubted it would be the billionaire who could have any girl he wanted.

I knocked on the bathroom door. "Lukas? I'm sorry, but I have to go back downstairs. I've been gone too long already. Don't come find me. This... we shouldn't have done this."

The water turned off on the other side of the door but I didn't stick around and wait for him to come out.

I ran.

CHAPTER 23

LUKAS

"So, how do you think the gala went, Mr. Holt?"

Rebecca Mills sat across my desk from me with one leg crossed under the other. She was dressed boldly in a matching ruby-red pantsuit. Her shoes were shiny black heels with red soles, and I noticed the curl of a cursive tattoo peeking out along the side of her foot.

I wondered what it said, but my mind was then occupied with thoughts about the gala to respond to her question.

How did I think it went?

Well, for starters, I'd had the best sex of my entire life that night in the Presidential Suite. I'd argue it had been more than just sex. It had been transcendent.

But as soon as Kayla and I had finished making love, she'd gotten dressed and bailed, claiming she had to go back downstairs to work.

To say I had been disappointed would be a gross understatement. After sex like that, I figured this thing between us had been solidified. In reality, it felt like Kayla and I were somehow even further apart. She was somehow even more unreachable.

I'd wondered over the past few days since the gala if Kayla's only priority was her work. It bothered me to think that it might be, and that was rich coming from me of all people, a type-A workaholic for over a decade. But seeing those same habits in someone else— someone I cared a great deal for—made me question everything. It made me realize how closed off I'd been.

"Mr. Holt?"

I glanced up at Rebecca and cleared my throat. "Sorry, got lost in thought for a minute there. I heard it went well and that we raised a lot of money. One hundred and fifty thousand was the last tally, I heard."

Rebecca smiled. Today, she hadn't brought a pen and paper but rather a recording device. She held it in one hand, her index finger poised over the red record button. "Actually last I heard, you were closing in on the two hundred and fifty thousand dollar mark. An impressive feat."

I plastered a smile on my face. "I'm happy people were willing to contribute and I could play a part in a successful charitable evening."

Rebecca eyed me suspiciously.

I frowned. "What?"

"I couldn't help but notice that you left the gala early. Very early."

My eyes widened. I hadn't even realized Rebecca was at the gala, but of course, it made sense that she would be there.

Rebecca carried on and I couldn't tell if she was playing games with me to get to the truth or if this was just how a reporter like herself conversed. "I'd been spending the evening with Lisa, who was introducing me to other CEOs and businessmen at the party. I wanted to get some background quotes about you, you see. Everybody likes an origin story. But by the time we went looking for you, you were nowhere to be found. Not one for late nights, or you just didn't want to stick around for a dinner that cost you five thousand dollars?"

I considered making up an excuse as to why I left the gala early but the thought made my chest feel heavy with exhaustion. I was tired of keeping part of myself tucked safely away. Wouldn't it be easier to just be honest? I didn't have to tell her about Kayla and me, but I could tell her what had been on my mind that led me to drag Kayla up to the Presidential Suite in the first place.

"I've never really been one for galas," I admitted, "or lavish parties of any kind really. I've attended more of them than any man should ever have to in my time and I think I got it in my head that fancy dinners with high ticket prices were the only way to be charitable. Or the most effective. But since working with Good Fellow's, I've come to realize this isn't the case. The non-profit gave me an opportunity to have some hands-on experience and now I can't go back to how it used to be before that."

"How did it used to be before that?" Rebecca asked.

"Removed," I said. "Galas let the rich feel good about themselves for a night. They let them think they're doing enough when they could do so much more. Now, I'm not saying everyone has to become a charity worker. I'm not saying that at all. All I'm saying is we could all do with a bit of a reality check. These kinds of fundraisers are too far removed from the real issues. Folks don't even know what the issues are that they're giving to half the time. And I used to be one of those people. I have a lot of regrets about that."

I was saying a lot of things I'd never said before and Rebecca was catching it all on her little recording device.

She leaned forward and draped an elbow over her crossed knee. "Why do you have regrets?"

I shrugged one shoulder and thought for a moment before answering. The response grew clearer in my mind. "I used to be the guy who thought the fundraisers were enough. But I realize now that I was foolish, which is especially ironic because I used to be the kid who needed the help so I didn't go hungry."

"Can you tell me more about that, Lukas?"

"I grew up in an apartment co-op. I had a single mother who worked tirelessly to provide for us, but when nobody wants to take a chance on you, it's impossible to get your foot in the door and make any real money. We struggled for a long time. As a kid, I thought I had it harder. You know how kids are, unwillingly self-absorbed. I thought about how I wanted more. How I wanted to be more. How I couldn't bear the thought of never getting out of those rundown condos. But I never thought about how hard it was on my mother until I was older. She was the one with the real worries. She was the one paying the bills and trying to put food on our table. She was the one who felt like she was failing on the nights when there was no food. I owe her a lot. I owe her everything."

Rebecca pressed her lips together and was quiet for a minute.

I didn't know where all of this was coming from. I never intended to share my past like this, especially with a reporter, but the words were flowing, and part of me suspected this meant it was time for the truth to come out.

There was no more time to hide the boy I used to be from the world.

"Do you think your past is what made you into the man you are today?" she asked.

I shrugged. "Sure, but isn't that the case for all of us?"

"I suppose you're right."

"I overheard a conversation last night that rubbed me the wrong way and I left before I spoiled the evening for everyone," I said. "There was ignorance in that room that made me feel ashamed because I used to—" I broke off and shook my head.

"Used to what?"

I used to be like Lewis and Ken. I was a damn bastard for it, too.

"It doesn't matter." I shifted in my chair. "The point is, those with less means are just as deserving of having their stories told, of being respected, as people who have everything. Or the illusion of everything."

"The illusion of everything?" Rebecca pressed.

"Fast cars, big houses, luxurious high-rise office towers. None of that matters. None of that equates to having everything."

Her eyes twinkled. "What does equate to having everything, Mr. Holt?"

I studied her and she stared calmly back. "I don't know yet," I said truthfully.

"But you're trying to find out?"

"I think I'm making a mess of things, but yes, I'm trying to find out."

Rebecca pressed the little red button on her recording device and leaned back in her chair. "I think people are going to like what you have to say."

"I didn't say it so they would like it. I said it because it's the truth."

"I know," she said, her dark eyes still twinkling. "And I respect it. You are not the man I took you for when we first met. Thank you for being so open with me. This is what makes good articles. Truth and insight. And a good picture, of course." She got to her feet and tucked her recorder in her purse. She paused and turned to me. "Would you like to grab a drink and talk a little more? Off the record, of course."

Her forwardness surprised me. Had Rebecca Mills just asked me out on a date?

She was beautiful, intelligent, talented, hardworking. She checked all the boxes. But she wasn't the woman I wanted. A few weeks ago, I might have said yes, even knowing that fact. I might have strung her along and indulged her in a drink or four, and then I might have taken her back to my place to show off my home and my bedroom.

But things were different now.

"Thank you, but I don't think that would be a good idea," I said, choosing my words carefully. "Let's keep our conversations on the record."

Rebecca gave me a pleasant but tight-lipped smile. "On the record, it is. We'll talk soon then. Have a good night."

"You too." I walked her to the door, let her out of my office, and closed it behind her.

I settled back into my chair behind my desk and spun to face the windows. In the distance, little white dots marked sailboats on the Puget Sound. A restlessness that had been burning inside me before the interview returned, and I knew there was only one way to silence it.

I needed to talk to Kayla.

Somehow, I had to make things better between us. I hated the thought of moving forward with Good Fellow's but not with Kayla.

Somehow, there had to be something I could do to repair the damage I'd done.

We had to talk openly, and the only way to do that was in person. I fetched my coat from the back of my office door and left, hoping to find Kayla at her Good Fellow's head office.

CHAPTER 24

KAYLA

Lisa frowned at the water cooler as it bubbled and burped while spitting water into a biodegradable six-ounce cup.

"You really need to get some upgrades done, Kayla." She straightened up when her cup was full and drained the contents in three sips. She tossed the cup in the garbage can beside the cooler and frowned when I arched a skeptical eyebrow at her. "What?"

"Those are compostable. I buy them for a reason. They go in the green bin."

Lisa looked down at the garbage can. "It's a cup."

"It's a biodegradable cup," I said. "The whole point is that it cuts back on waste and plastics. Please put it in the green bin."

Muttering to herself, Lisa bent over, retrieved the cup, and dropped it in the green bin beside the garbage can. "Better?"

"Yes, thank you."

She wiped her hands on her jeans. Today, Lisa was wearing a pair of dark-washed bell bottoms and red pointed-toe heels. Her black blouse was tucked into the jeans and part of me really envied her outfit. I would never know what it was like to rock an ensemble like that. The nicest thing I'd ever worn was the silk dress I wore to the gala, and that had been Lisa's. I didn't own anything glamorous enough to wear to a gala, so I'd had to ask her to borrow something.

At first, she'd tried to get me into a royal-blue fitted bodice with a full skirt. It seemed ludicrous to me and reminded me of a prom dress. There was no way as a grown-ass woman and the director of a successful non-profit that I was going to show up to a function in a dress made for eighteen-year-olds.

Lisa rested her elbow on top of the water cooler and her temple in her palm. "So we knocked it out of the park with the gala, huh?"

"We?"

"You and Lukas," she conceded with a knowing smile. "Sorry, sorry, I'm not trying to steal credit. But it went off without a hitch and you pulled in just over three hundred grand. That's wild! You must be proud of yourself."

"It's a good feeling for sure."

"And just think," Lisa said as she moved over to my desk and sat down in one of my chairs. "This will raise the company's profile among other tech companies in Seattle. Maybe it'll even engage a little competition. Competition always means good things for charities. Who doesn't want a bunch of people throwing money their way in the name of friendly one-upmanship?"

"It's beneficial for sure."

I was lying through my teeth. Yes, I was pleased about the amount of money we'd raised at the gala, but I wasn't all that pleased with the results of the fundraiser. Sure, the money was going to make a positive and necessary impact in a lot of people's lives, but the engagement with the attendees at the gala was low. In translation, all that meant was they didn't really care what charities they were donating to or what the cause of said charities were. About sixty percent of the people in attendance only showed up because it gave them something to do that night.

To add salt to the wound, I couldn't help but feel a little bitter toward Lukas, who'd insisted we host this gala and then ended up being equally if not more disappointed by it than I was. And I'd put in some serious work to pull it off. I'd skipped meals, missed shifts at the soup kitchen, and holed up in my office for an extra three hours a day to make that night happen.

"What do you think we should tackle next?" Lisa asked.

"Next?"

She nodded earnestly. "Yes. What, did you think we were going to stop there? I don't think so. Lukas needs all the help he can get, and even though the gala was fruitful, it's not exactly the best form of PR. We need more hands-on and engaging activities for him to throw himself into. Like the orchard. So tell me, what are some of your ideas?"

My tongue was glued to the roof of my mouth. I tried to speak, but all that came out was a muffled sound.

Lisa opened her purse and rummaged around. She paused to look up at me. "Pardon?"

I cleared my throat. "I don't know what's next."

Admittedly, I was afraid to spend any more time like that with Lukas. Time with him was what had gotten me in hot water in the first place. How was I supposed to keep my guard up if I kept getting thrown into situations like the orchard? That was the nail in the coffin for me. Seeing him with Angelica had softened the frost around his heart and torn down the walls I'd built around my own.

And now Lisa wanted me to do more of that?

Lisa found a tube of lip gloss, unscrewed the cap, and swiped it on her lips. It was shimmery and red. "Well, you'd better figure something out quickly. Rebecca Mills wants more material. She called the other day and told me she had an excellent interview with Lukas the other day. Apparently better than all the others. She claims he really got vulnerable with her."

"Lukas? Vulnerable?"

"Yep, I was shocked too." Lisa tucked the lip gloss back in her bag. "Apparently, it's quite the interview. Rebecca said I'll want to read it. I assume you will, too."

"Sure."

"Now," Lisa said, leaning forward and clasping her hands together on my desk. "Let's talk about how we can put that brother of mine to work."

My cheeks burned. *I have a few ideas of how I could put him to work.*

I was about to answer Lisa's question when the office door opened.

Lisa twisted in her seat and clicked her tongue when she realized it was Lukas blocking the sunlight streaming through the glass door. "Well, well, well," she said, "speak of the devil."

Lukas' jaw tightened at the sight of his sister and I knew immediately he hadn't expected her to be here, which meant he was here to see me.

Why? What do you want?

He swallowed. His Adam's apple slid deliciously up and down his throat. "What are you doing here?"

"Me?" Lisa asked, pressing an innocent hand to her chest. "Why shouldn't I be here? I'm visiting my best friend. Why are *you* here?"

Lukas' eyes darted to me. "I wanted to discuss the charity food drive with Kayla."

"Food drive?" Lisa twisted back to me. "You never mentioned a food drive."

"Lukas and I had only discussed it," I said. "We hadn't committed to it."

Lukas cleared his throat and rocked back on his heels as he slid his hands in his pant pockets. "I was just in the neighborhood, so I figured I'd pop in and say hello. We haven't seen each other since the gala."

I licked my lips. "No, we haven't."

Lisa looked back and forth between her brother and me. "Well, aren't you going to sit down then?"

Lukas shook his head. "No, you two chat. I couldn't stay long anyway."

"Then why pop in?" Lisa pressed.

Lukas scowled at her. "Has anyone ever told you that you're insufferably nosy?"

Lisa grinned. "All the time. It's part of my charm."

"Charm," he scoffed as he turned back to the door. "Keep telling yourself that, little sister."

I stood up. "Lukas, I—"

"I'll catch you around," Lukas said, and then he was gone.

I stood there like an idiot staring after him while Lisa frowned up at me.

"Did you do something to piss him off?" she asked.

"I don't think so."

She shook her head. "I don't know what's going on with him lately. I guess I never know. He's all over the map. One minute, I think I have him pinned down, and the next, he pops in to your office saying he was just passing through the neighborhood." She let out a sarcastic laugh. "As if anyone in their right mind would just pass through *this* neighborhood?"

I swallowed my frown at my friend's insensitive remark. Clearly, Lisa was becoming just as out of touch with her roots as Lukas had. Since when did she consider herself too good for this neighborhood?

My neighborhood?

"Anyway," Lisa said, leaning back in her chair so she could kick her red-soled high heels up on my desk. "Let's talk about what's next for you and Lukas."

"What's next?" I asked innocently. Ever since sleeping with Lukas, I was on high alert about everything his sister said. I couldn't help it. I constantly thought she was trying to suss it out of me that I'd hooked up with her brother—when in reality, she was just carrying on with life as usual.

"Yes, I want something with great visuals. Something that will photograph well. You know, like how the orchard did? We need something hands-on and exciting for Lukas to tackle. Something others haven't done before."

I chewed the inside of my cheek and considered what she was asking me for. "Hang on. I have a list of upcoming charity events. You can pick whichever one sounds like a good fit."

I rummaged through my filing cabinet drawers and did my best to ignore the look of judgment on Lisa's face. I could hear her own thoughts screaming in my head: *if you'd just clean your office, you wouldn't have to look for things.*

She didn't understand. She could never understand. I was busier than I'd ever been in my entire life and my mind was overflowing with information I didn't know how to handle—like how good Lukas was in bed.

"Here we go," I said as I pulled a yellow sheet of paper out of a file. I moved to the desk and laid it flat in front of Lisa. "The first twenty-four have already happened, so you can choose from the remaining ones left for the year."

Lisa pulled the paper closer and squinted down at it. "Toy drives, food drives, and Thanksgiving brunch at the soup kitchen. These are all so mundane. We need something colorful and vibrant. Something that marketing can really run with. Something like—" She broke off and grinned. "Here. This one."

Lisa spun the page around so it was facing me and pressed the tip of her red fingernail toward the bottom of the list.

I leaned over the page and read the word. "The haunted house?"

"Yes. The haunted house. Can't you picture it? Lukas dressed up in a costume, scaring kids, working in the house, making people scream? Better yet, if someone can get a good scare out of him. If that doesn't humanize him, I don't know what will. And look, the funds go directly to a local homeless shelter. It's the perfect event."

"It's not an event, Lisa. It's a fundraiser."

"Same, same."

I grimaced.

Lisa popped up out of her chair. "Okay, you know what to do. Make it happen. I'm going to call Rebecca and Meredith and make sure the duo is there to photograph and interview. Oh, shit!"

"What?"

"It's this weekend!"

"Yes."

Lisa rushed to the door. "Call Lukas. Make sure you can get him there. I'll handle the rest, okay?"

"Um, okay, but what if he doesn't want to go?" I found it hard to picture Lukas dressed up as anything but Lukas.

Lisa grinned at me. "Ask him nicely. For you? He'll go."

With that, my friend left me reeling in the truth of her words. If only she knew the full extent of what we'd done behind her back—and what I was still fantasizing about every night before I went to sleep.

CHAPTER 25

LUKAS

The tires bit into the gravel as I came to a slow stop in a parking spot in the middle of a field. I frowned and glanced at the GPS in my center console. This was it. This was the address Kayla had given me for the haunted house.

Up ahead was a transport trailer. There was a line of people outside it waiting for their turn to go up to the window. It was hard to see from where I was, but it looked like that was where the haunted house ticket sales were. I put the car in park, turned it off, and stepped out.

For once I'd used my foresight and opted for jeans, boots, and a leather jacket in favor of a suit. As I walked across the gravelly yard, I was thankful for that decision.

The air had a chill to it. It smelled like hay and dirt and hot chocolate, which I realized was coming from the window of said trailer. Not only were they selling tickets, but they were selling hot chocolate, brewed coffee, and cider as well. Parents with children made up the bulk of the line but there were a fair amount of teenagers too.

Almost everyone was in costume.

As I walked past the trailer and the line, I spotted vampires, clowns, werewolves, fortune tellers, fairies, kittens, dinosaurs, and ballerinas. I passed ninjas and mutant turtles and waved at a little girl dressed up like a ladybug. She promptly turned toward her father and hid behind his legs. If she was afraid to wave at me in jeans and a leather jacket, I hated to think how she'd handle the haunted house.

I proceeded down a dirt path flanked by wheat fields on either side. I hadn't been out to this particular country area before and it had taken me quite some time to find it on the GPS. Now that I was here, I could see why. It was quite literally in the middle of nowhere. The fields rolled on until they met darkness and the human eye could see no farther. Somewhere in the distance I thought I'd be able to see Seattle's city lights, but that wasn't the case. Fog hung low over the fields and made the air feel chilly and damp.

I tucked my hands in my pockets and bunched my shoulders up to ward off the chill as a structure took shape up ahead of me.

There it was. The haunted house.

It materialized out of the night and fog like a specter, and as I drew closer, I could hear haunting music pouring out of it accompanied by the sounds of teenagers shrieking with horror and glee. Children screamed in earnest, fathers laughed, and mothers? Well, based on the crowd of women I saw near the exit I assumed a great deal of them had no interest in going in the haunted house and had left their families to their own devices.

Kayla had told me to meet her in front of the house at seven in the evening. I was ten minutes early and I turned in a slow circle to peer around and see what else was around. There was nothing. I frowned.

Someone called my name.

I turned to the source. From around the side of the haunted house, a woman dressed as a creepy doll approached. Her hair was done up in high, messy pigtails, her face was painted white with high rosy cheeks, and there were stitches etched into her eyebrows and the corners of her lips. She walked with a lumbering, lopsided, messy gait, and I didn't realize until she was right in front of me that the doll was actually Kayla.

Laughter consumed me. "I did not expect this."

Kayla looked down at her costume. "What?"

"You look…" I trailed off. "Good."

You always look good, creepy stitches or not.

Kayla grinned like a damn fool and pinched the hem of her tutu skirt in her fingers so she could do a little curtsy. "Thank you. It took two hours to get this costume up to snuff. Freaky, right?"

"Very freaky."

She tilted her head toward the house. "Come with me. There's a costume trailer around back. One might call it a very low budget green room."

"Green room?"

"We have to get you dressed up too. Did you think you were going to get away with working a haunted house without having to dress up? Have you ever done Halloween properly?"

I followed her around the side of the haunted house. More screams tore out of the building and I chuckled. "What would you say if I told you I hadn't dressed up for Halloween since I was eight years old?"

Kayla stopped in her tracks and spun to look at me. Her pigtails whipped against her cheeks and her lips parted in an incredulous gasp. "Since you were eight?"

"Yeah, Halloween just isn't really my thing."

Her eyes narrowed. "I find it hard to believe any holiday is your thing, Lukas."

"Why's that?" I followed her as she started walking again.

"Because, holidays mean you're not spending time at work. And if you could have it your way, you'd spend every minute of every day in your office. Right?"

We rounded the back corner of the haunted house and just as Kayla had said, there was a trailer set up. The door was ajar and warm light spilled out onto the dew-covered grass. We moved into the pocket of light and Kayla entered the trailer. I followed and was met with the smell of glue and an old attic. When I spied the racks of Halloween clothes, I found the source of the smell. The costumes looked a little old, like they'd been toted around from event to event, and they'd collected a bit of a musty smell probably from spending three hundred and sixty or so days packed up in boxes.

"I don't know if I'd want to spend every day in my office anymore," I admitted as Kayla began sifting through the racks of clothes. "It's been kind of nice to get out and try new things."

She paused with her fingers resting on the elbow pads of an old tweed jacket and I willed her not to force me to put the monstrosity on. "Kind of nice?" she mused.

I shrugged. "Yeah."

She gave me a knowing smile and shook her head before going back to sifting through the costumes. "We have a station in that haunted house to get to in half an hour, so we have to make this quick. Do any of these speak to you?"

"Speak to me?"

"Do you want to wear any of them?"

I studied the racks of clothes. "Not particularly. You pick."

Kayla smirked and moved to the end of the rack, where she plucked a one-piece cream-colored thing from where it hung. From the back it looked like one of those terrible one-piece pajama sets that people had started wearing. When she turned it around, I realized it was not pajamas, but a one-piece clown costume with big multicolored pom-pom buttons, a jagged striped cuff on each sleeve, and a wide striped lapel that had been splashed in fake blood.

Kayla pumped her eyebrows. "What do you think?"

"Creepy killer clown? I think I can work with that."

Kayla turned to a chair that very much resembled that of a barber shop. It had the metal foot rest and everything, and it faced a wall of mirrors with a shelf over flowing with what appeared to be makeup products.

"Have a seat," she said. "Let's get you ready to scare the shit out of some kids."

Kayla and I were assigned to a room in the haunted house that, had I been the eight-year-old version of myself, might have made me piss myself. The walls and floors were black and the lighting was poor. Mounted in the ceiling above our heads was a black light that made the fake blood on my costume seem to glow. There were no mirrors in there but Kayla and I snapped a picture of ourselves to see how we looked under the lighting, and even though I looked like the world's most terrifying clown, I liked the picture.

I was glad we'd taken it on my phone so I could save it without having to ask her to send it to me.

Also in the room with us was a baby crib in which a deformed doll stood clinging to the bars. A soundtrack played on a loop of a baby crying while a woman hummed a haunting melody in the background.

In the far corner was a rocking chair, presumably where said humming mother would be rocking her child, and Kayla had taken up post there. She sat with her knees drawn to her chest and her arms wrapped around her shins while I stood with my back to the opposite wall, shoulders hunched, head tilted down, frozen in place.

Every time guests passed through, we'd let them see the baby. Let them creep forward toward the exit that they had to pass both of us to reach. Let them cling to each other and mutter worried whispers in each other's ears. Let them think they were alone in the room.

When the time was right, we'd spring to life and scream bloody murder at them.

Most of the kids screamed and laughed, the thrill they were seeking granted, and took off running to the exit to meet their fate in the next section of the maze. Others, mostly the adults, had a hard time walking past Kayla and me at all. Sometimes, we'd have to sink back into our positions and stay still in order for them to muster the courage to pass us.

After an hour and a half of delightfully scaring strangers, the house closed for a half-hour break. Kayla and I stayed in our room and she fished granola bars from somewhere out of her tutu. They were almond and honey bars dipped in vanilla yogurt.

"So what do you think?" Kayla asked.

"I think I'm having more fun than I should." I pressed my lips together. "Is that a little sadistic?"

Kayla giggled. "Maybe just a bit. But everyone here is signing up to be scared. It's a bonding experience. People love the adrenaline rush and the thrill, and they love having someone to experience it with. Someone to cling onto. It's kind of romantic, in a strange way, when couples come through."

"You have a strange mind, Kayla Goodfellow. A strange mind."

She stuck her tongue out at me.

She'd been effectively scaring strangers all evening, but to me, she looked adorable. I tried to consider her costume objectively. If I hadn't known her, would the doll ensemble be unsettling? Perhaps. But I did know her. And from where I was standing, the pigtails, red lips, pink cheeks, tutu, white stockings, and red sparkly shoes were cute not sinister.

"Have you done this before?" I asked as I leaned up against one of the walls and polished off the remaining bites of my granola bar.

Kayla shook her head. "No, I was supposed to last year but they had enough volunteers and didn't need me, so I took the night off. It was actually very lovely."

It was hard to imagine what Kayla was like when she wasn't working. Like me, she was a workaholic. "How did you spend the night?"

Had she not been wearing layers of white face makeup, I might have been able to tell she was blushing. She went back to her rocking chair and sat down. "I went home and ate an entire box of Halloween candy by myself, watched a movie, and went to bed before ten. It was glorious. Possibly the best night of all last year. Is that sad?"

"No, it's not sad. I get it."

Kayla ran her fingers through the fold of her white tutu, and for a moment, she looked sad, like a doll no child wanted to play with.

CHAPTER 26

KAYLA

It was embarrassing to admit that I'd spent last Halloween completely by myself locked up in my one-bedroom apartment that I could hardly afford. I'd eaten Halloween candy because I couldn't afford a bottle of wine, and I'd crashed early because I'd been so tired from working the last sixty-five days in a row that I hadn't been able to keep my eyes open.

I couldn't help but wonder what it might have been like to have someone with me that night. Someone to share the candy with so my belly didn't get hard with bloating, someone to watch a horror movie with instead of a romantic comedy so I could sleep easy, someone to cuddle and share warmth with before dozing off to sleep.

Someone to just be there so I wasn't alone.

"Kayla?"

I glanced up at Lukas. He was watching me with a furrowed brow.

"Are you okay?" he asked.

I nodded vigorously. "Yes, yes, of course I am."

He put his empty granola wrapper in his pocket and pushed off the wall to come stand beside my chair. "Aren't you going to ask me how I spent Halloween last year?"

I tilted my head back to look up at him. "How did you spend Halloween last year?"

He smiled, but it didn't touch his eyes. "By myself."

"What did you do?"

"I stayed at the office until ten thirty. Surprise, surprise. I only left when I realized I was holding up the night-shift cleaning crew who all had families to get home to. Otherwise, there's no telling how late I'd have stayed. When I got home, I had a drink, and then I went to bed."

I licked my lips. "Why are you telling me this?"

He crouched down beside my chair, and this time, he smiled earnestly. "I just didn't want you to feel bad about being alone. We're both losers, you see."

I hesitated before throwing my head back and laughing. "I am *not* a loser."

"Are you sure? Maybe just a bit? Because in recent weeks, I've realized that I am most definitely a loser."

"You're not a loser, Lukas. You're just very involved in your work. And so am I."

"Exactly. Losers. We have no social life. No commitments outside of our careers."

"That's not true."

He arched an eyebrow at me. "Name three social outings you have planned for the next three months."

"I—" I paused, frowned, and considered the question. "I don't have any. Do you?"

"No."

"Do normal people?"

He laughed and put his hand over mine. "With Thanksgiving around the corner? Yes, I would say most people have plans in the near future."

"Oh my God," I breathed. "We *are* losers."

"I tried to let you down easy."

I shifted in the rocking chair to get comfortable. It creaked and rocked softly. "Well, I guess we all make sacrifices for what is most important to us. My work is what's most important to me. The people

I help are what's most important to me. I don't think I'd change it. Would you?"

He searched my eyes for a beat before shaking his head slowly. "No, I don't think I would. I mean, maybe I'd spend more time with Lisa, and my mother, and you, but—"

A bell rang to signal the start of the next hour of haunting. The lights went out and a hush settled over us. I wanted to hear more of what Lukas was going to say but he straightened, rolled his shoulders, and moved to claim his place against the opposite wall. He shared a small, tight-lipped smile with me as we both settled in.

And waited.

We heard the screams coming and knew a procession of teenagers were on their way toward us. The haunted house took about fifteen minutes to walk through, and about eight of those minutes happened up ahead of us. Lukas and I were basically dead center of the maze, so when people came to us, they were vulnerable. They knew they had a ways to go and they'd already had a few good scares before reaching us, which made them easier to trigger.

The group of teenagers drew closer.

Lukas sank against the corner of the wall and I tucked my chin to my knees and watched the doorway the group would enter through.

The baby soundtrack shrieked and wailed and the mother hummed eerily in the background. For added effect, I began slowly rocking the chair.

Lukas gave me a thumbs-up and I hid my smile behind my bent knees.

The teenagers arrived. Two young boys entered first. They had to be around thirteen or fourteen years old. They walked shoulder to shoulder, muttering to themselves, trying to act tough, and then two young girls came in behind them. One of the girls looked truly terrified. She clung to her friend, her eyes wide with fear, her feet inching tentatively forward, her lips moving as she pleaded with her friend not to abandon her.

I wondered if Lukas and I should hold back with this group.

Lukas sprang to life in his corner. His arms shot up and he let out a bellow of a sound. The boys yelped and sprang forward to rush to the other door while the girls cowered at the entrance. I untangled myself from the rocking chair to tell Lukas to ease up, but I was too late.

The terrified young girl started to scream in earnest. There was no play left in her. This was genuine fear.

I rushed for the light switch.

Lukas beat me to it. He flicked the light on and killed the audio, and we simultaneously shielded our eyes against the glare of the lights. My ears rang from the screaming and the loud baby crying track.

Lukas unzipped the front of his clown costume to show the girl his T-shirt underneath. He rolled up the sleeves, exposing bare forearms, but did not move closer to her. "Hey," he said, his voice soft and warm. "I'm just a guy. See? Just a guy in a clown costume. Do you want to leave the house?"

The girl nodded with a trembling bottom lip. She still clung to her friend who, to her credit, had not left the girl's side.

Lukas turned to me. "I'm going to escort them out. Can you hold down the fort?"

"I'm coming with," I said. "I'll leave behind you and turn the lights out. If you go through the next hall, there's a door on the right. It's hard to see but it's there. It will lead outside so you don't have to finish the maze."

Lukas nodded, turned, and led the girls out. They followed hot on his heels and I waited until they were gone to turn the audio track back on and the lights. Then I hurried out after them and caught up with them along the side of the haunted house, where Lukas was smiling at the girls and speaking with them. I hung back to listen to what he told them.

"I'm not a huge fan of clowns either," he said. "Honestly, I never understood them and why people wanted to dress up as them in the first place. But listen, they're not that scary. They're unemployed. And weird."

The girls smiled at him.

"Thank you." The frightened one's voice trembled. "I didn't expect to lose it like that."

"Happens to the best of us," Lukas said earnestly. "I had to spend the whole night sitting across from her." He nodded at me as I hung back. "Now that's scary."

The girls giggled. He was charming even when wearing a creepy clown suit.

Lukas and I brought the girls to the exit where they met up with their friends, and we stood shoulder to shoulder as the group of four peeled off toward the parking lot, giggling like idiots.

"That was very nice of you," I said.

"I thought she was going to have a stroke."

"She might have," I mused. "She was pretty terrified."

Lukas got a devilish look in his eye as he peered down at me.

I frowned. "What?"

"I have a secret mission. Do you want to help?"

"A secret mission?" I asked suspiciously. I shook my head. "No, you've got that twinkle in your eye that I've only seen when we were kids and you were about to pull a prank on Lisa. I don't want anything to do with that."

"I'll write you a check for a quarter of a million dollars if you help me with this."

"A quarter of a million dollars?" I gasped.

"Yes."

"For a prank?"

"Yes."

I tried to hide my grin. "Let's go."

Lukas parked the Lykan at the curb half a block down from the duplex Lisa shared with her mother. Lisa lived on the left-side unit and her mother in the right. It was a lovely home with exposed brick on the first level and cream siding on the second. There were pumpkins on both doorsteps and autumn-themed wreaths hanging on the doors. I was struck with a sharp pang of envy that I resented as Lukas and I crept up the sidewalk in our costumes and broke off into the front yard to creep around to the back of the duplex.

I'd always dreamed of owning a place of my own one day. It would be nice to have a place that felt like home. My apartment was a messy, crowded, haphazard, and poorly decorated clusterfuck of mismatched items I'd acquired from thrift stores or friends and family who no longer needed their coffee table or bookcases. I didn't have the time or the money to create the atmosphere I wanted but I spent a lot of time daydreaming about what my future home might look like one day.

Hopefully, the dreams wouldn't always be dreams.

The damp grass made our footsteps silent as we rounded the back corner of the duplex and moved into the backyard.

A branch cracked under Lukas's foot.

We froze.

A dog barked, one of Lisa's mother's dogs.

"Oh shit." Lukas snickered in front of me.

I jabbed him in the shoulder. "Shh!"

He massaged the place where I'd prodded him. "Ow."

The dogs started barking in earnest. All two of them.

Lukas swore. "I forgot about the damn dogs."

"Do we run?"

A back-patio door slid open. Lisa poked her head out and peered out into the darkness of her yard. Lukas and I were crouched low, pressed up against the back of the house to her right.

Lisa saw us and shrieked.

Lukas bellowed at her and leapt forward. She fled inside and slammed the door behind her. The dogs in her mother's unit went absolutely crazy and the lights in the living room flicked on.

I grabbed Lukas's shoulder. "We have to go!"

He turned and pushed me back toward the front of the house. I took off running for the car with him hot on my heels, and before we even hit the sidewalk, I was laughing so hard my ribs hurt and tears were leaking out of my eyes. His laughter followed me, loud and free, and as I got in the passenger seat of his Lykan, he leapt over the corner of the hood and got behind the wheel.

If he hadn't been wearing a ridiculous clown costume, the whole thing might have looked quite suave.

He slammed the car into first and peeled away as more lights were flicked on in the duplex. I kept laughing all the way through the neighborhood, my ribs aching, my head spinning, and I didn't get the laughter under control until he pulled into an empty park overlooking the Sound.

"That was awesome," I breathed, slumping back against the seat. "I've never heard Lisa scream like that."

Lukas turned the car off and chuckled deeply. "Did you see her face? She thought we were there to cause some unholy hell or something. My sister watches too many horror movies."

"Her poor mother."

"A good scare keeps people on their toes."

I turned in my seat to face him. "Do you think we should tell them it was us?"

His eyes moved back and forth between mine. "Now why would we want to go and take the fun out of it? It can be our little secret."

I swallowed. We already had one of those and I felt guilty enough keeping it to myself. "Another little secret?"

He nodded slowly. "Do you think you can handle that?"

I licked my lips as he leaned closer. "I think so."

"I need a yes or a no, doll face."

I pinched my bottom lip between my teeth to stop myself from smiling. "Yes."

CHAPTER 27

LUKAS

For the first time in months—years—I felt full.

The way Kayla looked at me in the passenger seat of the car made it easy to see right past the creepy makeup and tattered doll clothing. All I saw was her. A kind spirit, a wise soul, a fierce friend, and a passionate lover.

She was the girl of my dreams, and right then, every fiber of my being pleaded with me to reach out and kiss her. Take her. Remind her what it was to be loved by Lukas Holt.

Kayla let out a breathless sigh and settled back in the seat. She closed her eyes and clasped her hands in her lap. "Tonight was so much fun."

"It was, wasn't it?"

She cracked open one eye and smiled at me. "I'm glad you came."

"Me too. I—"

"Oh, shoot!"

"What?"

"We never tracked down Rebecca or Meredith for an interview and photo op."

"Too bad for them, I guess. Although I think that's for the best. I hardly think this costume is me putting my best foot forward."

Kayla giggled. "It's not about the costume. It's about the willingness to get involved and participate. People like that, especially in a guy whose reputation suggests he doesn't possess those qualities."

"Are you trash talking me?"

She rolled her eyes, but her smile remained. "Oh please. I would never. I'm just saying. We should have gotten a picture at the very least, to prove you were there."

I pulled my phone out of my pocket and opened the gallery to show her the picture I'd taken of us back in the haunted room. "I have a photo."

Kayla leaned closer to me and looked down at the picture. "Can you send that to me?"

My heart pounded a little harder against my ribcage. "Of course."

She smelled like vanilla and spices and the leather seat creaked softly as she leaned even closer to peer down at the picture. "We look good, don't we?"

She glanced up at me, and I couldn't help myself. I cupped her chin and kissed her.

Kayla's lips curled in a smile against mine. She didn't protest. Instead, she clawed at my clown costume and worked to yank the zipper down. Once she succeeded, she plunged a hand down the front of the open suit and cupped it over my boxers.

"Someone's eager," I said breathlessly.

"I guess clowns really do it for me."

I laughed.

Kayla took her seatbelt off and went to her knees on the seat. She turned to face me, her small body making it easy for her to move around inside the car. She leaned over the console between us and pulled me free of my boxers. Things were moving quickly and I wondered if I was the only one who hadn't been able to stop thinking about our night in the hotel.

It would seem I wasn't.

Kayla bowed over my lap. She pressed her lips to the tip of my cock and her tongue traced a few gentle sweeping circles over me. My hips tightened and I gripped the sides of the seat as she worked me into her mouth deeper and deeper, until she held me in the back of her throat.

I let my head fall back and closed my eyes as she worked herself up and down. Soft sounds escaped her at first, but as she sucked me off, she fell more into the moment. Soon, she was moaning. Her knees spread farther apart on the seat. Her tutu inched higher up around her waist until I could see her hot pink panties through her white nylons.

Kayla never struck me as the sort of girl to wear bright pink like that. I liked it.

I reached between her thighs and rubbed her over the nylon material. Kayla paused to let out a soft sigh before descending on me again and worshiping me until I couldn't take it anymore. I gathered her hair off her face and used it to pull her up to meet me for deep, desperate kisses.

As we kissed, Kayla struggled to get her nylons down. She failed.

Unfazed, Kayla swung one leg over the console and slid into my lap. Her tongue plunged into my mouth and our kiss tasted like vanilla and honey from the granola bars. She whimpered against my lips and guided my hand between her thighs.

Desperate and in no mood to fidget with the nylons, I tore a hole through them.

Kayla yelped. The sound shot a jolt of need through me so primal my balls tightened. I gripped her hips and guided her over me. She lowered herself and took all of me. Her walls were tight and she gripped my cock all the way down. She was slippery wet and gloriously swollen with lust.

She draped her wrists over my shoulders and hung her head back as she slowly rolled her hips. I relished every second of watching her pleasure. I leaned forward as she rode me so I could kiss her throat and her chest. Soft sighs escaped her and I slowly bucked my hips beneath her until the softness of the moment passed and she pulled herself back up so she could cling to my headrest.

She bounced on my cock like it was an Olympic sport. Her thighs worked and flexed and slapped against my legs. Her ass hit the steering wheel so I pulled the seat all the way back. We slid about half a foot and I dropped the back of the seat to an incline. Kayla leaned over me, her pigtails grazing my chest, and ground herself on me.

I had to make her stop or I was going to lose it. I gripped her thighs and pushed down, forcing her to slow her movements. She gazed down at me, eyes burning with need, lips parted in a sigh, cheeks rosy from the effort.

"What is it?" she breathed.

"Condom," I grated. "I don't have a condom."

"Are you serious?"

"Yes."

She bit her lip. "We could pull out."

"No," I said, and it was the hardest *no* I'd ever had to give. I guided her up and let her sit straddling my lap. I ran a hand up her thigh and paused between her legs. "There are other ways."

Kayla gave me a cocky little smirk that made me want her more than ever.

I rubbed her in slow circles. She melted in front of my eyes. All the tension in her shoulders from holding herself up drained away. She rocked above me, grinding herself against my fingers until I finally gave her what she wanted and slipped a finger inside her. She whimpered and trembled above me.

With my free hand, I took a fistful of her hair and held her in place. She moaned, her eyes fluttered closed, and her thighs tightened around me.

I took my time and teased her when she got too close. I didn't want this to end before it had to. I had her right where I wanted. She was putty in my hands, mine to mold, mine to bring to the brink and mercilessly stop right when she was ready to come apart.

She grew more desperate. Soon, she strained against my grip in her hair. She growled at me to stop teasing her. Her fingers gathered in the front of my costume and her pussy tightened around my fingers.

"Please," she pleaded.

"Please what?"

Kayla pulled at my costume. *"Please."*

I leaned in close so my cheek was pressed against hers. I pulled her head back, using her hair as leverage, and trailed kisses along the side of her neck and up to her ear. "Please *what*? I want to hear you say it."

She trembled. "Make me come."

A growl escaped me.

We stayed pressed together as I gave her another finger and stretched her. Kayla gasped. Her spine arched and her body went rigid. I fucked her hard and fast, building momentum until I felt the pressure gathering at the tips of my fingers. She cried out, sharp and needy, and the next thing I knew, my fingers were slick and she was pulsing around me.

Her muscles relaxed and she released my costume. I nuzzled against her neck and rewarded her with more kisses as she slid to her knees on the car floor. How she fit down there, I had no idea. She took me in her mouth again and started off slowly. It didn't take her long to bring me right back to the edge, teasing me with her tongue, flicking it over my tip while she massaged me with her hand.

I bucked, pressing up against the back of her throat. She welcomed it and gazed up at me, her throat swollen, her lips sealed around my shaft. She moaned, and the vibration pushed me over the top. My release made my head spin. I clenched my teeth and gripped the seat and Kayla took all of me.

When we were done, I pulled her back up on my lap. She settled against my chest and closed her eyes. I didn't know how long we stayed like that but it was clear neither of us wanted to move.

Eventually, she slid back into the passenger seat. We tucked ourselves back into our costumes and she shared a knowing smile with me.

"I'm kind of glad you didn't have a condom," she said.

"Oh yeah?"

She pressed her knees together. "Uh huh."

I chuckled and started the car. It was late, almost midnight, and Kayla undoubtedly had an early start in the morning. "I'll take you home."

I pulled out of the parking lot and away from the Sound. Kayla gazed out the window at the passing streetlights as we wove around the outer road and made our way back into the city. I could see the reflection of her face on the glass and pretended not to notice that she was smiling—until suddenly she wasn't.

"What's wrong?" I asked.

"Did we make a mistake? Is this bad? Does this make *us* bad?"

"Look," I said gently. "There's obviously something between us. We've been fighting it and fighting it, but maybe it's a better idea to—I don't know—throw ourselves into it?"

Kayla stared blankly at me.

I smiled. "We can't keep ignoring how we feel, Kayla. At least I know I don't want to. I want to explore this with you."

She looked down at her hands in her lap. "I worry about Lisa. What would she think if she knew? Would she ever be able to look at me the same? When you came into my office last week and she was there, I felt like the walls were closing in on me."

How could we give this a fair shot when Kayla was going to be on high alert all the time?

An idea struck me.

"What if we get out of town?" I suggested. "We can go away just for a weekend. That way, we don't have to worry about running into anyone we know, specifically Lisa. We can talk openly. We can figure out what this thing is between us without having to juggle work and family and commitments."

"A trip? Just like that? Lukas, I'm not sure that's wise."

"We should go tonight."

"Tonight?" she asked sharply.

"Listen, Kayla. Working with you has changed a lot of things. It's brought up memories from my past that have been buried for a very long time. I keep pushing them back down, but when you're around, they resurface, and they don't hurt the way they used to." I paused and worried none of this was making a lick of sense. We took a right-hand turn onto her street. "I just want some time with you."

"I have shifts at the kitchen."

"I'll send someone to cover it."

"Who?" she asked.

"Someone. Anyone. Just look me in the eyes right now and tell me you don't want this chance. Tell me the truth, Kayla. Do you want to get away from it all? Do you want to see if this is real?"

I pulled over outside her apartment building. Kayla looked from me to the apartment, and back to me, and for a moment, I thought she might say no.

But she didn't.

"How much time do I have?" she asked.

"I'll send a car for you in an hour."

CHAPTER 28

KAYLA

This might be a mistake. No, not "might." This is probably a huge, horrible, bumbling mistake.

My mind raced a mile a minute as I crammed clothes into a duffel bag. I had no idea where Lukas planned on taking me for this whirlwind weekend getaway, so I had no idea what I was supposed to pack. Did I bring a bathing suit? Sweat pants? A nice pair of jeans? A winter jacket? Boots? Sneakers? How many pairs of socks did I need? Should I bother packing makeup and jewelry? Did I need hair tools?

With so little time at my disposal to properly prepare, I settled for comfortable items. I changed into a pair of leggings and boots with warm lining. I opted for a sweater with a hood and threw my denim jacket over it. By the time I'd managed to haul my bag to my front door, my phone chimed.

The driver had arrived.

I was not an impulsive person. I was the girl who meticulously planned every event, occasion, outing, date, meetup—everything. I needed to know how a thing was going to go in order to be comfortable doing said thing. I needed consistency and I hated the unknown.

This weekend held a lot of unknowns and all I'd had to prepare for it was an hour.

It simply wasn't enough.

But I was going for it anyway.

I turned off the lights, locked up behind me, and made my way out of the apartment building to the SUV parked at the curb. The driver was a familiar-looking man and I realized it was the same gentleman who'd dropped Lukas off at the orchard. He met me with a smile and a handshake and put my bag in the backseat before inviting me to sit up front with him. He said his name was Art as we drove away, and when I asked him where we were going, he just looked over at me and smiled.

"To the airport, of course," he said.

"The airport? Where on earth does Lukas plan on taking me?"

"It's a surprise, miss. He insisted I not let the cat out of the bag. Don't worry. It's not a long flight."

"Canada?"

He shook his head. "Nope."

I pursed my lips and settled back against the seat. Art told me all about his time working for Lukas and how much he enjoyed being his driver. I wondered if he was lying because I knew Lukas' mood swings better than most. There was no way Art hadn't been privy to at least a dozen, seeing as how he'd been working as Lukas' driver for nearly four years.

We arrived at the airport and drove straight out onto one of the tarmacs, where in the dead of night I spotted Lukas standing in front of a small passenger plane. He was illuminated from the light inside the plane spilling down the stairs onto the tarmac. He smiled when I got out of the car and met me with a kiss while Art retrieved my bags from the back seat.

"Where are you taking me, Lukas Holt?" I asked as I gazed up into his face.

He wore a smug smile. "Not far. Just someplace where nobody will recognize us."

"Are you taking me out of the country? Out of the state?"

"No." He chuckled. "I couldn't swing that exciting of a trip in one hour's notice. But I could swing this. Just trust me, okay?"

I crammed my hands in my pockets as a strong wind picked up. "Okay."

Lukas tilted his head toward the plane. "Let's get you out of the cold."

The flight was a smooth one despite the wind, and it was short. Quite short. Only about forty-five minutes or so. I appreciated that Lukas hadn't taken me too far away from home just in case something came up with work. I didn't want to bail on him but Good Fellow's had to come first. There were people who needed me, and Lukas would be just fine if I had to leave. He had his own private plane, after all.

But when we arrived at our real destination, every part of me hoped and prayed I wouldn't get called back to the city for work.

The plane landed on a small tarmac and another car took us from the small excuse of an airport to a resort on the island built right on a bluff overlooking the dark and magnificent ocean. Lukas claimed it was a rustic retreat of some kind but the cabins hardly looked rustic to me.

Clearly, he saw them through rich-people lenses. I saw them for what they were, glorious homes built amongst nature with simple creature comforts.

We checked in at the lodge underneath a massive chandelier made of deer antlers. There were twenty-five hotel rooms in the lodge and thirty cabins on the sprawling property. Our cabin was within walking distance, but due to the late hour and the chill in the air, the attendant in the lobby offered to shuttle us there in an enclosed golf cart.

Lukas and I gratefully accepted the offer.

A short while later, we were let into our more-than-just-a-cabin cabin. The attendant, a skinny wisp of a young man with reddish hair and cheeks that wouldn't likely see any beard growth for years to come, paced to the fireplace and offered to get it burning for us. Again, we agreed, and while he worked on the fire, Lukas and I explored our little homestead.

It was all one big room with cedar floors and walls. There was no overhead lighting, only sconces set in the walls, and the floors were covered in mismatching rugs that gave the place a homey, inviting, comfortable feel. The bed was a four-poster king. Red velvet drapes hung from each corner, and the bed reminded me of something royalty might sleep in.

The fire crackled and snapped as the attendant got it lit. When he was done, he straightened, wiped his hands on his pants, and asked if we needed anything else.

"I don't think so," I said.

"Wine," Lukas said.

The attendant nodded. "There is a room-service menu in the drawer of the nightstand. The kitchens and bar are open all night. Feel free to look through it and call to place an order. It usually takes about twenty to thirty minutes."

"Perfect," Lukas said.

The young man left and I warmed myself in front of the fire. "This isn't what I expected."

"No?" Lukas shrugged out of his jacket and draped it over the edge of the bed. "What did you expect?"

"I don't know. A posh hotel somewhere. Something fancy and glamorous, like the Monroe."

"I wanted to go somewhere nobody would stumble upon us."

I turned my back to the fire. "Mission accomplished. It's beautiful here. And so quiet."

"It is quiet, isn't it?"

There was no hum or roar of traffic outside our windows. Instead, there was the gentle rustle and scratch of tree branches scraping across the roof of the cabin. There was the steady crackle of the fire and, in the distance, the hushed roll of waves breaking against the bluff.

Lukas fetched the room-service menu from the nightstand drawer and dropped into one of the two chairs placed in front of the fireplace. Between them was a small table with nothing on it. I took the opposite chair and ran my hands over the armrests. The fabric was a deep burgundy velvet and it felt nice under my palms.

"What should we order?" Lukas mused, his eyes scanning the page.

"You pick."

He didn't hesitate. Within minutes, he'd placed an order to room service. While we waited, I stared into the fire and thought about his sister. What would Lisa think of us running away to steal some alone time together?

"Don't over think this," Lukas said, resting his head back against his chair. "We're here and we're going to enjoy ourselves, right?"

I nodded. "Right."

We chatted aimlessly about things that didn't matter until room service arrived. Lukas popped the bottle of red, and the first sip warmed my belly. The second and third were even more delicious, and soon, I was one glass of wine in with no food in my belly, so I dove into the crackers, jelly, pesto, and baked brie appetizer.

Lukas settled back in his chair with his wine in one hand. "You know, had you told me four weeks ago that I'd be dressing up as a clown for a charity, I'd have laughed in your face."

"I wouldn't have tried such a thing."

He chuckled. "Well, I'm glad I did it. I'm glad I've done all of this."

His words warmed my insides better than the wine. "Me too."

"I never would have expected these feelings to emerge from our working together, Kayla. These weeks have been..." He paused, the glint of a smile reflecting in his eyes as he gazed into the fire. "They've been better than most of the ones that came before."

At first, I thought he was talking about his feelings about me, and I almost told him I felt the same way, but he kept talking. The words poured out of him unabashed and I didn't dare open my mouth for fear of him never being so open with me again.

"I swore I'd never go back to that state, you know," he said, eyes still glued to the fire. "To being poor. I hoarded every dime I made, pinched every penny, and hustled to figure out how to collect the most interest. I figured if I could figure a way out of poverty, anyone else could too. I let that cloud my judgment. I fell so out of touch with reality, with who I was before the suits and the flashy cars." His expression darkened and he sipped his wine. "Now I realize the deck is stacked against most people. The wealthy have all the advantages, including their privilege and naivety. I used to be one of those assholes. Selfish. Ignorant. Blind. Whether it was on purpose or by default of accumulating wealth, I still don't know."

"I don't think you were ignorant, Lukas."

His gaze slid to me. "I was. It's okay. I accept it. I need to be better. To do better. You make that easy for me, Kayla. You've changed the game for me. Without you, I never would have realized that—" He broke off with a soft chuckle and shook his head.

"What?" I pleaded, reaching for him. "Tell me."

"You helped me realize that being poor isn't the worst thing in the world. Being lonely? Well, that might just be worse."

He was right. Being lonely was worse. I would know. For all the work I did and all the people I helped day in and day out, I still went home to an empty apartment.

"Thank you," he whispered.

I swallowed the tight lump building in my throat and willed myself to keep it together. "You have nothing to thank me for."

He ignored me. "Thank you for helping me realize what a lonely life I was leading. Thank you for showing me the wall I'd put up and teaching me how to take it down."

His words warmed me better than the fire ever could. I extracted myself from my chair and settled into his lap. Lukas wrapped his arms around me and I laid my cheek on his chest. He ran his fingers through my hair.

Finally, I was getting close to him. Finally, he was letting me in.

For the first time since meeting with Lukas in his conference room all those weeks ago, I felt like I was seeing the real him. Truthfully, he hadn't changed all that much from when he was a boy and we used to chase each other down the block. He was still introspective, smart, and caring. He was also protective and loving, and for him, being vulnerable wasn't easy.

I wasn't sure where things were going between us, but I knew in my heart that I loved this complicated man. I loved him for everything he was and everything he was not. There was no way to know if that would be enough. Maybe we would get lucky and maybe this would work. If not? Well, maybe he'd forever be the man I carried a torch for.

There were still things stacked up against us. But at least for tonight, I could sleep in his arms and pretend that he loved me too.

CHAPTER 29

LUKAS

It was impossible to pack a lifetime's worth of romance into a single weekend, but that didn't mean I wasn't going to try.

Kayla and I had a day and a half to soak up as much time together as we could on this remote little island. I wanted to give her a glimpse of what life would be like if she decided to share hers with me.

We started with an early morning storm and whale-watching boat tour on the Sound. And by early, I meant *early*. We were out of the cabin by five in the morning after having woken up at four to indulge in some passionate, sweaty, desperate lovemaking that left a pit of desire in my gut all day long.

The excursion out on the ocean was full of rain, cold, and glorious excitement as we saw humpback whales and orcas. Kayla had shrieked with giddy excitement when the first orca said hello by bursting into the air and plunging back into the water with a splash. He had only been the first, of course. After him came a chorus of other orcas in the pod, all of them sailing high into the air before plunging back down into the cold waters of their ocean home.

The highlight was easily how cute Kayla had looked all bundled up for the cold under her rain poncho. I'd snapped a couple of pictures without her looking, one of which was a shot of her when she saw one of the first whales jump. Her eyes were bright with joy and excitement, her hand outstretched, finger pointing as if I couldn't see the giant black whale leaping out of the water and defying gravity, her mouth open wide in a cry of glee. Raindrops clung to her cold-bitten cheeks where her hair was plastered to her skin. She'd never looked more beautiful to me.

After watching the whales, I decided to pamper her and warm her up with a trip to the lodge spa. I booked us an entire afternoon worth of treatments, starting with a dip in a hot mud bath together to warm up. Kayla had squealed and been repulsed by the sucking texture of the mud as we sank up to our chins in it, but as she experienced the weightlessness of it, she relaxed.

After the mud bath, we showered and went for full-body massages. We had facials done, including face massages, and I made sure Kayla was pampered with a matching manicure and pedicure. She chose dark red and gold for the autumn season after much deliberation. She told me as we left the spa that she'd never had a professional manicure before, or a massage for that matter.

Yet again, I was reminded of the differences between having it all and having what you needed. I had more than I needed and I hadn't been happy until Kayla came around.

Kayla had only what she needed, and from where I was standing, she was happy. Hell, she'd always been happy. She was the smilingest kid on the block back in the day and she was still the person to turn to if your day needed brightening.

Our last stop that late afternoon was to a winery on the island, where Kayla and I both indulged in a little too much wine. We were the obnoxious couple in the group who slurped every wine we tasted and descended into fits of giggles at the back of the group while the wine connoisseur bored everyone with details about acidity, sugar levels, and body. Kayla and I retained no information from the tour. Instead, we retained plenty of wine that made our heads fuzzy and our fingertips tingly as we rode back to our cabin, half slumped against each other, exhausted from our day of activities.

Back at our cabin, I stoked a fire while Kayla pitched face first onto the bed.

I glanced over my shoulder at her. "Tired?"

She nodded weakly and didn't bother opening her eyes. "Exhausted. Who knew being pampered and drinking wine could make you feel like you'd just run a marathon?"

I chuckled as an ember popped. I poked at the logs until the tinder underneath caught. "Have a nap. We don't have anything on the agenda for the rest of the evening besides spending time together. And dinner later."

"Can we eat here?" she asked softly. "I don't think I have it in me to go to the dining room in the lodge."

"Room service, it is."

"I want chicken strips."

I laughed. "Chicken strips? What are you, twelve?"

"Don't judge. Chicken strips are delicious. With honey mustard and fries? I can taste it now. Lightly breaded. Perfectly seasoned."

"All right, all right. I'll make sure you get chicken strips."

Kayla smiled and snuggled deeper into the bedding. "Thank you."

I straightened as the fire began to burn in earnest, and held my hands out to the flames. "I had fun today."

Kayla didn't answer.

I smiled. Sleep had taken her quickly. She wasn't lying. She was exhausted. We'd had an early start, after all, and gone to bed after midnight. A few hours of sleep weren't enough, especially for a woman who I doubted slept more than five hours a night anyway, based on how much she got done at Good Fellow's on her own.

I settled into one of the burgundy velvet chairs in front of the fire and pulled my phone out of my pocket. I had one interview remaining with Rebecca Mills and it was on the books for today. She was supposed to meet me at a coffee bar this evening around six o'clock, but obviously, that wasn't going to happen. So I decided to take matters into my own hands and give her a call.

I'd never hear the end of it from my sister if I missed the interview, and I didn't want to leave Rebecca hanging. That wasn't the guy I was. Not anymore.

Rebecca answered on the third ring. "Mr. Holt, nice to hear from you. Are we still on for our interview this evening? I was about to leave my office and head to the shop."

"Actually, I was hoping we could do the interview over the phone. I won't be able to make it into the city tonight. Something personal came up but I didn't want to miss our chance to wrap this up."

"Oh, sure," Rebecca said. I thought I detected a hint of disappointment in her voice. She banished it by clearing her throat. "Hold on. Let me put you on speaker so I can record you."

I waited and fidgeted with the stitching in the armrest of the chair.

"Okay," Rebecca said, her voice professional and collected. "Are you ready?"

"Let's do this."

"Let's start with the haunted house charity event. I went looking for you to catch an interview but you weren't there."

"I left early," I explained. "I was in one of the rooms but got a little too into the whole thing. I scared some poor girl senseless and had to escort her out. Then I got it in my head that it would be fun to drive down to my sister's house in my costume and scare *her* senseless. I used to pull a lot of pranks on her when we were kids, but you know how it is. You grow up, you forget that part of yourself, and your sibling relationships become adult relationships. There's less room for messing around and fun."

"But not that night?"

"Not that night." I chuckled.

"Did you scare her successfully?"

"Maybe a little too successfully."

Rebecca laughed. "Let's go back to the haunted house. Did you see any irony in the approach of using a haunted house tour to raise money for people who don't have houses of their own?"

I considered the question before answering. She was trying to trip me up like any good reporter would do. "I don't think it's about that.

It was about connecting with the community, particularly the young people. The whole idea was to encourage neighbors to help neighbors and to be creative about it. I think that's the trick. There has to be an element of fun to keep people coming back."

"And that's what the night was for you? Fun?"

"Yes," I said honestly. "And it might sound rich coming from a guy like me. But we don't have to label the right and wrong ways to help people. We're allowed to laugh and enjoy ourselves for a good cause. There's a time for fun and a time for seriousness. So long as you know when to make the distinction, you're in the clear."

"This all sounds very different from the man I first spoke to a month ago."

"I am different," I said. "Everything I've learned, I owe to Kayla, the director of Good Fellow's. She showed me how to be better, not perfect, and that it was enough so long as I tried. I never expected to enjoy the process so much. To be honest—and I know this might piss readers off—I wasn't the guy at the beginning of this journey I wanted Seattle to see me as. I was self-focused. I was motivated by material things. But after Kayla and her organization? Well, let's just say I'm trying to lay a new foundation for myself and start fresh."

Rebecca was quiet for a minute. "What's the next step?"

"I'm not really sure. I'll be donating two hundred and fifty thousand dollars to Good Fellow's to help the construction of a new shelter. After that? We'll see where I'm pulled."

"Can I ask you one last question?"

"Of course," I said, pausing to glance at Kayla, who still slept soundly on the bed.

"What is something you've learned on your journey into philanthropy that you want to share with readers?"

A good question. A very good question. I gave it a moment to think it over. I didn't want to give her an impulsive answer. I wanted to give her the right answer—*my* answer. Finally, it came to me. "I've realized that nothing happens in a vacuum."

"Can you elaborate?"

"I'm not a success because I built everything by myself. I used to believe that. I believed it so strongly that I didn't think anyone could bring value to my life that I couldn't provide myself. But now? I've learned that I've been successful in my life because I've had people around me to support me. Those people mean more to me than my wealth or my stability. It's important for me that I start supporting others as well. It's my turn to give back. It's been my turn for a long time and I've turned a blind eye. I know I have a lot to make up for and I'm ready to do that. The connections I've made with strangers who I otherwise never would have had a chance to meet have been life changing. I encourage anyone in a position to give to do just that. Give your time, your money, your hand. You have no idea how so little can go so far."

"Spoken like a true philanthropist."

"I wouldn't go that far." I chuckled. "Everything I've learned has been because of Kayla. She's the real superstar here. She's the one who's been giving anything and everything for years. She doesn't have interviews or reporters to impress. She doesn't have readers who will open to her story in a magazine or an online article and see all the work she's done. She does it thanklessly. Selflessly. And I want to be more like her. I think we could all stand to be a little more like her."

"So this Kayla," Rebecca said slowly. "You two have spent a lot of time together?"

"Enough for me to know I've met an angel on earth."

"It sounds to me like there might be more than just a friendship between you two."

I laughed. "Always the reporter, huh, Rebecca?"

"Always the bachelor, huh, Lukas?"

I chuckled but didn't answer.

"It's been good talking to you," Rebecca said. "We'll be in touch soon. Say hello to your sister for me."

We ended the call and I left my spot in the chair to join Kayla on the bed. She didn't move as the mattress groaned under my knees. I settled down beside her, wrapping her up in my arms and pressing a kiss to her cheek.

She moaned softly and mumbled that it hadn't been long enough.

"We can stay like this as long as you want," I whispered.

No part of me wanted to return to the real world after this weekend. Now that my interviews with Rebecca Mills were done, I should be done with my collaboration with Kayla, but I wasn't ready to give that up.

Or give her up, for that matter.

There was genuine fear in me that if I didn't work with Kayla anymore, we would start to drift apart. I couldn't let that happen. I'd fallen in love with her.

Madly in love.

Kayla didn't need to know my interviews were finished. Not yet. For now, we would exist in our happy little bubble, and we'd move on to whatever the next thing was back in Seattle.

Together.

CHAPTER 30

KAYLA

The college campus had been transformed into a spooky Halloween town for the night of October thirty-first. The lawn in front of the main campus building swirled with low-lying fog that curled in eerie tendrils. Smoke machines had been donated by the college theatre company to use for the special evening and it added that final touch of spook the event had been missing.

Tables and booths were set up with different stations in the Halloween town. One side of the lawn was definitely scarier than the other and tailored toward the older or braver kids. The other side was friendlier with smiling pumpkins, goofy ghouls, and friendly vampires.

Deep purple lights glowed around tables, and orange lights flickered inside carved pumpkins. Halloween music played from speakers mounted on light posts and rigged up by the lighting and sound team from the theatre company, who'd had a huge hand in making this event come to life. Good Fellow's had worked tirelessly with the students to ensure a night of carefree fun with safe activities, plenty of candy, and good old-fashioned scares.

The turnout was better than I expected.

Over the years, I knew parents had become increasingly less interested in taking their children door to door for old-fashioned trick or treating. There was a lot of trust being placed on strangers on a night like that, whereas at Halloween town, there was accountability. I'd had to pay an insurance company from my non-profit and there was an ambulance parked at the far end of the lawn just to be safe.

I had worked to put this event on for the past six years, and of all of them, this year definitely drew the largest crowd. It was a ticketed event, so proceeds went to Good Fellow's, but over the years, I'd pretty much barely broke even. This year, with some luck, I'd make some profits.

By seven thirty, we had nearly two hundred kids passing from table to table and participating in games or showing off their courage to their siblings and friends.

Lukas was supposed to arrive any minute, and as I stood in the purple glow cast by one of the tables, I searched the crowd for him. He'd promised to dress up but refused to tell me what his costume was. I'd told him to be on the lookout for a fairy princess.

My ensemble was complete with a pink sparkly dress, glittery fairy wings, and a princess crown. I'd curled my hair the way a princess might and pinned sections of it back. Little bobby pins with flowers were poking out of my locks, and tons of little kids stopped to talk to me and get some pictures. The bottom of my dress was already stained green by the grass from crouching down for so many pictures.

I spotted a man striding through the fog toward me across the lawn as I smoothed out my skirt and waved goodbye to the little girl who'd just stopped with her parents to say hello to me. He was dressed in what appeared to be a pirate costume. He was too far away for me to tell for sure. He walked with a committed swagger and the low-lying smoke on the lawn rippled around his knees. I realized that he was walking straight toward me.

He was ten feet away when I realized the sexy pirate was Lukas.

He flashed me a dashing smile that stretched his cheeks, which were painted dark brown to mimic a beard. "My lady," he said, his voice low and seductive. "Aren't ye a pretty lass?"

I giggled. "Oh no, the voice is so bad."

"Nonsense, ye scallywag!" He pumped his eyebrows before muttering in his usual cadence. "I'm at least selling it, aren't I?"

"You and I clearly have very different definitions of 'selling it.' I will admit though that you look quite handsome."

He gestured down at himself—at the loose white shirt, the brown vest, the ballooned pirate pants, worn boots, sash, scabbard, and black flag with a white skull and crossbones dangling out of his pocket. "This is what does it for you? Really? Poor hygiene and knee-high boots on a man?"

I nodded earnestly. "I think it's quite becoming on you."

"I feel uncivilized."

I leaned in and grabbed a fistful of his vest with a cocky wink. "You *look* uncivilized, too."

Lukas pried himself free. "Woman, this is a festival for children. Keep ye filthy hands to yerself."

"Please don't do the accent all night."

"It's that bad?"

"I hate it."

Lukas chuckled. "All right, all right. Fine. I'll stop. What's the deal for tonight? Where can I help?"

Lukas' costume certainly looked hot on him, but him asking how he could help was even hotter. He was the man I always knew he could be, and I was getting all hot and bothered under my sparkly princess gown. I willed those urges down, reminding myself what he'd said about this being a children's event, and pulled my phone out of a pocket sewn into my skirt. "We're the chaperones for a group of kids arriving at eight o'clock. I think there are five of them."

"Five kids and two chaperones?"

I nodded. "They have some special needs that can make navigating an event like this a little tricky. We'll have to be aware of certain sensory stimulations like flashing lights or too much smoke, but I have a list of activities we're going to do that I think they'll all really enjoy. Oh, that might be them there."

Lukas followed my gaze to the parking lot where a white van had just pulled up to the curb. A man and woman got out of the front seats and slid open the sliding door on the side of the vehicle. Several children came out, and the last was lowered on a lift off the back of the van in a wheelchair. We crossed the foggy lawn to meet them, and I hoped we would be able to think quickly on our feet to make sure she could still participate in all the games.

We met the workers driving the van who thanked me for hosting this event yet again. They told me the children had been talking about it for weeks now and that everyone was excited to be there.

I grinned as I shook all the kids' hands. "I'm so happy you're here, too. We have some new additions since last year that I think you'll love. My name is Kayla and this here is my friend Lukas. He's going to hang out with us tonight. If you're lucky, he might teach you some old-fashioned pirate terms."

Lukas performed a swashbuckling jig. "It's about time ye pipsqueaks got here," he crooned like a pirate. "The princess hasn't let me near any of the activities. Now that yer here, I can finally do what I do best."

The children, all roughly eight or so years of age, stared at him blankly.

Lukas straightened and blinked down at them. "Don't ye know what pirates do best, ye wee lads and lassies?"

I snickered into the puffy sleeve of my princess dress. "Wee lads and lassies?"

Lukas let my amusement roll off his shoulder as he planted his fists on his hips. "We cause trouble. That's what. Now, are ye ready to cause trouble with me?"

The children nodded. Their escorts returned to the van laughing to themselves while Lukas and I had everyone hold hands so we could make our way back across the foggy lawn together and to the first activity station.

Lukas talked to the kids the entire time, especially to the young girl in the wheelchair, who seemed the least intimidated by his costume. In fact, she seemed more intrigued than anything else. Like the rest of the kids, she was in costume. She wore a witch hat and a long black velvet dress. Her shoes had cardboard buckles taped to them that had been painted gold, and someone, a parent I assumed, had painted a mole on her nose. The socks peeking out between the hem of her dress and the top of her shoes were striped and it looked like she belonged at the end of a yellow brick road.

The four other children were timid and shy. They hung back behind me, all holding hands, and stayed huddled together for moral support. Coming out to such a popular event like this was a big deal, especially for kids who might be more susceptible to sensory stimuli like lights, fog, and scary noises. As we walked, I assured them that we wouldn't go anywhere scary unless they wanted to. For now, we were going to stick to some old-fashioned fun.

"Like what?" Addison, the young girl in the wheelchair, cocked her head to the side and nearly lost her hat. She set it back straight again.

Lukas turned to the first tent. Inside was a giant bucket filled with water. Beside the bucket were baskets full of apples. He grinned. "We're going apple bobbing."

Addison lifted her nose at that. "I don't want to get my hair wet."

Lukas swaggered out in front of her. "Fine then. I'll do it in your place. Sound fair?"

Addison shrugged.

"There's a surprise to be won, you know," Lukas said.

I opened my mouth to correct him that actually, there was no surprise. But he held a finger up to me and crouched down in front of Addison. The other children gathered around and he made eyes at them, the way a camp guide might while sitting around the fire telling ghost stories.

"If you get an apple," he began, "*if* you're lucky enough, of course, you'll have good luck for the rest of the night. You won't have to try to have fun because, well, you'll just be having it because of the luck. It's an All Hallows Eve tradition. So, what do you think? Who wants to go first?"

I watched, bemused and impressed, as the first young boy stepped up to the bucket of water and went to his knees on the stool in front of it. He was too short to go without the stool. He had shockingly bright blond hair that hung in tight curls around his temples. His costume, a superhero I didn't recognize, was half a size too big for him. I assumed it was an older brother's from the year before.

Lukas crouched beside the boy and asked him his name. He told Lukas his name was Carson, and Lukas shared some pro tips with Carson on how to successfully bob for apples. He told him to take his time and to have fun before Carson stuck his face in the water, mouth open like a gaping fish out of water, and tried to catch apples.

He was too short to have much luck, and when he came up for air, he massaged his chest where the rim of the tub pressed against him.

"I have an idea," Lukas said. "Can I pick you up?"

Carson nodded.

I watched as Lukas picked Carson up and held him upside down over the bucket of water. Carson started to giggle as Lukas lowered him down, his jaws unhinged like a snake, to catch the apples. Lukas pulled him up in a victorious flourish. Water sprayed from Carson's soaking-wet flat curls and whipped against the tent walls. Lukas laughed uproariously as Carson pulled the apple from where it was stuck to his upper teeth. He held it over his head, a tiny champion, and Lukas gave him a well earned high five.

Lukas pointed at Addison next. "Are ye ready to catch some luck, wee lady?"

Addison rolled into the tent. The wheels of her chair bumped against the edge of the tub.

Lukas pursed his lips thoughtfully. "How does the wicked witch want to do this? Her pirate servant can either hoist her up, like he did with the wee lad, or he can bob in her place."

Addison cocked her head. "What do you mean?"

Lukas pressed a hand to his chest and bowed. "I could bob for apples for ye, witch. I'll make sure I give ye the luck once I've caught it."

You're doomed, a little voice inside my head whispered. *Absolutely doomed.*

My heart felt like it was glowing in my chest as I watched Lukas bob for apples in Addison's stead. She cheered him on from her chair, clapping with delight and chanting his name along with the other kids who gathered around the bucket while Lukas made a show of struggling to catch an apple.

When he burst from the water, they all cheered and hollered, and he wiped the gently bitten apple on his shirt before he passed it to Addison. "My lady," he said with yet another deep bow.

I didn't need more reasons to fall more in love with him, but there it was, another reason, and it was a hard one to overlook.

CHAPTER 31

LUKAS

I never would have expected a Halloween night like this to be my favorite of the thirty Halloweens I'd seen. Over the years, I'd spent the spooky night doing one of three things: staying home, hooking up with a stranger, or working. As I looked back at the last three years, I realized I'd spent all of them in the office working away on new software or fine tuning the old stuff. No matter what it was, I could always find something to keep myself busy—and isolated.

But out there in the foggy Halloween town Kayla had created, it was easy to see what I'd been missing out on. Pure, honest, and simple fun.

Addison and the other kids moved with Kayla and me from activity to activity, and as promised, luck was on their side from their successful apple bobbing. They tossed darts at balloons set up on a particle board wall which was much like the kinds of games found at carnivals or amusement parks. They performed tricks for treats and were rewarded with little jack-o'-lanterns loaded up with mini chocolate bars and lollipops. They stopped for a bite to eat at one of the food trucks Kayla had reserved, and we sat with them at a picnic table half engulfed by fog while we ate.

Afterward, we only had time for a few more activities before the van returned to take the kids home. All of them were sad to leave, especially Addison, who put on a great show of pouting and wallowing in her misery.

I crouched down in front of her chair and stroked my chin and the painted-on beard that had all but washed off since the apple bobbing at the start of the night. "Don't be sad," I told her. "We'll do this again next year. Deal?"

Addison nodded. I held out my hand and she took it. She had tiny hands and cold fingers but a good grip.

I grinned. "It was a pleasure to meet ye, yer witchiness."

She rewarded me with a giggle. The other kids all got in the van after saying their goodbyes to us, and Kayla and I stood back as one of the drivers pulled the door closed and the other operated the lift to help Addison into the back of the van. Once everyone was safely inside and buckled up, they drove away.

Kayla and I stood side by side waving, and once they'd turned out of sight, I draped an arm around her shoulders and sighed. "That was more fun than I've had in a long time."

She tilted her head back and smiled up at me. "I'm glad. Halloween town is serious business for fun seekers."

"I'd say. I'm glad we got to stick to the happy-go-lucky side."

"What, you can't handle a bit of scary?"

"I think I had my fill at the haunted house." I chuckled.

Kayla rolled her eyes and I steered her back toward the lawn where the remaining kids and families were still having a blast. It was about nine thirty at night and we still had half an hour of the event to go. I asked Kayla where she wanted me to lend a hand and she told me the best thing we could do was walk around and get some feedback so we could keep requests or complaints in mind during planning and prep for next year.

As always, Kayla thought of everything.

We split up for the final thirty minutes of the night and talked to everyone we could about what they thought of the event. For the most part, all I heard were positive things but there were some people who had opinions about improvements. Most were well thought out, too.

So I pulled out my phone and frantically typed in what they said in one of my note applications so I wouldn't forget and I could pass along the message to Kayla.

People wanted more food options and, much to my surprise, an adults-only session later in the night, like after ten o'clock. I thought that was a brilliant idea. It would certainly increase profits having the event open a little longer—so long as the extra insurance costs and overhead didn't negate the increase.

Kayla and I reunited near the apple-bobbing station at the end of the evening as everyone started clearing out. Teams of students from the university swarmed the field to begin tearing down the stations, and Kayla and I pitched in where we could. It took over an hour to take everything down. Once the lawn was clear and the fog dissipated, we had one last task of making a round and collecting any garbage strewn about. Unfortunately, there was a fair amount of it.

"This is the only part about these kinds of events I don't like," Kayla muttered as she bent down and picked up litter with one hand to cram it into the bag she held in the other. We both wore plastic gloves. "I don't understand why people can't just use garbage cans. Look around. There are half a dozen of them!"

"People are lazy," I said. "Especially when they're enjoying themselves. They don't want to break away from the fun to put garbage in a can. I bet they're the same people who don't get out of the pool or lake to pee."

Kayla glanced up at me. "Eww."

I snickered. "I'm not wrong."

"Probably not." She sighed as she continued picking up garbage.

Other kids pitched in to help, and once the lawn was all clear, I found myself itching for some good old-fashioned adult entertainment. I turned to Kayla as she pulled the flower pins out of her hair. "We should go get a drink."

Kayla smiled as she tucked the pins in her purse. "A drink, you say? Where would you like to go?"

"Somewhere close by."

"All the bars around here will be filled with college students. It's Halloween night."

"What? Are we not cool enough to party with college students?"

Kayla smirked. "I never said that."

Kayla and I found a rocking bar not far from campus where we were probably the only people the bouncers let in without checking their ID. It made me feel only slightly too old to be there.

We pushed through the crowd and made our way to the bar, where I ordered us each a cocktail and a shot to get the night started.

Kayla leaned on the bar and looked up at me. "Did you just order a shot?"

I nodded and nudged her shoulder with mine. "I want to dance with you tonight and something tells me we need something to take the edge off."

The bartender placed two shots in front of us and began making our cocktails. Kayla lifted her shot glass up to the light and peered at it. "Why does it look like candy corn?"

The shot had layers of orange, white, and yellow, just like candy corn. "I thought we should do something Halloween inspired, you know, to stay on trend for the night."

Kayla grimaced. "I feel like tequila would have been better. Sweet shots are dangerous recipes for hangovers."

"Don't be a baby."

"I'm not a baby," she said, shooting me a glare. "I'm a princess."

I laughed. "All right, princess. Pull it together. Bottoms up."

We tapped our shot glasses together before throwing them back. She was right, of course. The shot was dangerously sweet. It was heavy on my tongue and I swallowed it as quickly as I could, resenting the cream liqueur as it inched its way down my throat.

Kayla shook her head and wiped her mouth with the back of her hand as she set the shot glass down. "See? Gross."

"You were right. Mistakes have been made."

"Nothing we can't fix." Kayla caught the bartender's eye when he set our cocktails down. "Could we please have two shots of tequila?" She pulled a five-dollar bill out of her purse and tucked it in his tip jar. "Thank you."

Based on the way he hustled to make our drinks, I suspected he didn't get many tips there. It made sense. Most of the customers were half-broke college students who could hardly afford to buy their own drinks, let alone give away money to the bartender. When our tequila shots were ready and we had our lime wedges in hand, we did our second round of shots.

Kayla's cheeks puckered as she sucked on the lime. She squeezed one of her eyes closed and let out a soft moan that did things to my man parts.

She put her half-sucked away lime wedge in her shot glass and left it on the bar. We ducked back into the crowd with our cocktails in hand and stood along the edges of the dance floor while we drank. Almost everyone was out in their Halloween costumes. The dance floor was packed with nurses, maids, vampires, fairies, werewolves, and monsters.

"Sometimes, I feel like I missed out by not having the college experience," Kayla said to me over the music.

"It's not all it's cracked up to be. Not all the time anyway."

She shrugged. "I think I would have liked it."

I smiled at the beautiful girl beside me as she sipped her drink and bobbed along to the music contently. "Yes," I said. "I think you would have liked it too."

She flashed me a charming smile. "Care to dance, loathsome pirate?"

"I've been waiting for you to ask me."

Kayla giggled and handed me her drink. "Wait here. I just have to use the ladies' room."

"I'll be right where you left me."

Kayla balanced herself on the tips of her toes to press a kiss to my lips before turning and vanishing into the crowd. She was a head shorter than most of the people in there, so I lost sight of her almost immediately. As soon as she was gone, however, several young women in the place seemed to catch sight of *me*.

I was approached first by a nurse and a girl in a costume that was basically just lingerie and bunny ears.

"Hi, handsome," the nurse purred. "What're you drinking?"

"Where did your friend go?" the bunny asked.

I pried an arm free from the nurse, who'd taken to trying to wrap herself around me like a snake. Alcohol made people stupid.

"She's coming right back," I said lamely.

The nurse giggled. "You should dance with us."

"You're so sexy."

"Are you a professor?"

"What do you teach?"

"Do you want to teach us something?"

I backed up with a nervous chuckle. "Ladies, I appreciate the flattery but I'm just not interested. I'm sure you could have any guy in this room you wanted. That guy just isn't me."

The nurse winked. "It could be."

The bunny turned and pressed her ass into my crotch. "We could show you a better time than that prudey princess you're with."

I extracted myself from the women with a shake of my head. "Leave me alone," I growled, and much to my relief, they didn't follow me into the crowd as I headed toward the back of the bar to look for Kayla.

She'd been gone longer than I expected.

And I needed to be saved from these women.

CHAPTER 32

KAYLA

When I pushed through the swinging door of the women's washroom, it got stuck and I walked straight into it. I smacked my nose on the door, quickly followed by my forehead, and stumbled back cursing my own clumsiness as someone out in the hall opened the door the rest of the way and apologized.

He was a young man, maybe twenty-five or twenty-six, and he wasn't wearing a Halloween costume. He wore a blue and white striped polo shirt and jeans, and he was flanked by two friends. All three of them had the look of football players, and all three of them looked me up and down as I massaged my aching forehead and stepped out of the room.

"Sorry," the guy in the stripes said. "The door jammed on my boot."

"It's all right," I told him. "I'm kind of clumsy anyway. I shouldn't have come out so enthusiastically."

He looked me up and down for the third time and I was thankful I'd worn a kid-friendly costume that showed no skin. "What are you supposed to be?"

I pointed at my tiara. "A princess. Obviously."

One of the other young men turned around to face me. He had a beer in his hand and his cheeks were rosy, a suggestion that this wasn't his first, second, third, or fourth beer, but more likely his eighth or ninth. "I haven't seen you around here before. What's your name?"

I turned sideways to squeeze past them and the wall so I could get out of the cramped hallway and find Lukas. "Sorry, I have to go. Someone is waiting for me and—"

"Have a drink with us, sweetheart."

I shot the guy in the stripes a dark look. I did not appreciate strangers calling me sweetheart. Hell, I didn't appreciate pet names from anyone who wasn't my partner. "No thank you."

"Oh shit." One of them snickered, patting Stripes on the shoulder. "She's feisty. I like that in a woman."

"I'm leaving," I said firmly.

"In such a hurry?" Stripes pressed. He stepped in front of me and blocked my path. "Stay a while. Tell us about yourself."

One of the others raised an arm over his head to brace it against the wall. "Yeah, tell us about yourself. Why'd you pick this dress? You've got a hot body. Why not show it off?"

I glared darkly up at them. "Get out of my way."

The three men snickered.

"Let us buy you a drink, babe," one said.

"Or two," another added.

"Let us show you a good time," Stripes added for good measure.

I held my ground. "If you don't get the hell out of my way, I'm going to scream bloody murder and I swear to God at least one of you will know the pain of having the toe of my shoes rammed so deep into your dick it will be inverted. Now *move*."

They didn't move.

Apparently, my grit and threats meant nothing to them. I was sharply aware of how small I was as they stepped toward me. Sharply aware of how poorly lit this hallway was, how far away from Lukas I was, and how a situation could go from bad to worse in the blink of an eye.

A familiar voice cut through my panicked thoughts.

"Hey!"

Relief rippled through me when Lukas broke through the tight wall of three men. I reached for him on instinct and he caught my hand so he could guide me behind him. I tried not to cower and instead peered around him to shoot dirty looks at the men.

"This your girl, man?" Stripes asked, nodding past Lukas at me. "We wanted to buy her a drink. We liked her costume. But she got all up in arms and—"

"You're very obviously making her uncomfortable," Lukas said, seething. He moved forward and closed the space between him and Stripes so that they were almost nose to nose. "When a lady says no, you back the fuck off."

"We just wanted her to loosen up," one of the guys said.

"No harm in a drink or two," the third added.

Lukas's eyes flicked between them. "Do you know who the fuck I am?"

None of them answered.

Lukas jabbed a finger in Stripes' chest. "I'm Lukas Holt, and if I hear so much as a whisper of you behaving inappropriately with any woman tonight, I'm going to have you arrested. Do you understand me?"

"Holt?" one of them breathed.

"Shit," Stripes said, backing up several paces. "We're sorry, man. We didn't mean any harm. We were just trying to have a good night."

"Go have a good night somewhere else," Lukas growled.

Just like that, the three guys took off running like dogs with their tails between their legs.

Lukas turned to me and put his hands on my shoulders as he looked deep into my eyes. "Are you okay?"

I nodded. "Yes. Thank you for coming to find me."

He pulled me in and kissed my forehead. "I'll always come find you. Now, about that dance. Are you up for it, or do you want to get the hell out of here?"

I nuzzled against his chest. My cheek met his bare skin where his white pirate shirt was unbuttoned. "It would be a shame not to dance to at least one song."

Lukas led me back out to the dance floor where we took a spot underneath a slow-turning disco ball that painted our cheeks and shoulders with fractures of light and rainbows. The music faded from an upbeat rock song to a slow ballad as if right on cue. He pulled me in close and we swayed together while singles left the dance floor and couples took their places. Lukas rested his chin on my head and I wrapped my arms around his waist.

I didn't want the night to end.

Every year before this, I'd gone home after working the Halloween town. I'd stop on my way to pick up some discounted Halloween candy if it was in the budget for that year and I'd overindulge by myself back at my apartment.

This was a far better way to spend the evening.

It was magical. I felt like a real princess in his arms. With any luck, I'd end up in his bed tonight, experiencing the intense pleasure that only Lukas could give me.

I tilted my head back and gazed up at him. He'd saved me from more than just three drunken idiots. He'd saved me from myself.

He caught me admiring him and smiled. "What is it?" he asked softly.

"Nothing," I whispered.

When the song ended, I was sad for it. I could have stayed in his arms swaying on the dance floor all night long. That wasn't in the cards apparently. The music picked back up and the dance floor flooded with young students looking to dance their hearts out.

I tipped my head to the door. "Should we get some fresh air?"

Shortly after, with bottles of water in hand from the bartender, we spilled out onto the sidewalk. There was a pleasant buzz in my head from the cocktail and the two shots, and I giggled about how much of a lightweight I was.

"When all you do is work, I suppose it makes sense that you'd have a low tolerance," Lukas said. He nodded at the unopened water bottle in my hand. "You should drink."

I took his advice and twisted the cap off. I drained half the bottle, only realizing how thirsty I was after the cold water touched my tongue. Some of it dribbled down my chin and throat and dampened the neckline of my dress. I caught Lukas staring at the trail of water glistening on my chest.

I smiled. "Like what you see?"

"Always."

"What are you going to do about it?"

He stepped in close and ran a finger along the neckline of my dress. "I'm going to take you home and have my way with you."

I giggled and hiccupped. "Don't you mean take me back to your ship?"

Lukas's brow furrowed.

I prodded him gently in the test. "Pirate, remember?"

"Ahh, yes." He chuckled deeply. "Prepare yourself for a terribly uncivilized night with this rogue."

I bit my bottom lip. I was ready. I was so ready.

Lukas moved to the edge of the sidewalk to hail a cab. As full ones passed us by, his phone started to ring. He frowned. "Who's calling me at one in the morning?" He fished his phone out of his pocket and lifted it to his ear. "Lisa? What's the matter? Why are you calling me so late?"

I couldn't hear what his sister was saying, but whatever it was, it wasn't good. Lukas' face fell. Color drained from his cheeks.

"I'll be right there," he said. He dropped the call and turned to me. "I'm sorry, Kayla. I have to go. You can take the first car home and I'll catch the next one. I'm sorry."

"Wait," I said, shaking my head. "What's going on? What happened? Is Lisa okay?"

"My mother is having a bad night."

"Oh." I cursed myself. That was the best thing I could think to say? Oh?

Lukas hailed the next cab and it pulled over. He twisted around to me after opening the door. "The facility tried to call me but I didn't hear the phone ringing in the bar, so they called Lisa. They can't get her to calm down. I have to see if I can help."

"I'm coming with you," I said simply.

"Sorry?"

"I'm coming with you," I said again as I slid into the back seat of the cab. I patted the seat beside me. "Come on. Let's go. Your mom needs you and you need someone in your corner. That's me. Get in."

Lukas got in the back seat. He told the driver the address and we pulled away from the curb as we put our seatbelts on.

I reached over and took his hand to give it a reassuring squeeze. "It's going to be okay."

Lukas looked at me like he never had before. I saw deep sorrow in his eyes and my heart constricted painfully in my chest. "My mother hasn't been okay for a long time," he said softly.

I swallowed. "I know."

"Ever since the car accident... well, she hasn't been the same since. She had a few good years after her recovery, but things went south pretty quickly after that. She started forgetting things. Weird things at first, you know? Like food in the oven or bills that needed to be paid. In the beginning, it was easy for me to step in and help with that kind of mundane stuff, but soon, I realized it wasn't just the little things. She'd forget to shower for days at a time. She'd miss appointments and meals. At first, we thought it was a side effect of the accident and her brain injury, but when I took her to see some specialist..." He trailed off. The rest of the story was clearly too painful for him to say aloud.

"You found out it was dementia," I finished for him.

Lukas nodded. "Yeah."

I unbuckled my seatbelt at a red light so I could move into the middle seat. I snuggled in close and didn't let go of his hand. "Lukas?"

"Yes?"

"I know you've been carrying this by yourself for a long time. But I want you to know you don't have to anymore. I'm here for you. And for your mother. Whatever you need. Okay?"

He closed his eyes and rested his cheek on my head. "Thank you, Kayla."

CHAPTER 33

LUKAS

We arrived at the facility around two in the morning. The cab driver drove off as soon as our feet hit the asphalt, and it started raining as we made our way up to the front doors. Kayla held my hand and I was surprised by how I felt supported by her, not pitied.

A huge reason why I never liked to talk to people about my mother was because of the way they would look at me. I never wanted people to feel sorry for me. But Kayla didn't look at me that way. She looked at me like she understood, like she wished things were different, and like she was determined to help. She looked at me like she loved me.

As soon as I opened the front doors to the facility, I heard my mother screaming. It was shrill and furious, and it instantly made my shoulders bunch up with tension.

Kayla squeezed my hand. "It's okay. If I was her, I'd be angry too."

Miraculously, her words helped me relax.

The night nurse working the desk knew who I was immediately. She bustled out from behind the desk with urgency in her steps and motioned for us to follow. As we made our way down the hall to my mother's suite, she gave me an update.

"Your mother had a really good day today, Mr. Holt," the nurse explained. She had shocking red hair and wore black scrubs with white cats all over them. "She was quite lucid and came to movie night, where the group watched that Halloween Charlie Brown movie. What's the name of it?" She looked over her shoulder at me.

I shrugged. "Beats me."

Kayla chimed in. "The Great Pumpkin Charlie Brown?"

"Yes, that's the one." The nurse nodded. "After the movie, everyone started getting ready to turn in for the night but your mother insisted on watching it again. We didn't realize that she'd had an episode, you see. She couldn't remember watching it in the first place. She felt ripped off, which made her furious, so we let her watch it again in her room. I'm afraid the cycle has repeated itself. She's furious, Mr. Holt. Nothing any of the nurses are doing is calming her down. Our last resort would be a sedative but there's the notation on your file not to—"

"No," I said firmly. "No sedative."

The nurse nodded. "Yes, sir."

We arrived outside my mother's door. The furious yelling and screaming was louder here, and I knew it would be so much worse when the door opened. I glanced down at Kayla. "Are you sure you want to be here for this? I understand if you want to wait at the front desk."

"Lukas," she said firmly, "nothing is going to scare me away, okay? I'm here for you. And your mother. Let's see if we can help."

Damn. This girl was magic. Absolute magic.

"Okay," I said, feeling a little more confident. I nodded for the nurse that we were ready to go in.

As soon as the door swung open, my mother's shrieks reached an all-time high.

She was standing in front of the window in her night dress. It was lilac colored and covered in bumblebees and flowers. The hemline was finished with lace. Her feet were bare, and her hair, permed a couple of weeks ago, was a wild mess. She looked around frantically until her eyes landed on me.

"You!" She pointed an accusing finger at me. "You tell them to get their act together! Tell them they can't treat me this way! Tell them I'm your wife and you're going to sue them for trying to keep me here!"

Wife. When my mother's episodes got really bad, she always thought I was my father, the damn bastard.

"David!" my mother shrieked. "Tell them!"

I felt like a fool standing in the doorway not knowing a damn thing to say. My heart hammered away in my chest as my mother refused and resisted the aid from the nurses who were trying to see her safely back to her bed. Kayla's hand still held mine, her grip tight as a vise, and I didn't dare look over at her.

One of the nurses spoke in gentle tones. "Mrs. Holt, that's not your husband. That's your son, Lukas. He heard you were having a hard night and he wanted to come see you."

My mother shot furious looks at the nurses. "Son? I don't have a son. David, tell them we don't have a son! Why am I here? Take me home. I want to go home."

My throat tightened.

My mother's gaze slid to Kayla. "And who's this little tart?"

"*Mom*," I said sharply. But it was no use. She didn't see me as her son.

Kayla cleared her throat. "Hi, Mrs. Holt. I'm Kayla. We used to live near each other in the co-op apartments. I was that silly girl who was always knocking on your door asking if Lukas wanted to come outside and play kick the can with me and Lisa and the other neighborhood kids. You liked when I showed up because you always wanted a reason to kick Lukas off his computer. Do you remember how much time he spent on that thing?"

Kayla's words were spoken warmly, like from an old friend. She had the presence of mind to keep her cool and her kindness in the face of what always made me freeze.

My mother blinked at Kayla.

Kayla gestured at the chairs in the room. "Do you mind if we come in and sit with you for a little while?"

My mother looked at the chairs and back at us. "I think that would be fine."

I wasn't sure how Kayla had so effortlessly diffused the tense situation, but she had. She guided me by the hand into my mother's room and the nurses slipped past us. They told me to come get them if we needed anything, but with Kayla by my side, I doubted we would.

We took our seats.

Kayla sat on the end of my mother's bed. "It's been a really long time since we last saw each other, Mrs. Holt."

"Call me Ally," my mother said. "I always used to ask you to call me Ally. You were the girl with the pigtails and the skinned knees."

Kayla grinned. "That was me, yes."

"Your mother gave us apple pies on Sundays."

"Yes, she did." Kayla nodded. "I always thought Lukas ate them all before he brought them home to you. I'm glad he resisted and shared."

My mother actually smiled. "Yes, he was always a good boy. He's been taking care of me for as long as I can remember. Where is he, Kayla? Where is my son?"

Her words hit me like a freight train.

Kayla leaned closer to my mother and held out her hands. My mother reached for her and let Kayla wrap her hands around her own. Kayla ran her fingers over my mother's knuckles.

"Ally?" Kayla started. I could tell she was struggling to find the right words. "A lot has changed since we lived in those apartments. I have my own apartment now. I have a good job doing something I love. And so does Lukas. He's grown up to be a really good man. You should be proud."

My mother's eyes shone with tears. "He was always such a good boy. Always trying to take care of me."

"Well, he's still taking care of you," Kayla said. "He comes to visit you here all the time. I know it's hard to remember. I forget things too. One day bleeds into the other, you know? But it's important you know that he comes here all the time, and when he's not here, he's thinking of you. And you know what else?"

My mother sat in rapture listening to Kayla talk about me. Meanwhile, I stood by, heart hammering in my chest, hating this disease that made it so my mother didn't see me even though I was right there, and loving the girl who was saving us both a little bit of pain by sharing her kindness. The storm raged inside me.

"What?" my mother breathed.

"He helps strangers, too. He volunteers a lot of his time to help people in need. And well, he helps me too. I was very lonely before your son and I started growing close again. Now I feel better. I feel happy. Because of Lukas."

My mother smiled. "Lukas."

"Mom?" I asked.

Her eyes slid up to me. "Our son is a good boy, David. Did you hear?"

Kayla licked her lips and averted her gaze.

I nodded. "Yes, I heard."

Sometimes, it wasn't worth trying to correct her. Sometimes, it was best to roll with it and pray like hell the next time I came to see her she'd know who I was.

"Lukas and I went trick or treating with some other kids tonight," Kayla said. When my mother's eyes lit up, Kayla told her all about our evening, and she painted the night like I was a kid again so as not to confuse my mother. At first, it stung a bit, but as I sat and listened, I realized that even though she was remembering the me from twenty years ago, she was still remembering *me*. And that was a treasure.

At the end of the night, my mother no longer wanted to watch her Charlie Brown movie. She let us help her into bed, and once she was all tucked in, I leaned over her and kissed her forehead.

"Goodnight," I whispered.

My mother closed her eyes. "Goodnight, David. See you in the morning."

Kayla and I slipped out into the hall. Neither of us said a word as I leaned against my mother's closed door. Kayla sniffled.

I looked down at her and found tears streaming down her cheeks.

"Please don't cry," I whispered.

She wiped her tears away with frustration and shook her head.

"I'm sorry. This isn't fair of me. I just... I didn't know, Lukas. I truly didn't know that you were dealing with this all this time. I wish you'd told me."

"Sometimes, it's nice to pretend this part of my life doesn't exist," I said. "It might sound cruel but it's true. Now you know. The cat's out of the bag. It's not like this most of the time, but when it is..." I trailed off, unable to find the words to describe the hurt and the pain this caused me. To be forgotten by your own mother was a cruel fate that I wished on no one.

Kayla wiped the last of her tears away.

"We should go," I said. I didn't want to be there anymore.

CHAPTER 34

KAYLA

I turned on Lukas' shower and held my hand under the water until it was hot. Steam rose in billows in the shower stall that reminded me of the fog on the campus grounds earlier that evening.

Halloween town felt like it had happened such a long time ago. All the events of the evening had all muddled together, leaving both of us reeling in the aftermath of coming face to face with Ally's terrible disease.

Lukas hadn't said a word since we got in the taxi and rode back to his place. I didn't push him. If our roles were reversed and I was in his shoes, I doubted I'd have anything to say, either. He was hurting. That much was obvious. And all I could do to help was show him that I was there.

Sometimes, the best way to do that was to help them do the little things that seemed like so much effort when they were drowning.

So once the water was hot, I started peeling his Halloween costume off him.

Lukas let me. He stood still, eyes cast down to the floor, his mind probably playing a reel of memories where his mother knew him as her son, and I stripped his vest off. His shirt came next, followed by the sash, plastic sword, boots, and balloon pirate pants. When he was down to his boxers, I turned him around to face the spray of water. I fetched a face cloth from under his bathroom cabinets, got it wet, and gently began wiping the makeup from his face.

He muttered a hollow thank you.

I ran the cloth over his eyelids. He kept his eyes closed in the wake of the cloth and I went to the tips of my toes to kiss his jaw, cheeks, and chin. I hoped he understood my silent way of telling him I loved him.

Once his makeup was wiped away, I stripped him out of his boxers and guided him into the shower. Lukas didn't protest, but he didn't start washing himself either, so I discarded my costume as well and joined him under the hot stream of water.

It felt good standing there naked under the water. I pulled him in close and wrapped my arms around his waist. He hesitated for a brief moment before engulfing me in an embrace and bowing his head so his cheek rested against mine.

I turned my face to his and kissed him. He kissed me back, slow and gentle, and I turned him around so he was under the water. It ran down the sides of his face and settled in the corners of our mouths as we kissed.

When we broke apart, I took his hand and pumped a dollop of shampoo into his palm. I told him to massage his scalp, and while he did that, I washed his body. The whole shower smelled like cedar and oranges.

When I was finished, we stayed in the hot water and kissed. His body felt good against mine, but not in the way it had felt before. The lust wasn't there like it used to be. Instead, I felt close to him. Painfully close. Each kiss left me wanting more of him—more of his heart, soul, and spirit. He poured more of himself into me as he backed me up against the glass shower wall.

I almost said it when we broke apart. I almost muttered those three little words to him in that moment. I knew I loved him. But this hardly seemed like the right time. He was hurting deeply. I could see it in the permanent furrow in his brow and the depths of his eyes that the pain he felt was deep and sharp. I could tell he needed healing, not promises of love that he might not be able to return in his state.

I turned off the water. Lukas let me towel him dry before I dried off too. I tied my wet hair in a tight knot on top of my head and followed him into the bedroom, where he collapsed onto the bed with a tired sigh. I pulled the blankets up over him and kissed him.

He caught my wrist when I turned away. "Stay."

I ran my fingers through his wet hair. "You need to sleep."

"And I will," he said. "But please stay. I don't want to be alone tonight."

He rolled over and I climbed into bed beside him. I had barely fluffed my pillow when he caught me for a kiss, his hand cupping my cheek, his other hand reaching down to grip my thigh and pull my leg up to hook it over his hip.

I pressed in against him and reached down to stroke his cock. Lukas' breath hitched in his throat and his pulse fluttered against my fingertips as I ran a hand along his neck. I worked him over slowly as our kisses deepened and our bodies began to take over. I rolled my hips, desperate to be touched, and Lukas responded by rolling over and pinning me beneath him.

In the dark bedroom, I could just make out his eyes. He watched me for a moment as I lay beneath him. For a moment, I thought he was going to say something but he descended on me for kisses instead. He dropped his hips. His cock rubbed against me and I moaned softly. A plea for more.

Lukas worked his way down the length of my body and got comfortable between my thighs. I watched as he licked and tasted me. He gripped my thighs as I reached my hands over my head and clung to his headboard. A rumbling sound of satisfaction rippled through him as he suckled and teased until my head buzzed with euphoria after my first release.

He crawled back up and over, reaching across to the nightstand where he retrieved a condom. I watched him roll it on and spread my legs for him. He went to his knees, pushed my legs back, and slid inside me. I gasped.

Lukas bowed over me and went to his elbows. He rolled his hips, his body grinding against mine, and I wrapped my legs around his waist. I used my heels against his buttocks to guide him deeper. He groaned against the side of my neck as he worshiped me with kisses, and as I grew breathless beneath him, he stole kisses.

The sex was nothing like the other times we'd been together. This was slow and sensual, intimate and steady.

We were making love.

I clung to his shoulders. My nails pressed into his skin and I pressed my head deep into the pillows, exposing my throat. He rewarded me with more kisses as another orgasm rippled through me. My toes curled and my pussy tightened. I was swollen and sensitive, and Lukas maintained his steady rhythm. He stroked my hair and kissed my forehead. He cupped my cheek and ran his thumb along my jaw. He watched me as I came, the sorrow I saw in him before now gone.

Our lips crashed together as he closed in on his climax. I held him as he groaned and strained. My world slipped away and there was nothing but Lukas as he gave in to the pleasure. The kisses deepened until we could hardly breathe, and we fell apart, both of us lying on our backs staring up at the ceiling.

I closed my eyes when he got out of bed to take off the condom and clean up, and I waited for him to slide back in and wrap me up in his arms.

I woke to birds chirping outside Lukas' bedroom window. My hair was still a bit damp from being tied in a bun all night, so when I got out of bed and went to the bathroom, I let it down. It fell in loose curls around my shoulders and smelled like Lukas' citrus shampoo.

I crept out of the bathroom while Lukas slept and I put on his bathrobe that I found hanging off the back of his bedroom door. It was plush and dark blue, almost indigo, and definitely too big for me. It probably hit him mid shin, but on me, it nearly touched the floor.

I headed for the kitchen and struggled to find light switches as I went. His home was a sprawling masterpiece and I still wasn't familiar with where everything was. As I explored his kitchen looking for things to make breakfast, I realized this might be quite the challenge. He had so many cupboards it took me ages to find his frying pans and even longer to find a cutting board. Once I had all my supplies lined up on the counter, I ventured to his fridge, which was stocked full with everything I needed to make us omelettes and toast.

I pulled red peppers, onion, mushrooms, cheese, eggs, and the carton of milk out of the fridge. As I was balancing it precariously in my arms and carrying it to the counter, I heard footsteps from around the corner.

"Good morning," I called as I caught a runaway egg that tried to roll off the counter. "I was going to surprise you with breakfast in bed. I didn't think you'd be up so early. Do you want a cup of coffee? I can—"

I broke off when I looked up and realized the footsteps I heard weren't Lukas'.

They were Lisa's.

Oh shit.

Lisa stared at me in her brother's bathrobe, standing in his kitchen like a domesticated housewife about to make him breakfast. Her mouth opened and formed shapes, but no words came out.

My heart raced and my stomach rolled over.

"Lisa," I said. "I can explain. I know this doesn't look good."

"What the hell are you doing here?"

I swallowed. How could I explain this to her without her feeling like I'd driven a knife in her back?

I walked around the kitchen island toward her. "Lisa, I'm so sorry. This isn't how we wanted you to find out."

"*We?*"

I looked at my feet. "Me and Lukas."

"You and Lukas?" she asked incredulously. "There's a you and Lukas? What the fuck, Kayla? Are you fucking my brother?"

My cheeks burned and my palms started to get clammy. "It's not about the sex, Lisa."

"So that's a yes? You are fucking my brother? Where is he? Lukas!"

"Lisa, please," I begged. "He had a really rough night. Let's not do this right now. He's not the one you should be mad at. I am. I'm your best friend. I'm the one who crossed the line."

"You're damn right you crossed a line," Lisa seethed. "I can't believe you!"

I heard the bedroom door open. My insides twisted into a tight knot as I heard Lukas coming down the hall. He rounded the corner in nothing but a pair of sweats. He rubbed his eyes and still looked half asleep when he dropped his hands and spotted his sister. He looked from her to me, and back to Lisa again.

"What the hell are you screaming about, Lisa?" Lukas asked.

I groaned. That wasn't the right approach at all.

"What am I screaming about?" Lisa planted her hands on her hips and laughed without humor at the ceiling. "I've just discovered that my brother and my best friend are fooling around behind my back. I never expected this kind of betrayal from either of you."

"Betrayal?" Lukas asked. He shook his head in disbelief. "Lisa, I don't owe you an explanation about who I'm seeing. I can't help who I—"

"Don't give me that shit, Lukas," Lisa spat.

My mind spun. What was he going to say? He couldn't help who he *what*?

"You two are unbelievable," Lisa said. "How can I ever trust either of you again? Why did you do this, Kayla? So he'd give you more money? Are you just like all those other sluts who want to be part of his life?"

"Lisa," Lukas said sternly. "You're out of line."

She rolled her eyes and marched for the front door. "I'm not the one out of line. You two are. Screw you both."

The front door slammed behind her. To me, it felt like the whole house shook.

My eyes started to burn as tears began to build.

Lukas sighed and raked his fingers through his disheveled hair.

"Well, I guess we don't have to worry about trying to figure out how to tell Lisa about us anymore."

I swallowed past the lump in my throat as Lukas walked over to me.

He put a hand in the small of my back and smiled. "Were you going to make me breakfast?"

I shook my head. "I have to go."

"What?"

I turned from the stove and made my way to his bedroom, where I dropped his robe and put on my princess costume. Talk about the walk of shame.

"What do you mean, go?" Lukas asked.

My heart was breaking into pieces. "I think it's best if we don't see each other for a little while."

"What?" Lukas shook his head. "No, come on, Kayla. Lisa is over-reacting. She doesn't get a say in who we choose to be with. Stay."

"I can't," I managed to say through tears that wouldn't stop falling. I turned to him and searched his eyes. Was I really about to walk out on him after everything? "We have to make things right."

He reached for me. "They're right when we're together."

I stepped back. He let his hand fall to his side.

"I'm sorry," I breathed.

CHAPTER 35

LUKAS

The black screen with lines of code and commands taunted me. I hadn't been able to get a single thing done over the past few days. Usually, the office was the place for me to find solace when things in my life were piling up and becoming too much.

But this week?

There was no comfort in those lines and chains.

I sighed and leaned back in my chair. I was too distracted to be productive. My thoughts were consumed with concerns and worries about my mother and her condition. Since Halloween, I'd gone back every day for four consecutive days to check in on her, and none of those days had been as bad as the night Kayla and I went to visit her.

My mother had been in high spirits for the last couple of days. What was more, she knew my face when she saw me, and she knew I was her son, not her good-for-nothing husband. I'd forgiven her, of course. It wasn't her fault that she remembered me as someone I hated. And it wasn't her fault that she was hurting me.

Even though Kayla hadn't said those words, she'd shown me that my mother still loved me simply by how she'd got her talking about me. There was nothing in the world I could ever do to thank her enough for that.

Even if I could, it was hard to thank a person who went dark on you.

I hadn't spoken to Kayla since she rushed out of my home the other morning after the confrontation with Lisa. My sister had sent her running for the hills and it was clear to me where Kayla's loyalties really rested.

With Lisa.

It hurt. It hurt a lot. But I also couldn't hate her for it. Lisa and Kayla had been best friends since they were old enough to play hopscotch. Sure, I wished Lisa had the emotional maturity to be happy for me and Kayla rather than shame us for falling for each other, but apparently, that wasn't in the cards.

Kayla and I had been doomed from the start.

I should have known better. I should have stopped things before they went too far. I should have listened when Kayla expressed concerns about Lisa. At least the pain wouldn't be so bad if we'd put a pin in things early on. I might wonder what might have been, but part of me wondered if that was better than knowing what I knew now.

I was in love with Kayla Goodfellow. Madly, wholeheartedly, desperately in love with her.

Part of me wished it hadn't been so easy for her to walk out on me that Sunday morning. Part of me wished she'd said screw it all and thrown herself at me, deciding she loved me more than she needed Lisa.

But then she wouldn't be the woman I loved.

I loved Kayla because of how good she was and how she cared for everyone. I loved her because she was kind and generous and she would never hurt someone. I loved her because she knew how to repair things, how to pour love into things, and how to save people from nightmares of their own making.

And she did it all with grace and no judgment.

No, if Kayla had been able to turn her back on Lisa, she wouldn't be the woman I thought she was.

Even though I knew all these things, it didn't make it hurt any less.

I was relieved for a distraction when my assistant knocked on my office door and popped her head in. "Mr. Holt? Rebecca Mills just published her article about you. Would you like to read it?"

"Sure, why not?"

My assistant came in and put a newspaper flat on my desk in front of me. My face was on the front page. It wasn't the usual sort of picture I was used to seeing of myself on the front page of anything editorial. Normally, the image was posed. Normally, I was in a suit and tie. Normally, there was professional lighting to capture my best angles.

But this picture wasn't that.

It was candid.

I was laughing, half turned away from the camera, facing Kayla, whose head was thrown back in laughter as well. She had a hand on my arm and an apple in her other hand. The backdrop was the orchard farm, the place where I'd first started to have genuine feelings for my sister's best friend.

"It's a very good picture of you, sir," my assistant said.

"Thank you."

"And she's very pretty."

I smiled as I gazed down at the black and white image of Kayla. "Yes, she is."

My assistant left me alone to read the article. I flipped a couple of pages in after reading the first page to finish the rest of the piece, where Rebecca had compiled all our interviews into one story where she concluded that the subject of her stories had changed a great deal in the time of our working together.

In the article, she described me as someone introspective, sympathetic, and changed for the better.

For the first time in a long time, I felt a sense of pride.

But what really stood out to me in the article were all the snapshots of Kayla and me. I wondered if readers would notice that she was in almost every frame with me, and in each shot, we were smiling like idiots at each other. There were pictures from the gala, from the orchard, and from the Halloween town. I hadn't even known pictures were being taken there. There were shots of me with my head in the bucket bobbing for apples and a picture of me holding Carson above the bucket by his ankles while Addison cheered us on.

Had Kayla seen the articles? Did she think it was well written? Did she think it was accurate?

Or would she refuse to read the article because she didn't want to be reminded of me?

I sighed and got out of my chair to go to the window and look out at the city.

In each and every one of those pictures, it was clear on my face that I was looking at a woman I loved.

Suddenly, it struck me.

Kayla was looking at me with the same look in her eyes in all those pictures. She had genuine feelings for me, just as I did for her. If I was hurting now, how must she be feeling as the one who had to put a pin in things all for Lisa's sake? Was she questioning herself? Did she resent Lisa for this? Did she want to call me more than anything and explain it all?

Did it matter?

I loved her. That was what mattered. And I was quite certain she loved me, too.

I've come too far to give up now.

I loved my sister. Lisa was one of the most precious people to me in my life. But she didn't get to choose who I fell in love with or wanted to spend the rest of my life with. She didn't get to tell me no, and she didn't get to stop Kayla either.

No, I refused to let her stand in the way of the best thing that had ever happened to me. I wanted Kayla.

And at the end of the day, I was still Lukas Holt. The new and improved Lukas Holt to be sure, but I was still the guy who went for what he wanted. I was still the guy who put it all on the line even in the face of rejection.

Now was not the time to throw in the towel and go soft.

CHAPTER 36

KAYLA

"Lisa, pick up your phone," I said into Lisa's voicemail service. I'd called several times a day for the past four days and she'd sent each and every call to voicemail. I'd texted and emailed and received no replies. "We need to talk about this. You can't ignore me forever. I understand that you're upset and that I hurt you, but please, give me a chance to tell you what happened. You know me. You know I wouldn't do this to you on purpose. Things just… I don't know. They got away from us. Please. Call me back."

I hung up the phone.

I knew she wouldn't call me back. Lisa was as stubborn as her brother. Once she'd been wronged, or felt like she had, she would stick to her guns and hold a grudge against her enemy until the end of time. I never thought I'd be on the receiving end of that stubbornness but there I was.

Suffering.

I wanted my best friend back. I also wanted my lover back. But I couldn't have either of them.

The guilt and shame that I'd felt on Sunday morning had long since morphed into despair and, to my surprise, anger.

I was angry at Lisa's reaction. I was angry that she didn't seem to care about Lukas' happiness, or mine for that matter. She could only see this thing from her side, and for some reason, she thought it was all about her. It wasn't.

It was about me and Lukas and how happy we made each other—how much better we made each other. Couldn't she see that? Couldn't she see through her own cloud of fury long enough to realize that this was real?

I wouldn't have risked our friendship for something that wasn't real.

I raked my fingers through my hair as I sat at my desk at the Good Fellow's head office. I had so much pent-up frustration because she wasn't giving me a chance to speak my piece. I needed to get it off my chest. I needed her to hear me. Otherwise, I was going to be stuck in this lonely place for eternity.

I wanted my relationship back with Lukas but I knew I wouldn't sacrifice my friendship with Lisa for it. Somehow, I had to get her to understand how I felt about him. I had to get her to listen.

I grabbed my purse and left the office, locking up after myself. Clearly, the phone calls and virtual messages weren't working. I needed to take drastic action.

I hopped on the bus and rode it to the closest stop near Lisa's duplex. There was no way to know if she'd be home, but I figured she'd be trying to spend as little time as possible at Lukas' office that she could. So, naturally, the first stop was her house.

After walking six blocks from the bus stop to her duplex, I found myself standing at her front door feeling more than a little nervous.

I'd thought of everything I wanted to say to her on the bus but now my mind was blank. There was nothing but white noise up there.

It doesn't matter. You need to buck up and knock on that door and make her listen to you. If you're not willing to put it on the line, then you never deserved Lukas in the first place. Right?

My fingers tingled as I lifted my hand to the door and knocked.

To my surprise, the door swung open and Lisa stood there with her phone pressed to her ear. Her eyes narrowed on me as she spoke to the person on the other line. "I'll have to let you go, Mrs. Weiss. Can I call you back in an hour?"

She hung up the phone.

"Lisa," I started.

"What do you want?"

"I want to talk."

"Talk?" she scoffed. "You had plenty of time to talk to me before I found you in my brother's house half naked cooking him breakfast."

I rubbed my lips together. *You can do this. Don't let her intimidate you.*

"I didn't spend the night with Lukas to hurt you, Lisa. I know it might feel that way but I swear to you what happened between me and him had nothing to do with you. Can I come in so we can talk properly?"

"No."

I nodded. "Okay. Fine. Can we—"

"I don't want to hear anything you have to say, Kayla. There's nothing you can do that will make this better. You were sneaking around with my brother behind my back. How long did it go on? How many times did you smile in my face and pretend that you weren't screwing my brother? Huh?" Lisa shook her head in disbelief. "Nobody should ever do that to the person who is supposed to be their best friend. Ever. Especially when you know how I feel about people taking advantage of my brother."

I adjusted my purse strap on my shoulder. "Lisa, I wasn't taking advantage. It just happened naturally."

"Oh? Naturally? It did, did it? How does that work? One minute, you're picking apples, and the next, you have his tongue down your throat and then the pair of you are making a pact to keep it a secret from me?"

"You know that's not true."

Lisa laughed. "I don't know what's true anymore. How could I when the two people who mean the most to me have been in on a lie for the past month?"

She was overreacting. I wanted to tell her so. I wanted to scream at her that she was acting like a spoiled brat. She did not get to call the shots where Lukas was concerned. He was a grown-ass man who could do what he wanted.

And what he wanted happened to be me.

"We never conspired against you, Lisa," I said calmly. "Lukas and I spent a lot of time together—time that you orchestrated for us to spend together, I might add. And that's how these things work. You spend time with a person and then you realize you like them more than just a friend, you know?"

"He's my *brother*," she said.

"Do you seriously think I don't know that? Do you think I threw myself into this thinking fuck Lisa, I do what I want? I'm not that person and you know it. I fought this, Lisa. I fought it as best I could. I told him no. He knew we shouldn't have let things get too far. We both did. But—"

"But you got in bed with him anyway," Lisa said. "Words are just words, Kayla. You betrayed me. Plain and simple. You went behind my back and deliberately kept it from me. You're just like all the other girls who are always throwing themselves at my brother. What was it? You realized how easy it was to get close to him and you thought you'd try your hand at getting in his pockets? I know he has a lot of money and there's a lot of good you could do if you got your little claws on his billions."

I blinked. Was she seriously accusing me of sleeping with her brother to try to get his money? *Who does she think I am?*

"I did not go for your brother to get to his money," I said, my tone developing a sharp edge. "I can't believe you would even suggest that.
"

Lisa crossed her arms and arched an eyebrow. "I've been there to pick up the pieces of my brother's bad decisions for years now. That's all this is. A bad decision. He let you get in his head."

"Why am I the bad guy here? This took two of us."

"You knew better. You knew better and you went for it anyway without caring what it would do to me."

"Lisa!" I practically yelled. "This isn't about you! I didn't do this *to* you. I didn't do it to hurt you. Holy shit. Since when did you become so damn self-absorbed? Do you think I chose to fall for your brother? Do you think I wanted this extra complication in my life? No, I didn't. But we don't get to choose these things. Sometimes, they just happen to and for us."

"Are you trying to make me feel bad for you now?"

"No," I said, shaking my head. She was impossible. She didn't want to be reasoned with. She wanted to stay angry and bitter because it was easier than forgiving and moving forward. There wasn't a damn thing I could do about that. "I wanted to apologize."

"For what you did to me?"

"No, for hurting your feelings. I didn't do anything to you. But I hurt your feelings, and for that, I am deeply sorry. We should have told you when things first started to get serious between us. I regret that now."

Lisa searched my eyes, but her body language remained stiff and angry. "Our friendship can't come back from this. I think you should go."

That stung. I flinched under her words. "So that's it? You're going to let a twenty-year-old friendship die because I have feelings for your brother?"

"No, I'm going to let it die because you didn't trust me enough to tell me."

"Would you have wanted to hear it?"

"That's not the point."

"You're impossible, Lisa. You want to be angry. You're just like Lukas used to be. He wanted to be alone. He wanted to be shut off. It was easier for him. But as soon as he let go of those old ways, he changed. He grew. Hate me if you want, but I promise you, this will only cause you more pain down the road." I turned and hurried down her front steps to the sidewalk, where I faced her one more time. "If you change your mind, I'll be ready to talk anytime."

Lisa closed and locked her door.

I walked back up to the bus stop in tears. How had I lost my two best friends all at once? How had we gotten here?

CHAPTER 37

LUKAS

When I arrived at the office that morning, the first thing I noticed was that Lisa was in the conference room with my assistant. She was standing, the lights were out, and she was pointing to the pulldown screen where a projector was blasting a chart of some sort onto it. My assistant was nodding where she sat at the table and taking notes while Lisa talked.

I made for the conference room with a determined stride. Lisa didn't see me coming until I opened the door and joined their meeting. I took the seat across the table from my assistant, who looked back and forth between me and Lisa when my sister fell quiet.

"This is a private meeting," Lisa said.

"With my assistant?" I asked as I crossed one leg over the other. "What meeting could you possibly have with my assistant that you couldn't have with me?"

My sister licked her lips. "I didn't want to waste your time."

"No, you didn't want to have to see or talk to me because you're mad at me."

Lisa's mouth twitched. "So?"

I smiled at my assistant. "Could my sister and I have some privacy?"

I'd never seen a person leave a room quicker.

Lisa and I stared at each other in stony silence. Neither of us were willing to speak first.

Finally, I bit the bullet. "We need to talk about me and Kayla."

Lisa rolled her eyes and started collecting her things. She had notebooks open on the table and a couple of pens. Normally, she would put everything in its spot in her bag, all separated and organized by dividers and pencil cases. This morning, she just dropped it in the open mouth of the purse carelessly.

"There is no you and Kayla," she said flatly. "There can't be."

I arched an eyebrow. "Why? Because you say so?"

My sister prickled, slung her purse over her shoulder, and picked up a coffee cup with an imprint of lipstick on the lid that matched the fuchsia shade she wore this morning. "Yes."

My sister had always been stubborn. She was used to getting her way just like I was. But I'd never seen her quite this hostile.

It pissed me off.

"You're mistaken," I said. "There most certainly will be a Lukas and Kayla because I intend to marry that girl, and you need to get on board."

Lisa stared blankly at me. For a moment, I couldn't read her expression, but when her brows drew together and her bottom lip quivered, it all started falling into place. She felt betrayed. Her anger was a deflection. "Why didn't you tell me you were seeing her?"

"Things moved quickly," I explained. "At first, there was nothing to tell. Kayla tried to shut things down time and time again, but every time we were thrown together for an activity to put on a good show for Rebecca Mills, sparks flew. We could only pretend there was nothing between us for so long, Lisa. Then, I don't know. We both gave in. We stopped fighting it. We stopped letting outside sources make our choices for us."

"You could have told me."

"And have you react like this? Why would I?"

"I only want to protect you," Lisa said firmly.

"Protect me? From what? I'm a thirty-year-old man. I don't need protecting."

"Everyone needs protecting sometimes, Lukas. I don't want you to get hurt. You've never been in love before and it scares the hell out of me to think about how badly things could go. How they could end. You've been through so much. I don't want someone else to hurt you."

I got to my feet. Someone had clearly hurt my sister in the past and she'd never opened up about it with me. I intended to find out who that someone was and how they'd hurt her, but right then, I just needed to settle this.

"Kayla isn't the type to hurt someone and you know that," I said softly.

"She hurt me."

"Not on purpose. She was trying to protect you. See how that bit her in the ass? Just like you trying to protect me would bite you in the ass."

Lisa crossed her arms. "Those aren't the same thing."

"If you say so. Listen, Kayla is a good friend. She's the best person you and I know. She made a mistake because she was afraid of how you'd react when you found out she was happy with me. You need to forgive her."

Lisa didn't say a word. She could hardly bring herself to look at me.

"And for the record," I added, "you shouldn't be upset. If you really want me to end up with a good woman, one we know isn't after me for my money or any ulterior motive, then Kayla is the right choice. She's made me a better man, Lisa. An infinitely better man. You can't deny that."

"Maybe that's because you were getting laid."

"No," I said, irritated. "She taught me that I don't have to sit on my pile of gold like a dragon. She showed me how to help people and how to effect real change. She's made me vulnerable. Open. Generous. Do you know how good it feels to be this guy instead of the guy I was before her? I was so angry, Lisa. I was angry all the time. And I was so tired."

Lisa swallowed hard. Her eyes grew glassy. "I know you were."

"And now I'm not. Now I'm home. I'm me. Isn't this what you wanted when you hired Kayla in the first place? Wasn't this the whole point?"

"I did not push you two together."

"You pushed me to grow, Lisa. That's all. And Kayla was part of that growth. I didn't know it at the time but she was. I've never met anyone like her."

Lisa nodded slowly. "Yeah, me neither."

"So?"

"So what?"

"Are you going to stop being mad at us and storming around the office like a furious cat, or are you going to be happy for me?"

Lisa sighed and peered up at me from beneath her brows. "Are you sure she's the one you want?"

"There's not a doubt in my mind."

"How can you be sure? How can you be *that* sure? It's only been five weeks!"

"I love her," I said simply. "I do. I love her."

My sister stared at me like she was seeing me for the first time. "You love her?"

"That's what I've been trying to tell you," I said, taking my sister's hands. "And I'm pretty certain she loves me too."

"Then she'd be here with you."

"No, because she's torn. Kayla never wanted to hurt you, Lisa. Do you know how much turmoil she must be in that she can't make this right with you? How many times has she tried to call you?"

Lisa looked down at her feet. "Over sixty. And she showed up at me place."

"She did?"

"I said some mean things."

I sighed. "Nothing that can't be forgiven, I'm sure. This is Kayla we're talking about."

"She probably hates me," Lisa whispered. "I'd hate me."

"Kayla doesn't hate anyone. She wants her friend back."

234

Lisa looked up at me and I wiped a tear from her cheek. "I want my friend back, too," she whispered.

That was what I wanted to hear.

I smiled at my sister and kissed her forehead. "Then what do you say you and I make things right?"

"How?"

"Follow my lead, little sister."

CHAPTER 38

KAYLA

My fingers flew over the keyboard as I typed out yet another apology letter to Lisa. The words *sorry* and *forgive* were starting to look strange and I had to use spell check just to make sure that they were in fact spelled correctly. A quick glance at the time on my computer told me I'd been at this for two hours and hardly made any progress, so I slapped my laptop closed and slumped down on my sofa, pouting.

"She's never going to forgive me," I muttered to my empty apartment.

Nobody spoke back to me. Nobody offered any encouraging words. Nobody told me to stick to my guns. Nobody came and sat with me and told me not to waste any more energy on this.

Of course, the only person I wanted by my side telling me those things was Lukas. But I'd gone and botched that, too. I abandoned him hours after he had to go through a terrible night with his mother. Chances were he hated me too.

"You've successfully alienated yourself from both the Holts. Well done, Kayla." I clapped for myself bitterly. It didn't make me feel better.

Desperate to feel something other than regret and guilt, I got up and put the kettle on to make myself a cup of tea. I chose a ginger and honey tea because my stomach had been bothering me due to all the nerves. As the kettle boiled, I stood by the counter slouched over, the sash on my robe dangling precariously close to the floor.

I heaved a dramatic sigh and willed the kettle to boil faster.

It didn't.

"Why hasn't he come to see me?" I asked the tea kettle. That was a question that had been playing over and over in my mind.

Lukas hadn't bothered to reach out. Even if I'd hurt him, part of me assumed he'd push back a little. It was in his nature. He'd done it at the beginning of our relationship. He wouldn't take no for an answer. But this time? The time I desperately wanted and needed him to step up and push me a little, he was nowhere to be seen.

That hurt.

I gave my head a shake. *Nonsense.*

Was I seriously upset with him for respecting my wishes? I'd told him we shouldn't see each other for a while. So naturally, he wasn't seeing me. He was doing what I asked. He was following through.

And clearly, it wasn't what I'd actually wanted.

What I wanted was my best friend back. And my man.

Why couldn't we all just coexist? Why did Lisa have to care? Why did she have to paint me with the brush that I was the same as all the gold diggers who'd pursued her brother before? Why did she have to make me feel like a movie villain for falling in love with her brother?

"All that's missing is superpowers and a cool costume," I mumbled.

The kettle finally started to whistle and I poured hot water into my teapot. The smells of honey and ginger wafted up on the steam until I put the lid on and set the timer on the stove for four minutes.

It was after the first minute had passed that there was a knock on my door.

I frowned and looked over my shoulder. Who would be dropping by my place? I didn't get visitors. Not ever. *Probably a neighbor looking for sugar or salt. Or eggs.*

I considered ignoring them, but it wasn't in my nature. With a tired sigh, I shuffled barefoot across the kitchen floor to my front door. I looked a mess and whoever was knocking was going to regret what they were about to see. My hair hadn't been washed in approximately three days and had existed in the same messy bun on top of my head for that entire duration. It was oily, and the bun had come loose, so it had settled a little off center. My skin was oily and my robe was stained from food and drinks I'd managed to eat over the last four days.

I mustered up the energy to open the door.

And there he was.

"Lukas?" I breathed.

He smiled. He looked good as always. He was wearing a pair of dark jeans and black boots. He had a gray hoodie under a black leather jacket, and the hood and shoulders of his jacket were speckled in raindrops. He held a bouquet of red roses in his hand. The petals glistened with tiny drops of water.

"I brought these for you," he said, holding out the roses.

I blinked at the bouquet and looked up at him. "How did you know I still lived here?"

The subject had never come up, so I never mentioned to Lukas that I still lived in the very same apartment I'd grown up in just down the road from where he and Lisa lived.

"I talked to my sister," he said.

Right. Of course. "How is she?" I asked.

"She's good."

"You talked to her?"

"I did."

"And she said that herself? That she's good? Because I'm not good. I am *so* not good. I think I might be falling apart a little bit. I've been trying to get her to talk to me but she won't talk to me, Lukas. And I don't know what else to do because I don't know who I am without Lisa in my life."

"Hey," he said softly, stepping forward to cup my cheek. "Take a breath. Everything is okay. You're okay. Lisa's okay. We're all okay."

I swallowed. "Okay." The word was beginning to sound strange, just like *sorry* and *forgive*.

He smiled. "Are you going to invite me in, or what?"

"Oh." *You're a bumbling idiot, Kayla. The hallway smells like Kraft Dinner and wet cardboard. Get the poor man out of there.* I stepped aside and gestured for him to come in. "Sorry. Clearly, my mind is a little jumbled."

Lukas brushed past me and stepped into the kitchen. I closed the door behind him and set the roses on my kitchen island right as the timer on my stove went off. I padded over to it. "Do you want a cup of tea? It's freshly brewed."

Lukas tucked his hands in his pockets. "Sure. Why not?"

I took two mugs down from the cupboard beside the stove and filled them with piping hot tea. I passed one to him and we moved into the living room to sit down.

Then I remembered how much of a mess I was.

I paused as he took a seat and looked up at me. "I should shower," I said.

"What?"

"I should shower," I said again, like that would help clarify things for him.

That little frown formed between his eyebrows. "Right now? Why? Can we talk first?"

Priorities, Kayla. Priorities.

"Yes." I sat down and gripped my mug in both hands. "Yes, we can. I'm just... I'm all over the map. I look like a mess."

"You don't look like a mess."

"I feel like one."

"It hasn't been an easy week."

"No," I admitted. "It hasn't. What do you want to talk about?"

"Us."

"Us?"

God, I was starting to sound like a fool. Everything he said, I repeated back to him or stammered over.

Lukas smiled graciously. "Yes. Us. You and me."

"There can't be a you and me. Lisa forbids it."

"I spoke with my sister."

My heart began to thump wildly in my chest. "You did?"

"Yes. It wasn't easy, and it took some time, but I got her to come around and finally understand how I feel about you."

How he feels about me? I put my mug down on the coffee table as my hands started to shake. "How do you feel, Lukas?"

He smiled like he had a secret he was about to let me in on. "I'm head over heels in love with you, Kayla. I told Lisa I wasn't going to give you up."

He did? "You did?"

"I did." Lukas nodded. "Lisa admitted it was wrong of her to be so upset. She's given us her blessing, Kayla. So, if you'll have me, I want to start over."

I couldn't believe what I was hearing. Was this real? Or had I passed out while I was waiting for the kettle to boil and this was all some cruel dream?

If I woke up Lukas-less, I was going to blow my top.

"Say something," Lukas said.

"Are you positive this is what you want? That *I'm* what you want? We're from different worlds, Lukas."

"I'm certain. And we're not from different worlds. We're from this world right here. This neighborhood. This town. You and me? We grew up the same. I've never been more certain about anything in my life."

"Me neither," I breathed.

I fell toward him. Lukas met me in the middle of the sofa. He engulfed me in his arms and lowered me down onto my back. His lips sealed over mine, and every single nerve ending in my body sang to life. After feeling numb and hollow for nearly a week, the rush of emotions and joy was almost overwhelming. Tears spilled down my cheeks and Lukas wiped them away with his thumbs while he kissed me.

A kiss had never tasted so good, like honey, ginger, and hope.

"Wait," I stammered, breaking away.

His eyes darted back and forth between mine. "What?"

"I need to tell you something before we go any further."

"What is it?"

I smiled. "I love you too."

Lukas grinned. "You're a shit disturber, you know that? I thought it would be something bad."

"It is bad," I teased. "I'm not supposed to end up with you. I'm supposed to end up with the safe-choice guy. The guy in the khakis who likes to barbeque but doesn't know where he leaves his car keys. The guy who doesn't care about driving a minivan to take our kids to swimming or piano lessons."

"Rodney?" Lukas teased. "Are you talking about Rodney?"

I laughed as he nuzzled his way to the groove of my neck. "Poor Rodney."

"You snooze you lose, Rodney."

I held his face in my hands. "Why are we still talking about Rodney?"

"I don't know."

I kissed him hard. Lukas' hands wandered all over my body and began pulling my clothes off. I relished the feeling of his fingers grazing my bare skin and I fumbled with the sash on my robe. Realizing I needed to shower, I extracted myself out from underneath him and led him down the hall. He followed me like a lost puppy dog and I relished the power I held over him.

I slipped into the bathroom with him hot on my heels and turned on the water. I dropped my robe and he looked me over, his eyes filling with desire.

"Want to know something wild?" I asked.

"Tell me."

"I've never had sex in this shower before."

Lukas grinned like the devil himself. "I think it's time we change that."

CHAPTER 39

LUKAS

I took her in the shower.

Kayla gasped as I filled her up. She hooked a leg around mine and held herself up with one arm draped around my shoulders. The other gripped the wrist of the hand I had planted on the tiled wall at her back. She moaned softly and closed her eyes. Shower water clung to her lashes and left streaks down her cheeks, and I was quite certain in that moment that I'd never laid eyes on anyone more beautiful.

She was like a starry night sky in the country where city lights didn't compete for attention. She was a canvas of oil paint capturing the epitome of beauty and depth. She was everything and anything in between, and I couldn't understand how she'd chosen me back.

She was an easy woman to fall in love with.

But me? I was not.

I'd given her hell in the beginning. Some days, I'd been cruel. I'd been difficult. I'd been a bully.

But she saw past all that. She remembered the boy I was and knew the man I was supposed to be, and she'd pulled that out of me.

Not only did I love her, but I owed everything to her.

Kayla ran her fingers through my wet hair and trailed kisses across my jaw and throat as I thrust deep inside her. She was tight and greedy and her skin was slippery from the water. Her breasts, full and perky, were crushed up against my chest as I rocked my hips and made her thighs tremble until she could hardly stay on her feet.

I wrapped an arm around her lower back and held her up as I fucked her harder. Kayla let her head hang back. Water rained down from the ends of her hair. Her chest swelled as she took a deep breath. I kissed between her breasts and licked her flesh, wanting to taste and savor every inch of her.

I pulled her back up and spun her around so I could pin her against the tiles. She giggled when I took her hands behind her back and held her wrists in place with one hand. She squirmed, testing my strength, and I held fast.

She spread her legs without me having to ask and pushed her ass back.

She had a glorious body.

The curve of her spine did things to me, and so did the two dimples in her lower back above her ass. Her thighs were full and strong, her calves defined, her waist trim, and her hips thick enough to grab onto. She had taut flesh, the kind that dared a man to squeeze.

So I did. I squeezed her hips as I pushed my cock back into her and took her from behind.

Kayla pressed her cheek against the tile wall and sighed with pleasure. I rocked against her, fucking her deeply, and she clawed at the tiles. Her nails bit against the grout until her hands curled into fists and she whimpered for me to show her mercy and fuck her like I meant it.

I took a fistful of her hair. Kayla gasped in surprise as I pulled her head back sharply, forcing her to look up at the ceiling and rest her head on my shoulder. A smile curled her lips as I tightened my grip.

I thrust deep inside her. Her expression molded into one of ecstasy. Watching her pushed me to the brink. Her smile stayed on her lips as I pressed in deeper, harder, faster. Soon, she could hardly keep it together. Her thighs shook furiously and her knees nearly gave out. She cried out my name at the ceiling, her eyes fluttered open, and she came hard.

I pressed a kiss to the side of her neck. "Good girl."

My girl.

I wrapped her hair around my fist like it was a rope. Kayla bounced on my cock. The shower water did not spoil how wet she was. She was slippery and swollen, just how I liked her, and I knew I was going to lose control soon.

She reached back with one hand to cup it around the back of my neck. Her eyes opened and met my gaze, and her lips parted in a contented sigh.

"Come for me," she whispered. "Let go."

Her words did me in. I clenched my teeth against the strain as the pleasure mounted until it broke. I pulled free and released onto her lower back. Kayla wiggled her ass for me and let me guide her under the water to wash her off. Only then did I release her hair.

She smiled at me as I soaped up her tits.

"What?" I asked, my head still spinning from the best sex of my life.

"There are a lot of other places in this apartment I haven't had sex before, you know."

"Oh? You don't say? What sort of places?"

"Well," she said seductively. "There's the kitchen counter. The sofa. The living room floor. The balcony."

"The balcony? You are a freak, aren't you?"

She giggled and stepped in close for more kisses. "Only for you."

To say Kayla and I were spent by the time nine in the evening rolled around would be an understatement. We christened every corner of her house—and we did it with vigor. Now we were both exhausted, not to mention hungry, and as we lounged on her sofa waiting for the delivery guy to show up with pizza, I pulled her close and breathed in the coconut scent of her shampoo.

"I've learned so much since you came back into my life," I said softly. "I think I have a lot more changes to make."

"I like you just the way you are."

"Like?"

She giggled. "You know what I mean."

I let her get away with it. "I'm going to start giving away most of my fortune. I think it's time that I learn how to be without it. I'll need your help finding the right places to give it."

She propped herself up on her elbow. "You want to give it all away?"

"I'm not a psychopath." I chuckled. "I worked hard for what I have. I'll keep enough where I can give us a more than comfortable life. But Kayla, you really have no idea how much money I have to my name. I have so much I could give away that I'd never be able to spend my way through anyway."

"You're a good man, Lukas Holt. A very good man."

"Because of you."

She smiled and tucked a strand of still damp hair behind her ear. "You were always good. You just needed help letting that part of yourself to take the driver's seat."

"Well now that he's behind the wheel, I want a lot of things I never thought I'd want."

"Things like what?"

"A family," I said.

My quick answer surprised her. She blinked and cocked her head to the side. "A family?"

"I want to make babies with you. I want to raise humans who are as kind and as good as you. I want to share something with the world that it needs. More good people. I want to watch them grow while we get old together. I want to have holiday dinners with our grandchildren, maybe even great grandchildren."

Kayla kissed my cheek. "I never thought I'd hear the grumpy billionaire I started working for say these kinds of things."

"I'm not afraid to admit when I've been wrong."

She cuddled in close. "Well, these changes are looking real good on you, Lukas."

"You know what else looks real good on me?"

"What?"

"You."

Kayla laughed and rolled her eyes. "I should've seen that one coming."

We laughed and sank deeper into the sofa. Her stomach growled and I checked the time. The pizza would be there any minute.

"We'll have to figure out how to spend time away from work, you and me," I said. "We'll need to find a way to relax and enjoy each other's company without feeling tied to our jobs all the time. There are more important things than making money, or giving it away for that matter. Like spending time with you. And we'll spend some of that money of mine on each other. We'll travel. See the world."

"That will be something to get used to. I can't remember the last time I had any real time off. Or spent money on myself."

I looked around her apartment. "Well, it's about time we changed that."

I looked forward to spoiling her. She deserved it.

She sighed and settled into the groove of my shoulder. "You know, I've never really wanted much for myself, but I have to admit, your beautiful home on the Sound is a little nicer than this dingy old apartment."

I chuckled and rolled into her to pepper her with kisses. "The only thing my house has been missing is a pretty girl in it."

"Check that off the list."

"Already done."

I kissed her deeply and left her panting with red cheeks when the door buzzer rang and the pizza arrived. She scolded me as I left her on the sofa hot and bothered to run down and grab our food.

Silly girl. She should know by now. I'd never leave her hanging again.

EPILOGUE

KAYLA

One Year Later

L isa lifted my veil gently and let it fall into place down the back of my wedding gown. She clapped her hands together, clearly satisfied with her flair for the dramatic, and hurried out in front of me in her lilac-colored bridesmaid dress.

"Any last minute doubts?" she asked.

I laughed and shook my head. "Aren't you supposed to ask me something a little more positive?"

"You're right, you're right," she said. "Are you sure you want to marry that idiot brother of mine?"

Snickering, I nodded. "I'm absolutely positive."

Lisa smiled tearfully. "You look so beautiful, Kayla."

Butterflies took flight in my stomach. "Thank you. I couldn't have done this without you."

"No, you couldn't have," she said.

We shuffled and shimmied up to the swinging saloon doors that led from the kitchen of the soup kitchen out into the hall. I knew it was a weird venue for a wedding, but for me, it fit right, like the perfect shoe.

Lukas had told me we could get married anywhere I wanted. He even suggested the Monroe Hotel, the very same place Lisa had landed for us by cashing in that favor with the owner, Stephen Edmonds. Apparently, Lukas had some pull there as well.

But I wasn't one for flashy or glamorous events. I was a simple girl who liked to stick to her roots.

And this place was my roots. My bread and butter. My home.

And the people there were my family.

Our guests were made up of family, friends, and soup kitchen regulars who'd all been invited to our ceremony. We'd decided on Thanksgiving Day for the wedding so that the caterers could feed everyone a hearty turkey dinner. Lisa had joked that a lot of the guests were probably there for the turkey, not the wedding, and if that was the case, I didn't mind at all.

The chairs would be filled with smiling faces of people I'd helped and who'd helped me. They deserved to be there today.

And so did Rodney, who stood off to the side of the doors with a tight-lipped smile on his face.

I knew this hadn't been an easy day for him. When Lukas and I first made our relationship official about a year ago, I'd told him my very first shift back at the soup kitchen. He'd told me he wasn't all that surprised. He'd suspected something was going on between me and Lukas and he'd told me he knew he couldn't compete.

I'd assured him it had nothing to do with competing. When I explained that I'd known Lukas since I was a little girl and we grew up together, Rodney felt a little less sorry for himself. I knew this still wasn't the best day for him, but he was my friend, and that was how he'd shown up for me on my special day, as a friend.

He'd handled all the catering details, telling me I had other things to worry about as a bride. He'd been a great help and the event wouldn't have gone as smoothly without him.

He tipped his head to me as I inched closer to the door. "Lukas is a lucky man," he said.

I smiled. "Yes, he is."

Rodney patted my hand before letting it go. It had been a full year since he'd given me one of those a-little-too-personal hugs. A full year since he draped an arm over my shoulders and teased me for being short. A full year since he so much as flirted with me.

I had a lot of respect for him.

On the other side of the doors, music started to play. My breath hitched in my throat as I realized I was going to be Mrs. Holt in less than twenty minutes.

Lisa stepped up beside me and looped her arm through mine. "Ready, babe?"

I nodded. "Ready."

"Let's get married."

We pushed through the doors, and as we walked, Rodney fanned my dress out so it fell dramatically behind me. The train flowed out beautifully and grazed the red carpet that had been laid down for me as my aisle. All the soup kitchen chairs formed neat rows facing an archway of white roses under which Lukas stood.

We locked eyes.

Emotion I'd never felt before rushed through me. I knew it was probably all just the usual emotions of the day, but there was something else that probably made it more intense. The hormones, of course.

I was six weeks along in my pregnancy. Nobody knew but me and Lukas. It had been an incredible early wedding gift to tell Lukas that I was pregnant. I'd never seen him cry before, but he'd cried that day. He'd gone to his knees in front of me, wrapped his arms around me, and held his cheek to my stomach while I ran my fingers through his hair. He'd talked to the baby every day since. In fact, I couldn't get him to shut up sometimes.

I resisted the urge to put my hand on my stomach as I walked down the aisle to meet my future husband. For now, the little baby was our special secret.

Lukas smiled and tugged at the sleeves of his suit jacket as I came to him. We walked slowly and I felt the eyes of every person in the room land on me. Some people waved. Others sniffled and dabbed their eyes with tissues. Up in the front row, Ally, Lukas' mother, turned and smiled at me. She wore a shimmering light blue dress and bolero jacket, and she had a fresh perm. She looked beautiful and healthy. Her cheeks were rosy and full and her lips were pink and glossy. She'd been lucky enough to qualify for an experimental treatment for patients with dementia, and she'd been lucid for the last couple of months. Sure, sometimes her memory still slipped away from her, but most of her days were good ones, not bad ones.

Like today.

Today was a good day.

Today, she got to see her son get married.

I met Lukas at the end of the aisle. His eyes were glassy, and when Lisa passed me off to him, he stood back and looked me up and down.

"You look incredible." His voice was hoarse with emotion.

"You clean up real good yourself," I said.

The music slowed to a gentle tempo and the crowd fell into a hush. Our officiant stepped up between us, a leatherbound book resting open in the palm of his hand, and he addressed the room. "We are gathered here today to celebrate the union of two remarkable people. Kayla Goodfellow and Lukas Holt."

As the officiant performed the ceremony, I gazed into the eyes of the man I loved more than anything else in the world. I thought about our future together, our upcoming honeymoon to Belize, the baby in my belly who was already so loved, and the people sitting in the rows of chairs who had come to celebrate our special day with us.

I was the luckiest woman alive.

Later, after the vows were exchanged and our pictures were taken, everyone gathered back in the kitchen, which had been transformed from the ceremony setup to a banquet hall with dining tables and a head table for Lukas and me.

It was a full-service meal and waiters brought everyone their plates of food. Pitchers of gravy steamed on tables next to crystal bowls of cranberry sauce. Dinner rolls overflowed from wicker baskets lined with floral linens, and sunflowers poked out of vases. It was simple but perfect.

After we ate, we received our guests, who came up to the head table and thanked us for inviting them. Some offered me special words, thanking me for everything I'd done for them with Good Fellow's. To say I was a basket case during the whole thing would have been an understatement.

Finally, the gratitudes were over and I was left to recover. I dabbed under my eyes to try and wipe the tears away and Lukas leaned in close. "I have a gift for you," he said softly.

"I thought we said no presents?"

"It's not a traditional present," he said. He reached under the table and pulled out a stack of paperwork. Every third or fourth page in the stack was marked with a sticky tab. There had to be at least forty tabs. He slid it toward me. "Here."

"What is this?"

"Read it."

I watched him out of the corner of my eye suspiciously before turning over the first page and reading what was marked beneath. My eyes widened. "This is a contract. A developer's contract."

Lukas nodded. "I bought the condos. Our condos. I bought all of them."

My eyes slid up to meet his. "You did?"

"Yes." He pulled his chair closer to mine and flipped a couple more pages over. "Some were abandoned. Others had renters, and a select few had owners living in them. We're going to invest in the neighborhood, repair it, and build things up. We're going to save it from zoning. The city wanted to tear it all down but I beat them to the bid."

I flipped through pages as emotions swirled inside me. "Lukas, this is... perfect."

He smiled and rubbed a hand across my back before draping his arm on the back of my chair. "I have mock-ups to build a community center and a village for people without a roof over their head. Somewhere they can sleep and feel safe and get warm. It's only the beginning stages and I didn't want to dive too deep into it without bringing you onto the project with me."

"Really?"

"Really. This is ours, Kayla. It's always been ours."

A tear slipped free and I wiped it away. "I love you so much."

He kissed me deeply. "I love you too."

Somehow, Lukas had made me even happier than I'd been just minutes before. That was what he did. He upped his game every day and I knew I had a bright future ahead of me with a man like him by my side.

Great things were in store for us and the people of Seattle.

And for the baby in my belly.

I put a hand on my stomach and Lukas put his hand over mine. We shared a secret smile before someone tapped the side of their glass with a knife and bellowed for a kiss.

Naturally, we indulged them, and the room echoed with cheers as I smiled against Lukas' lips. It was the best kiss of my life, second only to the one that would come later in a storage closet where the soup kitchen kept extra chairs and linens. And that one would be defeated by the kiss we shared in our hotel room later that night as Lukas stripped me out of my dress.

That was how it was with him. Everything just kept getting better.

The End

ABOUT THE AUTHOR

Chloe is a hometown girl from Tennessee who loves a great short romance, drinking coffee most of the day, and hanging out with family. When she's not writing, she can be found playing the piano or surfing Facebook!

Having been a reader all her life, she's hoping that you'll find yourself lost to time, laughing and falling in love all over again with her books.

OTHER BOOKS BY C. MORGAN

Take Me Back
My Uptown Girl
Tell Me No Lies
Ringing in New Years
Stealing His Sister
Santa's Favorite Elf
Opposites Attract
Keeping Score
Drive Me Crazy
Hometown Hotshot
Your Secret is Safe
Make Me An Offer
Singles Retreat
Accidentally On Purpose
Dating Dr. Wright
Hot Summer Nights
Model Student
Guarding Her Assets
Accidentally In Love
Romance Rivals
Don't Walk Away
Wash Over Me
Whatever it Takes
Mountain Man's Secrets
Mountain Man's Girl
Mountain Man's Fake Fiancé

Made in the USA
Middletown, DE
06 November 2020